The Flight of the Ilyushin 76

A Historical Novel

Herbert Leonard Cohen

D1738891

ISBN: 979-8-3915-6658-8

For my family

Also by Herbert Leonard Cohen

The Washington Triangles
Eric Porter
The Message And The Messenger
Sleepers Awake
The Hilton On The Moon

I wish to thank the several United States Air Force Staff Judge Advocates under whom I had the honor to serve and apply international law. The importance of their work in the Pentagon E wing is not fully appreciated. The character Air Force Major General Jeffrey Levy Staff Judge Advocate was inspired by my service.

In Vienna, Austria, in July 2015, the issue had not changed. Should the Islamic Republic of Iran be allowed to become a nuclear power? After twenty months of negotiations the United States, United Kingdom, France, Russia, and Germany finally negotiated with Iran an interruption to its nuclear ambitions, the Joint Comprehensive Plan of Action, JCPOA, along with an inspection Roadmap Agreement with the United Nations International Atomic Energy Agency.

Critics described any JCPOA agreement as next to worthless because the Iranians, determined to have their atomic bomb, could buy uranium and plutonium from North Korea.

The critics were right. North Korea would agree to sell, and Iran would buy.

CHAPTER 1

September 5, 2016

Farah Habig considered himself an essential part of the United States Central Intelligence Agency, an essential part of the United States government. At fifty-two, thin, with graying hair combed straight back, bifocal glasses, a certain tightness around the eyes, and a limp, he always dressed neatly and thought of himself as professional. He worked at the CIA campus at Langley, Virginia, 9 miles and twenty minutes from Washington, D.C. via US 29 S and George Washington Memorial Parkway.

The CIA headquarters building was in plain sight in Langley. It had been so for many years. Virginia highway signs directed traffic to the campus, and tourist busses stopped for photos of the big building and parade of men and women in ordinary clothes coming and going. There was less activity for the tourists to see on holidays, nights, and weekends. Inside the building operations were being planned. Elsewhere around the world CIA agents watched, made contacts, and prepared encrypted reports to send back to Langley. Habig earned his living carefully considering some of those reports involving atomic matters, and producing his own reports for those above him to consider and have others act on.

Within the CIA Habig thought of himself as professional in a way that made him a part of what he considered a small community of extraordinarily competent, underappreciated, and vastly underpaid national security experts. Within the CIA officer structure he was a tier three senior operations officer, well below tier one, the Director and his executive staff, and tier two, the branch chiefs and their executive staff.

His native languages were Arabic, French, and English because his Algerian mother spoke Arabic and French, and his American soldier father spoke English. Under several names, in several countries, with different occupations skirting different laws, he lived in the Middle East until he was a young adult. Egypt, Jordan, Lebanon, Syria. On and off during those years he worked for Russian traders in aircraft equipment and learned to speak and read an imperfect Russian. At Langley he adopted the name Farah Habig. Everyone just called him Habig.

With his new employer's sponsorship he took several years of George Washington University language and business courses: Russian, Korean, Persian, corporate finance, and accounting. For electronics and cryptology he was paired for months with teams of experts. He showed remarkable ability working with stealth computers, was given more and more opportunity to work on his own, and granted higher and higher security clearances.

On his own he further developed his ability to work with his sophisticated computer to penetrate foreign computers and other electronic devices known, believed, or suspected, of being connected to atomic activities. Mining and refining uranium ore, manufacturing centrifuges or reactors, operating centrifuges and reactors. Also, the computers and electronic devices of foreign government officials who did not go near centrifuges, reactors, or atomic warheads but controlled the money and signed contracts.

Habig was proud of his security clearances, his prizes, as he thought of them, but he knew that they were not like a George Washington University degree because they could never be framed and displayed, and unlike a college degree, his employer could take them away without any recourse from him. He knew what his security clearances were because his supervisors told him they existed on some computer memory somewhere. Existed for the time being. Without them continuing to exist in good order somewhere he could be shoved out the door and there would be no evidence he could produce that any of his prizes ever existed.

He knew that everything depended on his complete and patriotic loyalty, good work, and good behavior as seen by his supervisors, his haughty *masters,* as he thought of them. They treat themselves like generals and admirals, he thought, and treat him like a lowly lieutenant when they should treat him respectfully and pay him like a colonel.

When he urgently, sometimes passionately, disagreed with them about the importance of some new information he brought them, sometimes they reminded him that all his security clearances could be taken away, revoked, with a single keystroke. One impetuous keystroke and so would go his prizes, his job, and, important for him, so would vanish the years ahead he needed to build his pension high enough to pay for a comfortable retirement. His masters knew it, and he was certain they sometimes achieved some perverse delight in putting him in his place.

He was also an amateur scientist, historian, and philosopher. He read Blaise Pascal, Immanuel Kant, Gottfried Leibniz, Arthur Schopenhauer, and Baruch Spinoza. He accepted with the European philosophers that there had to be a cosmic cause for the existence of the cosmos, but he could not agree that there had to be predetermined unchangeable history because he was convinced that specialists like him at CIA contributed to continuing change that became part of what was historical change. The good, and not so good, historical change. He read and reread Albert Einstein's layman's explanation of the time and space aspects of relativity. He could not accept that time and space have 'substance' (Einstein's English language word). He was not ready to decide that Einstein and his followers were wrong, but he was satisfied that they could not prove time and space 'substance' to his satisfaction.

Farah Habig had become something of a twentieth century Renaissance man in his philosophical thinking as well as an accomplished CIA twenty first century computer sleuth. And he had a very special CIA value. He had information about atomic activities he could share, and using continuing opportunities he developed a personal relationship with Lev Marloff, a high Russian government official who was also keeping track of changes in atomic weapons and the people in a position to control them. To better understand the Russian mind of His Excellency, Lev Marloff, he read Russian history, Russian novels, Russian newspapers and magazines. Habig understood he needed his master's permission to contact Marloff by telephone or internet, or any other way, and he needed their travel money to go see him in Moscow.

Farah Habig also developed a certain sophistication about American culture, literature, theater, highly educated women, fine hotels, gourmet food, and fine wine. He could afford bouquets of flowers, theater tickets, good hotel rooms, and gifts like a string of Mikimoto pearls, but he controlled his more expensive desires, like a romantic week at a Hawaiian resort. Over several years he achieved romantic relationships with several women taking courses with him at George Washington, but he never found one willing to go to bed with him twice, much less let him put his ring on her finger. And with his CIA spy work, his limp, and the kind of accomplished left leaning woman he wanted, he knew better than to continue to wish for what he could not have.

Disappointed, discouraged, watching his bank account plummet with each failed romance, he gave up trying, stopped dating, and started dreaming. With his stealth computer he acquired and started admiring a picture of Lev Marloff's niece, Elena, when she was graduating from her gymnasium. She had an expressive face with blue eyes and reddish brown hair. Habig thought she was beautiful, a true Russian beauty. Smitten, he progressed from one picture of Elena to admiring pictures of her graduating from St. Pyotrsburg State University and graduating from the Diplomatic Academy of the Ministry of Foreign Affairs. He progressed from collecting pictures of her to loving her from afar. Not so strange, he thought. Petrarch did it, wrote about it, and is famous for it. He realized he would probably never meet Elena Marloff.

Habig's file at Langley showed a twisting history, a trail back to his Syrian employer's connection to Russian intelligence. It also showed Habig working with customers from several countries to get around import and export restrictions for aircraft electronics. It showed that a CIA officer encouraged, then helped, him come to Langley. It showed that Lev Marloff had taken an interest in him, and it showed that Habig's connection to Lev Marloff was valuable even though the scraps of information Marloff gave him could not be taken as accurate.

Sitting in his dimly lit four by six cubicle with his computer Habig looked up at the clock. It was near six, half an hour beyond his normal workday. He tapped the end of his pencil on the number keys. He was calculating hours of flight time and thousands of kilometers from Pyongyang, North Korea to Tabriz, Iran. FNJ to ULN in Mongolia for refueling, and on across Central Asia and the Caspian Sea on to TBZ.

He worried about Iran developing large and small atomic weapons. He worried about Iran's missile program developing missiles to carry nuclear warheads to targets a few hundred to several thousand kilometers beyond Iran's borders. Tel Aviv, Bagdad, Cairo, London, Moscow, Los Angeles, New York, Washington. He worried about Iran's aging Supreme Leader, Ayatollah Ali Khamenei, continuing to stir chaos in the Middle East, trying to resurrect the Persian empire of Cyrus the Great that a millennium before Christianity ruled from the Aegean Sea in the west to the Indus River in the east.

Iran had been his top concern for years, but July 14, 2015, was special and he thought truly historic. On that day the United States, the European Union, and Russia finally signed the long negotiated atomic arms agreement with the Islamic Republic of Iran. In exchange for the United States and the European Union lifting stiff economic sanctions on Iranian industry and banks, the Islamic Republic of Iran agreed to severely limit its nuclear weapons program. Not abolish, but limit. The agreement required Iran to freeze its efforts to produce, or otherwise obtain, weapons grade uranium or plutonium, to export to Russia most of its stockpile of enriched uranium and stop producing plutonium at its Arak nuclear reactor. Iran also agreed to allow continuing inspection of its nuclear facilities by the International Atomic Energy Agency, IAEA, to verify compliance. The Iran uranium and plutonium freeze, along with the IAEA inspection, was to last ten years.

Habig was not surprised that Supreme Leader Ayatollah Ali Khamenei continued to publicly insist that nothing in the agreement, negotiated and duly signed by Iran's diplomats, prevented him from continuing to assert that Iran had the sovereign right to make, and if it considered it necessary, to use atomic weapons, and nothing restricted his right to continue to declare at prayers *Death to Israel, Death to the Great Satan.* The Ayatollah's devout worshipers, and his secular detractors, all understood that the Supreme Leader was continuing to call for the destruction of the State of Israel and threating the United States of America for supporting Israel. Habig noted, again, that the Ayatollah did not travel outside Iran, and did not meet with foreigners.

Habig was particularly anxious about an approaching Iranian atomic bomb because his most recent computer probing strongly suggested that North Korea's Supreme Leader, Kim Jong Un, had agreed to sell, and deliver, weapons grade uranium and plutonium to Iran. The reality, he was near certain, was that beyond the public negotiations this was an agreement between the Chief of Staff of the Iranian army and the Chief of Staff of the North Korean army, that the Ayatollah had approved in principle but had not been asked to approve the complex financial and logistical arrangements.

Habig worried that in the Congress a number of senators and representatives with power over the CIA thought they knew more about North Korea's nuclear program than he did, more than his masters, and from time to time they would go over the President's head and dabble in changing history to their liking. He had been allowed to become an American citizen despite his checkered background. He knew that, too, could be revoked, and he could be deported. He was not about to complain about any American politician.

Habig thought that his CIA masters had remarkable memories for events, time, and names. They were, he thought, very shrewd, analytically and politically shrewd, but less skillful in dealing with computer experts like him trusted to work alone in four by six cubicles with stealth computers. They had to trust him to bring forward to them what he considered important, and just as important, to keep the rest forever to himself. When he demonstrated a credible danger, and urgently needed help outside the building, his masters grudgingly let him get around to the Pentagon for an office meeting or an evening meal in a home or restaurant. From time to time when he developed something of great concern they managed to find the money for a short trip to

Moscow. Out of the country he was all business, concerned that if he got himself in trouble and landed in a jail cell his masters might not pull strings to get him out.

Habig was not comfortable dealing with CIA psychiatrists. They all had framed diplomas on their office walls and high security clearances. As high, or higher, than his. He thought they diligently studied the latest professional literature about personality disorders so that they could expertly interview and then write expert reports on people who had high security clearances and did research, planning, or traditional spying. Habig appreciated the more secret the research, planning, or spying, the more important it was that there be regular and reliable psychological checks on him, and interviews and reports on all the other very valuable people involved in their very secret work.

As Habig saw it, there was an insurmountable problem. The very valuable person with the very secret work could not be allowed to tell his, or her, secrets to the psychiatrist, and the psychiatrist could not be allowed to follow up evasive answers with suggestions of a bad report, and so by intimidation wheedle out deep secrets. If it were otherwise the psychiatrist might learn too much that was very secret, and so become a grave security risk. Although continuing evasive answers to probing questions strongly suggested a personality disorder, or worse, the psychiatrists all knew that they could not afford to send in too many bad reports. Certainly, they could not afford to send in bad reports on their professional colleagues who, he thought, had a variety of personality disorders of their own.

As he saw it, they all knew the rules of the game, and so most of the time the psychiatric interviews had to be carefully routine, the reports they wrote had to be full of meaningless professional jargon, and they all kept their well paying jobs. Habig was certain his astute masters decided long ago not to rock the psychiatric boat, and they were not going to change now.

Habig spent his days, and some of his nights, in his four by six cubicle with his computer following his master's assignments looking for strings of information in two areas. For countries without nuclear weapons, any and all activity that suggested an attempt to acquire nuclear weapons or defend against an atomic attack, and for any country with atomic weapons, any increasing capability of making an atomic attack, or defending against an atomic attack. He used a highly classified software program, a version of a computer program called Pegasus, which allowed him, and others around the world like him, unauthorized no-click entry into other computers and a variety of other electronic devices. He recognized that his own computer might also have been penetrated, perhaps many times, without his knowledge, and that his highly sophisticated encryption may have been expertly pierced. If he was a spy to others, he considered himself above that. In his mind he was an elite professional in a new kind of worldwide electronic warfare.

Habig sent a report to his masters on the first working day of each month explaining what he had been doing, what he had found, and what he believed it might mean for them.

Often he turned in a single page reading, *Nothing significant to report.* When his masters called him in and complained he usually responded that he reviewed all current available reports, that he was continuing to search for new strings of useful information, he attempted to follow the old strings, but none of them became active, so there was nothing useful to report. Usually, he was right and truthful.

Over the years Habig had several successes. He found information relating to atomic activity that was important to his masters. He realized that his masters often had the same intelligence from other sources, but his confirmation, or lack of confirmation, was also important to them. Over the years he also made what he called unfortunate left turns, some of which he was told resulted in unfortunate consequences. Exactly whatever happened, where, how, to whom, he was not told, and he did not need to know.

At times he thought that his masters were keeping him far away from some highly secret operation. Without telling him why, they gave him highest priority assignments that took great amounts of time with little hope of turning up anything he believed valuable. At other times they ordered him to stop following a particular string, or several strings, that he believed had a good possibility of turning up very valuable information. He knew better than to question their orders because they could be following someone's orders and he didn't need to know anything about what happened at the highest level of the CIA.

All in all, he believed that his astute masters kept him around at a good salary because they realized they needed him.

Habig came to Langley with a limp. He had it because he was shot in the left leg by an Israeli border guard. It was just after dawn, he was wearing a stolen Lebanese army officer's uniform, and during the night he had driven the stolen officer's staff car through half a dozen checkpoints from downtown Beirut to the Israeli border. The Israeli guard stopped the car and ordered him to get out. When the guard asked for his military identification card he pretended not to hear, gave a friendly wave, and started to walk away. The soldier could easily have killed him but thought that a very young army officer with a staff car might be more valuable alive.

CHAPTER 2

Elena Marloff was the child of a moderately wealthy Russian family that lived in a solid big house in Moscow between the Garden Ring and the Boulevard Ring, an area of fashionable restaurants, shops, and museums. The Marloff family had a Moscow history that went back generations. On holidays members of the family, near and far, gathered there for memories of things past, news of what was happening now, and hopes for a good future. At New Year there were toasts to everyone for a good life, for good health, and by family tradition, because they had all gone through the best, and less than best of Russia, a toast *To Russia, to the best of Russia.*

From the beginning, Elena had so much going for her. She was quite pretty and naturally vivacious. She delighted in all sorts of music. On the intellectual side she was very bright and had an ear for foreign languages. Both her parents were intellectuals, both spoke English and several European languages. Her mother, a professor of chemistry at Moscow State University, stayed far away from government affairs. Her father, an economist, the opposite. For many years he held a responsible position with the Russian equivalent of the American Export-Import Bank.

Elena's uncle, His Excellency Lev Marloff, was a Deputy Minister in the Ministry of Foreign Affairs. During his career he served in important posts in the Russian foreign service around the world, and being a seasoned diplomat, economist, and skilled politician all rolled into one, he negotiated, with other senior diplomats, several trade agreements. He had an ornate office on the twenty-sixth floor of the Ministry of Foreign Affairs building, and he enjoyed the perquisites that came with his status. For the most part his decisions were final because he had the authority to make final decisions, and when the situation was of unusual importance and went up to the twenty-seventh top floor for approval, he usually prevailed there. The people below him knew better than to try and go around him.

Lev Marloff was proud of his service and proud of his ancestry because his father served with distinction in the Russian diplomatic service, as did his paternal grandfather, and he looked to an unbroken line of distinguished Marloff diplomats for generations still further back.

He always hoped that Elena would follow him into the diplomatic service. From the day he first held her in his arms and admired what he was sure was her Marloff intelligent face, he planned it. He kept in his study books about Russian history going back to the turbulent time of Pyotr the Great. He had maps of every country in the world, current maps and old maps, and after Elena was old enough to understand he would visit the Marloff home at least once a month and after each trip abroad say a few words about his recent journey. Often he would show photographs of historic monuments and new high buildings and leave a theater or museum program. Before leaving he would invite his niece and her mother and father to come over to his house. His wife, always happy with the visits, would serve tea and little cakes she baked herself, and he would again talk about his travels, show photographs and maps, all to explain what was happening in the government offices in Moscow and beyond Moscow, in the world beyond Russia.

As Elena grew older he would talk to her about her school work, first history, and then if she was at his home what books she was reading. Always there was a suggestion, and if it was not in her library, he would pull down a copy for her to take home and talk about next time. If there was a visitor he would proudly introduce Elena to the minister of this department or the chief of that division.

Lev Marloff's wife, Angelina, warmly hugged Elena at every meeting at her home. The dear woman died much too young. It was an accident. A drunken driver. Too much vodka. Elena's mother was in the car, she was hurt, not seriously, but she was grief stricken. After the funeral she went to church, Russian orthodox, and took Elena with her. She told Elena that she went to church when something of great importance to her happened, and that Angelina's death was one of those times. That, she told her, was the time for prayers. Prayers in church with the priest and prayers alone. Spoken prayers and silent prayers. All this sank deep into Elena's consciousness, and so Elena learned that life was precious, death was a fearsome thing more powerful than government ministers and more powerful than her parents and Uncle Lev.

When Elena was fourteen Uncle Lev first talked to her about going into the foreign service. He had talked to her mother and father about it several times during the past year, and this time he came to her house in the late afternoon in a light snow carrying a package. Elena helped him off with his coat and gave him a kiss on his cold cheek and put the package on the table by the piano. He talked to her mother, as he always did, about what Elena was studying at school and about her piano lessons. After tea Elena played her Bach and Schubert for them, they smiled and applauded, and then her mother left him alone with Elena. Elena looked at the package and said with a knowing smile, "Uncle Lev, what did you bring me from Egypt?"

"Elena, why Egypt?"

"Last time as you were leaving you made a joke that you may have to learn how to ride a camel."

"So?"

"Camels are in Africa. There are camels in many places in the northern part of Africa, and the country with camels that you would be going to had to be an important country. Important for Russia. Important enough for you to go there. Egypt is the most important country in Africa with camels, so it was Egypt."

"Yes, I brought you a little present from Egypt."

"Thank you. You are very kind."

"Tell me, what do you know about Egypt?"

"I have been reading the encyclopedia. Egypt has a very old

civilization. It goes back three thousand years. It has ancient stone pyramids. For thousands of years it has always had farming along the Nile River."

"What do you know about the Nile River?"

"The Nile River has two parts, the big part, the Blue Nile and the smaller part, the White Nile. The Blue Nile starts in the rainy mountains of Ethiopia, and it flows down through a big country called Sudan to a place in Egypt called Aswan where Russia has built a big dam for Egypt, and then it flows down by the capital city and ancient big pyramids into the Mediterranean Sea. When I read about the Aswan Dam I thought that you must have helped make it possible. Did you?"

"I was involved in arranging the financing of the Aswan Dam, and I had a small part for several years overseeing how the money was spent. Do you know the name of the capital city of Egypt?"

"The capital city is called Cairo, and there is a famous Mediterranean seaport close to Cairo called Alexandria."

"What else do you know about Egypt?"

"Egypt grows much cotton. It didn't used to. It used its fertile land by the Nile River to grow wheat and corn and barley. It was what the people relied on for centuries, but now Egypt imports most of its food for its people because it uses much of the fertile land all along the Nile River to grow great amounts of cotton. It has factories that make the cotton into all sorts of textiles and cotton clothes, so I think that you have brought me something to wear from Egypt."

"Yes, I have. It is a cotton dress. The best Egyptian cotton. Your size, I think."

"You went to Egypt to help Egypt get along with Russia. That is what you always do. Tell me about how Russia gets along with Egypt."

"It is complicated because Egypt wants to stay on good terms with all the countries in the Middle East, and beyond, and it would take a long time."

"It is complicated. That is why you went. Tell me."

"Egypt is a big country with many problems. It has many very poor people, and some very rich people, and it has many difficulties dealing with other countries, including Russia."

"I know. I read the newspaper. And you know all about it.

That is why you went."

"Go put on the dress, see if it fits, and we will talk."

"No, that will take too much time. Please, tell me about Egypt. Tell me why you went to Egypt. Is Egypt our friend? Did you make Egypt our friend? Tell me."

"I will but go put on the dress."

When she came back she walked little ballet steps up to her uncle, smiled, and twirled around. He smiled, told her that she should keep up her ballet lessons, and that she looked fine in her new dress. She thanked him for the present and with a serious look asked him to explain more about Egyptian cotton, and what it meant for Russia.

"It is very complicated. Egypt is not the only country that grows cotton and wants to send its cotton goods to Russia for Russian companies to buy."

Elena persisted and it took Uncle Lev several minutes to answer her questions about how Egyptian cotton was coming to Russia in competition with other country's cotton coming to Russia, and then he told her that he had to leave.

"I will get your coat, but please don't get up. There is something I have been thinking about for a long time."

"Tell me."

"I have been thinking that when a very important diplomat like you goes to a foreign country, and then in order to be accepted as the official diplomat that he is, he has to go to the palace, and when he goes there he has to dress up a certain way, and he has to carry some special papers in special envelopes with all sorts of official wax seals, and he has to ask to see the king's official that meets ambassadors, and then he goes into a big inside room with great carpets on the floor, and all sorts of huge paintings of men on horseback on the walls, and there he meets the king himself, or the king's official, and then he bows from the waist, not smiling, just bows, no handshake, he just bows from the waist, and he says, in French of course if he is in Paris, he bows, and then he says, I am Lev Marloff, or whatever his name is, and then he adds his title and goes on, I have the honor of presenting myself to Your Excellency as the ambassador of the Czar of Russia with the request that you receive my official authorization from the Czar of Russia to act as his ambassador to the king of France, and I request that Your Excellency permit me to advance to your person and to present these documents affirming my office to you."

"Elena, you know that we don't have a Czar anymore. What you have been reading about went on years ago. It is more informal now."

"I know, and if I had the chance to do it now I would just walk right up to the king, and smile at him, and tell him why I was there, and like a good modern king he would smile back, and even kiss me on the cheek."

"That, Elena, would be going too far, even now. But then, it depends on the king, and how you do it."

"Tell me, what was it like for your grandfather when he made trips to other countries for his Czar. I think about him in years past going off in a very big boat across the ocean. I think of him on a long train going across Europe to do his work. I think of you now flying to Paris in a big airplane and presenting your credentials in French. I am learning French. I have a book, and I have a recording that tells me how to pronounce the words. After I learn French better I am going to learn English better. I will get a recording for English, too. Uncle, when you were an ambassador, you had to speak many languages."

"Elena, I was a diplomat, I worked with many ambassadors, but I was never an ambassador."

"Why not? You should have been an ambassador."

"It is complicated. Early on in my career I saw that ambassadors have a great deal of prestige, they have influence, but they are not much involved in deciding, in hammering out, the important things. Diplomats sometimes can help make important government decisions. Sometimes they can help people who need help because of what their government is doing. I preferred to be a diplomat."

"Being a diplomat is a very great honor, and being a diplomat runs in our family. Whether it is for one Czar, or for other Czar, or whoever rules the country now, it is a very great honor, and it runs in our family."

"And so, Elena, you want to be a diplomat, you want to continue the family tradition?"

Elena responded with a smile and the twinkling eyes of a happy Russian girl who is getting ready to meet the world. "I do, and you want me to do it. I know that you do. You must help me."

"Elena, I would be proud, very proud, if you could carry on the family line. And as it happens, there is something you can be thinking about."

"Tell me."

"There is a government program for very bright and talented young men and young women to guide them into the government's foreign service, including the diplomatic service. The first step is that you must graduate from your gymnasium near the top of your class. Next, you apply for university admission. You must be accepted, you must take difficult courses that prepare you to go further, and you must do very well at the university. Part of that is getting along well with all sorts of people you have never met before. Then at graduation, if you want a career in the foreign service, and you have done very well in undergraduate studies, there is a graduate school scholarship at a special college in Moscow. It is on Ostozhenka Street, and it is named the Diplomatic Academy of the Ministry of Foreign Affairs. Usually, it is just called the Foreign Service Academy. There is a distinguished faculty, and you go to the Academy for two years. Longer for some. Not everyone completes the program. Those who graduate, if they are recommended by the head of the school, go into government service according to their ability and training and where they are needed. So not all the graduates are taken into the diplomatic service. All the graduates must serve where they are placed for a number of years."

"And you are telling me about the Foreign Service Academy because you went there."

"Yes, I went there."

"And because the graduates go into the Ministry of Foreign Affairs."

"Yes, many of the graduates do go into the Ministry of Foreign Affairs and they have lifetime careers with that work. Others go into important positions with other parts of the government and have careers there. You are too young to be concerned about applying now."

"I am too young now, but I should get prepared to apply. You must help me."

"So, if you were graduating from university with very high

grades, and very good recommendations, you would apply, and you would write in your application about the difficult courses you mastered, and you would write what you want to do as a career. Would you like to travel and speak, read, and write many languages? Would you like to live with all kinds of people in all sorts of places where everything is different?"

"Is it hard to learn many languages and to live with all kinds of people?"

"Some find it very difficult. They learn the different languages and different customs, but they don't like the country, how the government rules the people, and how the people live. They don't like the hot climate, the different food, the crawling and flying insects everywhere. They complain but they go anyway. They become lonely being away from their wives or husbands. Others like to travel to foreign places. They adapt to the conditions. Not everyone can. As you get older you will learn more about yourself that way."

"I will learn, and I will prepare myself. I will do it."

Elena graduated from her gymnasium with honors and was accepted to attend Saint Pyotrsburg State University.

CHAPTER 3

Pyotr Suvorov was graduating from his gymnasium with honors and ready to apply to attend the university at Pyotrsburg. His history teacher, Sophia Akhatova, was sitting across the desk from his gymnasium's dour headmaster, Nikolai Dimitriev.

With the top button of her blouse unbuttoned she leaned halfway across the desk and said earnestly, "You, Nikolai Andreievich Dimitriev, you have the responsibility. Pyotr will be graduating at the head of the class. You must make the decision to recommend him for admission. He wants to go to Pyotrsburg, and he needs a stipend scholarship."

"Sophia, I know very well that Pyotr is graduating. I know that a stipend would be helpful for him, and I hear you very well. Sophia, I know all that. Please, sit back."

"As you wish, I am sitting back. Nikolai, I am only here to help you."

"Help me? What you mean is that I should decide the way you tell me to. Admission to Pyotrsburg is very competitive. You are asking a lot because Moscow looks at these admissions, and they may know there are problems with that boy. You don't see them, but others will, and if I send in the recommendation for his admission then I am responsible. Sophia, for you to recommend, that is easy. For me to decide, that is a big decision. You must remember we are not a class one gymnasium. I am not the headmaster in a class one gymnasium. Pyotr is not a graduating student from a class one gymnasium."

"This is an excellent gymnasium! Excellent in every way! *You*, Nikolai, you are the reason for that. Everyone knows. You are so good in everything you do, and so you have such a fine reputation."

He gave her a sober look. "So you say. This is a class three gymnasium, Sophia, because we are in a small railroad town in the middle of nowhere, the very middle of nowhere, and that is how Moscow wants the town to stay, and how it wants this gymnasium to stay. My office is like a broom closet. That is how the people in Moscow treat me, that is how they think about me, that is how they think about this gymnasium. In Moscow they remember that there have been agitators from this area, violent agitators that had to be put down by force, again and again, all the way back to the 1900 railroad strikes, and that's why there has never been a student accepted for a Pyotrsburg scholarship from this gymnasium. Not one scholarship, never."

"You have only recommended… twice."

"Recommended twice and denied twice. You say I have a fine reputation, perhaps so here, but I tell you, Sophia, my reputation in Moscow is like a crab on the bottom of the ocean ready to crawl into a trap box."

"With Pyotr you have a sure winner. He is the best student ever. This time you cannot go wrong."

"So you say. Moscow pays, Moscow watches, and Moscow decides."

"The application goes to Pyotrsburg, not Moscow. Even if a fool in Moscow looks at the application, you cannot go wrong. Let me read to you your part of the application."

"Moscow does not have fools. Moscow will look, Moscow will decide."

"Nikolai, please, just listen."

"Alright, go on, I am listening."

"This is how it reads. *To the Admissions Committee, St. Pyotrsburg State University*

Pyotr Suvorov is an exceptional student and exceptional person in every way. He has a natural interest and ability for science of every kind. He has the highest scores in all his science courses, including advanced calculus. He has a wide knowledge of Russian and world literature. He reads texts in English and German. He has written several short stories about using computers for adventures in space. However, this is recreation for him. He does not intend to become a professional writer. Pyotr is well liked by other students, both boys and girls, but he does not attempt to be the center of a party.

Politically, Pyotr is a solid Russian in every way, the exceptional child of a thoroughly Russian family, and in my opinion, and that of the entire gymnasium faculty, Pyotr Suvorov is the finest candidate for admission this gymnasium has ever graduated.

Pyotr is frugal and the state living stipend should be entirely adequate for him at St. Pyotrsburg State University.

Signed Nikolai Dimitriev, Headmaster"

The headmaster frowned. "Pyotr is a good student, he has good ability in science, and he has a knack for languages. He is well liked. But for his politics, how do we know? The best I can write is that he doesn't talk about politics here. Will he stay like that? Or will he change? He dreams of making the world better. If he becomes a radical, which he well might, I will get a terrible black mark."

"Like so many young people he has these dreams. Just dreams. That doesn't mean he intends to do anything radical. Nikolai, talk at his age is cheap, we all know that."

"He might already have a political record. Not long ago they purged all the universities. They threw out all the radicals, administrators, faculty, and students, from top to bottom. Top to bottom. And they do not allow radicals in now."

"Pyotr does not have a political record."

"So you say. How can you know?"

"Nikolai, believe me, I know him, and he is too clever for that."

"He has a Jewish ancestry, a Jewish radical ancestry. They keep records, they know it."

"His grandparents were never revolutionaries. They were business people, so naturally they were suspected of being against the revolution. Perhaps, like many other shopkeepers, they were against the revolution, but that's long ago, that's not important now."

"And if he is asked about his religion, then what?"

"Why would he be asked? His family doesn't have a Jewish name."

"Not now. Jewish names have been changed. What if he is asked?"

"If he is asked about religion he will say that his family does not practice religion, they do not have any religious books, they do not talk about religion, that he respects people with religion, but he has no religion. If he is asked other questions, he will know how to answer. He is more than school smart, he is street smart."

The headmaster scowled again and shook his head. After a long silence he put his chin in the palm of his hand and said, "So, if I decide to recommend Pyotr, I will need a letter written by Pyotr. Not too short, not too long. By Pyotr without your help. You will talk with Pyotr the right way."

"I've talked with Pyotr. I talked the right way."

"All right, Sophia, have Pyotr write his letter. You can help him in a general way, but he must write it himself, and I must be able to say that he wrote it himself. Get a new photograph to go with it. I will look it all over, and if I approve, I will send it in."

Sophia leaned over the desk again and with a knowing smile said, "Nikolai, you are a wonderful man. You will look it all over, you will be pleased, and so you will send it in with your recommendation."

"I will be pleased?"

"Yes, Nikolai Andreievich, you will be quite pleased."

Nikolai smiled. "And you will be pleased?"

Sophia smiled, stood up, and gave his hand a little squeeze.

Back at her desk she took up her latest draft of the application for the university science program, made a few small changes, one by one took them all out, thought again, and one by one put them all back in. Pyotr, she decided, would write his own application, he would write in his own words, he would only follow her outline and it would be outstanding! As for Nikolai Andreievich and his miserable *games*, that old *bastard*, from time to time it has to be done.

CHAPTER 4

Supported by his state stipend Pyotr Suvorov was looking forward to graduating from Pyotrsburg in May. In his electrical engineer class, of the one hundred and sixty-eight mathematics and computer mavens, only seven were above him in hardware, and only two in software.

Elena was also one of the thousands of students at the campus. She took courses in foreign languages, economics, history, the humanities, and a single computer science course.

Near the middle of their senior year Pyotr sat next to Elena at lunch in a student cafeteria and they talked over sandwiches and coffee about student life, housing, meals, occasional entertainment, and what courses they were taking.

Pyotr said he envied her. She was learning about economics and world history, and with music and art she was going beyond Russia and exploring the world. He told her he was immersed in computer engineering, physics, and mathematics. He went on that he was also interested in economics and history, but he had little time for them. She thought of Pyotr as interesting, rather attractive, very bright, and a little shy. He thought of her as very pretty, more than pretty, beautiful, very bright, very appealing, but in so many ways beyond him. Far beyond him. With his limited finances he could not reach out and touch her for more than as a cafeteria friend.

It was a short meeting, less than an hour. There were students milling all around, but they didn't see or hear them. It was long enough and private enough for both of them to know that it was more than an ordinary lunch chat, that it really wasn't about the school, it was about them, and that something more could happen.

They met again several times at the same cafeteria. Oblivious to what was happening around them, they chatted about the courses they were taking and then activities they might attend on campus. He saw something in her face and heard something in her voice that told him he could reach out. He took a chance and reached out. She understood, took a chance, and responded. They had a date for a movie, then another. And another...

Elena told him that after graduation, in September, she would likely go on to the Foreign Service Academy program in Moscow. She had asked for a recommendation from the head of her department. She should have it in a few days, and with it she could send in her application. Did he know about the Foreign Service Academy? Did he know there was a special program at the Academy for electrical engineering graduates? He answered that he had read about it. There was a notice on his department's bulletin board. She asked, "What did it say?"

"It said that graduates in electrical engineering may apply to go there for graduate work in information technology. They split their time on foreign service international communications programs and fundamentals of foreign service work."

"What else did it say?"

"It said that all foreign service careers involve security clearances, lots of travel, and living abroad for extended periods."

She asked him if he was interested. He answered that international communications systems might be interesting. Elena looked at Pyotr seriously, intently, leaned forward, put her hand on his, held it tight, and told him that she was applying to the Foreign Service Academy, and that if he was also interested in the Foreign Service Academy, and interested in her, he had to apply right away. "People make their own destiny," she told him. "They don't wait, they do what they need to do! And they do it now!"

He took hold of her other hand and told her he would need a recommendation from the head of his department. She told him to go to his professor and do it now!

That afternoon Pyotr asked the head of his department for a recommendation to attend the Foreign Service Academy in the fall with a living allowance. The professor responded that he was making a mistake. The Foreign Service would be glad to nab him, to bring him into their communications and cryptology work, very worthwhile, but he could do much better in space science. Pyotr replied that it was very kind of him to think that he could do better elsewhere, but he really did want to go to the Academy. The professor shook his head and asked if it was because a girl was going to the Academy. Pyotr answered that she was graduating with him, and that she was applying. Was he entirely sure he also wanted to apply? Yes, he was sure. The professor nodded, nothing would change a lovesick mind.

He wrote that Pyotr Suvorov was an excellent candidate for the Foreign Service Academy communications program and added that the candidate was also well suited for advanced engineering work in space sciences. Living allowance fully justified. Copy to department file and candidate file.

Pyotr understood that the government controlled his future. The government paid for his education, his elementary school, his gymnasium, his university education, and it controlled every step of his future. Even so, his professor had agreed to sponsor him, and so his first step after graduation could be the Academy. Likely, it would be. Hopefully, almost certainly, Elena would be there with him.

Elena saw him at a distance a few days later. He was bent over carrying a bag of books over his shoulder. She caught up with him and asked him about his application. Pyotr told her his professor had written a very good recommendation, he had completed the application, he was on his way to make a copy and mail it. She told him she should look it over with him. He agreed, and she kissed him.

During the summer Pyotr worked at low paying jobs. It was a stiff dose of Russian economic reality. Most of his meager earnings he gave to his father to help with family living expenses. Away from Elena, away from the university computers that solved exotic equations in split seconds, he spent his spare time reading Russian classics and a magazine for engineers and scientists. It was a summer of miserable work, old Tolstoy and Turgenev, and new high tech.

In the first week in August he received a notice from the Academy that his application had been approved and he would be notified when and where to come in September. He went back and forth between joyous elation and despairing moods. He would be with Elena again. He would go with near empty pockets. He worried that Elena might respond to his advances and then, without the money he would need to treat her the way she expected to be treated, deserved to be treated, she would make excuses, leave him, and find another Academy cadet. One with brains, smiles, good family, good manners, and lots of ready money. Then he determined to try to stop worrying so much. Elena didn't want some handsome fellow with brains and lots of money, she wanted him, as he wanted her, and with only a little money he had a chance.

CHAPTER 5

Elena wanted to make the most of her summer before starting two years of Academy world history, foreign languages, diplomatic protocols, and whatever else the Academy program had waiting for her. A week after university graduation Uncle Lev called and invited her to lunch with him the next day. It was a good restaurant near his office, she would enjoy it. They could talk about her summer plans.

The maître d' guided them to a reserved table laid with a spotless cloth, sparkling wine glasses, gleaming silver, and linen napkins. When the waiter left with their orders Uncle Lev smiled and said, "In the next two months what would you like to do to get ready for the Academy?"

Smiling broadly, Elena clapped her hands together. "Have I been accepted?"

"Yes, of course!"

"I haven't heard. How do you know?"

"The Rector is an old friend. He called me. He had a story to tell me about you."

"A story about me?"

"Yes, nothing serious, but first things first, for the summer, what do you want to do?"

"I have been thinking about it. I want to travel. One, maybe two, tours with university students and faculty. Not expensive. but decent food and lodging for faculty and serious students. I want to travel around Europe. I want a week or more in Paris and a week or more in London. I want to try out my French and English."

"Excellent. I know just the travel agency for you. What else for the summer?"

"I want time to read. I have a list, books we touched on in different classes."

"Good. Tell me about them."

"Classic works: Rousseau, *The Social Contract*; Locke, *Of Civil Government*; Darwin, *The Moral Sense of Man and the Lower Animals*."

"Excellent. I am impressed."

"The rest of the list are twentieth century American and English novels: Hemingway, Huxley, Fitzgerald. I might fit in a French novel."

"No Russians?"

"I have had years of the Russians. They saw the world with Russian eyes. That's good, but you can understand I want to go beyond them and the old world they wrote and dreamed about."

"Enough about summer." He smiled again. "While we are waiting for our fish there is something more important we should talk about."

"Oh?"

"Pyotr is also being admitted to the Academy. You should both get the letter to enroll in in the first week of August."

She joyfully clapped her hands together. "That's so wonderful! How do you know about Pyotr?"

"The Rector told me. He told me he had your excellent application, and he also had an excellent application by Pyotr Suvorov. He said that both of you are fine graduates from St. Pyotrsburg, and you must know each other. He said that the application styles are quite different. His style is lean, like an engineer, and yours is flowing like a humanities scholar. The styles are so different, except for the long closing sentence in both applications, which is almost identical. For you it is about working for eternal Russia in the best traditions of the Russian foreign service. Pyotr left out the eternal part. Could you have been Pyotr's tutor for such a good cause?"

"Dear Uncle, because of you it was fated that I was going to the Academy. After I met Pyotr, and got to know him, it was fated that he was going to the Academy with me, but his application needed a little help."

"Well done, my dear. Well done. Now I can do my part and give you the traditional foreign service warning not to think of traveling around the world too soon at government expense. That will take time and work on your part."

"I understand."

"Good. Go at it with a will and you will find most of it satisfying and meaningful. What do you say to champagne and Napoleon cake?"

Pyotr reported to the five story Academy on Ostozhenka Street in the late afternoon. He showed his identification and admission letter and was told he would take lodging and meals at a nearby house for Academy students. He went to the house where the bursar had him sign and date a form, took his fingerprints, took a photograph, gave him a sheath of papers and said, "Read all the instructions on house rules, meals, and medical care. The cafeteria, offices, and supplies are here on the first floor, the women are on the second floor, the men on the third floor. There are pay telephones on every floor. Your stipend doesn't pay for a telephone in your room. Be back here tomorrow afternoon for your Academy identification card."

Pyotr nodded, the bursar assigned him a room, handed him a key, and told him there would be fifty new students in the house, twenty-seven new men and twenty-three new women. Smaller, but much better, he said, than the bigger houses. The bursar wished him good fortune at the Academy, and with a wink, good fortune with the girls.

Pyotr found his way to his room, heard rocking music inside, opened the door, saw two beds and two chests, a closed window, and the back of a thin fellow in a rustic shirt and jeans keeping the beat by shaking his shoulders back and forth. He went in and after a moment recognized his old college roommate. Pyotr flung his duffel bag on the bed by the window and bellowed, "Hello, Alex, good to see you again!" Alexsandr turned around, after a moment gave him a broad smile, spread his arms wide, and shouted over the music, "Pyotr! Very glad to see you again!" He turned off the music and added, "Two years ago we were roommates for a year at Pyotrsburg, and here we are going to be together again! Couldn't be better! You want the bed and chest by the window again?"

"You remember."

"They're yours. I'll get my stuff off in a bit."

"Take your time. Alex, you left me. What happened to you?"

"Pyotr, my good friend, I left you, but I didn't forget you. You remember, like now, I used to tinker with electronic stuff?"

Pyotr glanced over the equipment. "This is a different kind of electronic stuff that's spread around the room. Why?"

"A professor at Moscow State took an interest in me. He got me a part time job in his department, and I transferred and completed my electrical engineer degree there."

Pyotr looked more carefully over the equipment being unplugged and shoved into a corner. He waved his arm and said, "All this must have cost somebody a small fortune. Back then you had nothing like this. Three or four pieces of what you called electronics junk, cheap junk."

"True, a few pieces of obsolete electronic junk, but they all worked."

"This all looks new and expensive. Back then you were always broke."

"Not true. Near broke."

"Where did you find this stuff?"

"I was helped, and I looked here and there."

"Alex, you were helped with the central processor, you lifted this modulator here, and you stole that transponder there?"

"Not quite."

"There's a phone on the wall. How much does that cost?"

"Pyotr, it is sort of complicated, and right now you don't need to know about the phone."

"Am I going to be paying half?"

"No, not now. Maybe later."

"So, where's the money coming from?"

"I have help from my Moscow professor. He helps me, and he wants me to have a telephone in my room."

"Why?"

"He knows me, he knows what I am able to get into. He tells me what to do, and I do it as best I can."

"You are obligated to find time to help, to work, for your friendly faculty advisor."

"In a way, true."

"Alex, the Academy is a professional school for diplomats, and for engineers to set up the communications systems that keep the diplomats useful around the world. For the engineers, in addition to learning the foreign service lines of command and studying foreign affairs, there will be learning about the international electronic network, becoming proficient in foreign languages and special cryptology. It will take up all your time. Have you thought of that?"

"I will concentrate. I will miss some sleep. For exams at Pyotrsburg, you used to do the same."

"True, true."

"Put your stuff away and we'll go to dinner. At eight there is a newcomer mixer in the cafeteria. You have to go and meet the girls."

"How about you?"

"I have things to do."

"I'm thinking, Alex."

"Always dangerous, Pyotr."

"Alex, I'm thinking that you got yourself into this Academy program because you thought there would be a girl here you are interested in."

"True. I met Veronika in a statistics class. We got to know each other. She is deep into economics. She applied, so I applied."

"Veronika is here with us?"

"She is."

"It was arranged?"

"She very much wanted to be here, and she deserves to be here. For Veronika, it is all about the world food problems that the Foreign Service deals with, all the arrangements among countries that make imports and exports work."

"What does that mean for her?"

"*It means a lot.* She wrote an impressive paper on Russia moving from being a large importer of grain, soybeans, and soybean meal during the early Soviet period to a major grain exporter as the agricultural economy moved from a small farm planned economy to a cooperative large scale market economy. It's a short hop for Academy graduates to the Ministry of

Agriculture and Food. She deserves to be here, and I don't want to lose her."

"She means that much to you?'

"She does. She really does."

"I'm thinking your faculty advisor talked to someone who set this up for both you and Veronika."

"She was at the top of her class in economics, and she would qualify on her own merits."

"I'm thinking that you made a deal with your faculty advisor that if you were accepted you would work on satellite orbits."

"On space projects, entirely possible."

"So now I'm also thinking that it is no accident that I'm here arguing with you."

"Pyotr, we're not arguing, but you could ask for another roommate."

"No, I'll stay."

"So, stop thinking so much and get ready to meet the girls after dinner. You already have one in mind."

"It's possible."

"And her name is Elena Marloff."

"How do you know?"

"She has been asking around whether you are here. Everyone on the Academy staff, and a lot of the students, know who Elena Marloff is."

"What do you mean, everybody knows who she is?"

"They know because they know who her uncle is. Elena Marloff is the niece of Lev Marloff, who is a deputy minister to the head of the foreign service. Maybe it is a different title, probably is, but her uncle is way up there in the foreign service. He is at the very top of the foreign service."

"I didn't know."

"She is looking for you. You know her, she knows you. How could you not know?"

"I didn't know, but it makes no difference."

"It makes a *big* difference. She must be used to a good life, and that will cost money. Unless you have robbed a bank recently that kind of money you don't have. Whatever money you saved up will go fast."

"True."

"Suppose you want to take her on a date. A nice restaurant, good seats at the theater, or after a few dates a nice hotel room. And, of course, you need to rent a car. No car, no girl. So, you need money."

"You need money, too. You need it for your Veronika. What do you have in mind?"

"I am going to repair computers. Small business computers. The telephone is for my professor and for contacts."

"You mean customers."

"Same thing. Contacts, customers. Customers, contacts. The telephone company doesn't care as long as it is not a regular business and the bill is paid on time every month."

"And if it's not?"

"The only thing that will happen is they will yank the phone, and I will have to pay a deposit to get it back."

"You really think you can stay in school and make this work on the side?"

"I think so, but I may need your help. Actually, I think I probably will. There are many small businesses near the Academy that have computers. The computers develop problems, and with good work, fair pricing, and assurance of complete confidentiality, we will become successful."

"We?"

"We both know computers. We both need the money. No money, no Veronika. No money, no Elena. Are you in?"

"I need the money. I'm in if I can find the time."

Alex went over to Pyotr and put a firm hand on his shoulder. "Pyotr, we are in the same boat. Where there are girls there is a will, there is a way."

"If it were only that simple. Do you have any real life business experience?"

"I've seen a couple of other fellows do it. About twenty hours a week. They didn't get rich, but they treated their customers right and they put good money in their pockets. We can, too."

"You are probably right. Give me a couple of weeks. Let's see how it goes."

CHAPTER 6

There were fifty talented young people at the house party, mostly slim and good looking. The cafeteria tables and chairs were pulled back to make an open space in the center of the room. For the girls, no fancy clothes, for the fellows, no ties. Recorded music, Russian standards, French and American standards, blues, ballads, all to a slow dance beat. Wine, soft drinks, talk, more talk, smiles, dancing. With some renewing university friendships hands were gently squeezed and there were teasing smiles and light kisses. The others, just getting to know each other, there were friendly smiles. A few mature faculty members were also there looking over the new crop, introducing themselves, not staying with anyone too long. A few junior faculty members were looking over the new crop for romantic possibilities.

Afterwards Elena told Pyotr that it was fated that they would meet again that evening, and it was fated that they would dance and fall head over heels in love. It was fated, she told him, that he would come over with glasses of wine as soon as the music started, they would talk and then he would ask her to dance. She told him she loved to dance, always had, waiting for the right man to dance with. It was fated he would hold her in his arms, look intently into her loving eyes, and come back all evening.

As Pyotr remembered it, Elena came over to him, reminded him with a smile how she helped him with his application, and coaxed him onto the dance floor. As he remembered it, when the set was over, and he didn't get more wine, she told him that would be the right thing to do. As he remembered it, Elena had already won his heart, and when she danced with him there was no turning back.

Pyotr dove headlong into his studies learning foreign service basics, and the basics of setting up, maintaining, and using the foreign service worldwide communications network. Not complex and fascinating like space engineering, but worldwide, complex in its own engineering way, and with its adaptation to many languages, fascinating.

It took him a full week after that evening of budding romance to come over to Elena in the cafeteria. She remembered that it was at the end of the evening meal. Everyone was getting ready to leave. Could he join her? Would she take a stroll around the area with him?

They talked about life at the Academy, how similar, and how different, it was from the university, and as she expected, he finally got around to asking her for a weekend date. She was both pleased and peeved. Waiting a week she could understand, she, too, had been immersed in getting to know her roommate, getting settled in, and starting with a will on challenging class assignments. All the acceptable reasons for waiting. Even so, a full week just to hold her hand while they walked and ask for a date, too long, and after the way she showed herself at the dance, he should have known it. What kind of a date? Elena accepted the invitation to go out to a movie, something like that, even though it meant for this first date getting there and back on the bus. Walking stiffly back to their Academy lodgings from the bus stop, not even holding his hand, she suggested that if there was ever going to be a next time, she suggested in a way that to Pyotr amounted to a demand, he would have to borrow a car, or rent one, or buy one. Seeing his crestfallen face she decided to lighten the blow and spur on his efforts with a long goodnight kiss. Having learned his lesson well, please her or lose her, Pyotr decided that he had no choice, he either had to rob a bank or make time to join Alex with the computer repair business. Alex, he thought, had better get busy finding paying customers.

As it had always done, the Academy imposed itself on its cadets as a unique professional school with its own methods and patriotic values. There was much to study and learn to appreciate. The

Russian Ministry of Foreign Affairs, like every government's diplomatic corps, has its vertical and horizontal lines of command for its diplomatic staff. Learn it, respect it, and faithfully follow it. There are the special terms of diplomacy: the Note, the Memorandum, the Official Letter, and the Aide-Memoire. All historic diplomatic tools. One had to study carefully many examples of each that had been used by Russian diplomats, and their opposing diplomats, for many historic situations. More than careful reading, one had to appreciate every carefully chosen word and phrase. An official Note that began, *The Ministry of Foreign Affairs conveys its respects to the Ambassador of Sudan and has the honor of notifying his Excellency*, did not necessarily mean that Russian officials respected the checkered diplomatic background of the current ambassador of Sudan. An agreement between Russia and Sudan, described as *The Agreement of the High Contracting Powers to open exploration of Sudan natural resources to Sudanese and Russian companies equally*, did not mean that the Kremlin considered its contracting partner in mineral prospecting worthy of respect in mineral contracting matters. The student had to recognize the importance of the clause providing that Sudan's reports of operations will be examined and verified by the Ministry of Foreign Affairs before any compensating rubles are paid into the Sudanese treasury.

At the Academy Russian history was everything. By the end of the first six months the students were expected to know well the problematic history of the Czars, the peasant revolts, the rise under Lenin of the Communist opposition, the 1917 revolution, the complicated economic and social transformation of the country in the 1920's, the Stalin purges of 1936-1938, and the long history of Russian war and peace. They had to study the victories, defeats, and peace treaties, the causes and results of Russia's wars with its historic enemies, north, south, east and west. Among the chapters: the Mongol invasion in the 13th century; the Muslim conquest in the 16th century; the Swedish invasion in the 18th century; the French invasion under Napoleon in the 19th century; the British and French incursion in Crimea in the 19th century; the Japanese wars in the Pacific area in the 19th and 20th centuries; and the devastating battles with Germany and its Balkan vassals in the First and Second World Wars.

Elena immersed herself in the peace treaties of the Czardom of Russia, those of the following Russian Empire, then the Union of Soviet Socialist Republics, and the present Russian Federation. There were also individual projects. Elena, spurred by Uncle Lev's interest, critiqued the Comprehensive Nuclear Test Ban Treaty. Veronika, taking advantage of her economics degree, critiqued the International Sugar Agreement. Alex and Pyotr were directed to study the diplomatic structure and technical implementation of the Space Station Intergovernmental Agreement.

Pyotr joined Alex in their computer repair work. They quickly developed satisfied customers who brought in other customers, all of whom appreciated their good work at reasonable rates and assurance of confidentiality. For Alex and Pyotr there was money to rent cars for weekends, money for good restaurants, and now and then little extras. Nothing ostentatious. A colorful wool scarf, a nice pair of gloves. Not needed, but so much appreciated. The Kirov ballet was performing Swan Lake in Moscow and Elena insisted they had to see it. Pyotr had never seen a professional ballet company perform with an orchestra. He was delighted. With her family Elena had been to the ballet many times. She was enthralled with the Kirov production, the brilliant dancing to Tchaikovsky's music, the prince's sexual bending of the willing swan in her strikingly revealing costume, the death and resurrection of the lovers.

In a few short weeks Pyotr and Elena drew close. Elena offered to share expenses, but Pyotr refused. During those few short weeks with money for good small hotels they progressed from long embraces and passionate kisses to passionate intimacy. They were happy slipping into each other's arms. Why should the Rector be concerned? Should they be married before or after graduation? As long as they could be entwined wouldn't it be best to wait? Their families would want that. By graduation the wedding date would be set. Meanwhile, like other Academy couples, they would be discreet.

For Alex and Veronika it was much the same. They made the commitment of marriage, and discreetly waited for graduation.

For the Rector, so long as the couples were progressing well, and were discreet, why interfere? For faculty members discreetly making advances to uncomplaining students, why interfere? It had always been that way.

The Rector knew about Uncle Marloff and his family tradition of service in the diplomatic corps, so for Elena there was really no question, she was headed for the diplomatic service. It would not be confirmed until graduation, but the Rector had no doubt, and Elena had no doubt. For Pyotr and Alex, the Rector knew about the arrangement to have them work on space station technology. He expected that at graduation they would both be inducted into the army as first lieutenants and posted to an army base outside Moscow that dealt with space technology. He hoped that after some army service they would be put in the reserve and shifted over to the foreign service that would give them good careers in international communications using their space age expertise.

The day after graduation Pyotr proposed again, and Elena with a kiss and embrace again accepted. So with the blessing of their families and Uncle Lev, two weeks after graduation Elena and Pyotr were married in Moscow. It was a simple civil marriage at Elena's home with both families, Uncle Lev and Sonia Lyadov, his devoted personal assistant, beaming on. After a brief honeymoon they were ready to embrace the world awaiting them.

Alex and Veronika also married shortly after graduation. Elena and Pyotr heartedly congratulated the bride and groom. After a short honeymoon they were ready to embrace the opportunities, joys, and sorrows of the changing Russian world.

Uncle Lev had expected that Elena would marry some fellow from the Academy. There were hundreds of Academy marriages, and if he was likely to have a diplomatic career and came from a good Russian family, so much the better. Pyotr was not from a traditional good Russian family, and he was not on the diplomatic track at the Academy, but so what? As for Pyotr's Jewish heritage, he was not practicing any religion, neither was Elena, and it was long past time to break the prejudice. Besides, the family history could not be ignored. In 1914 great grandfather Dimitri Mikhailovich Marloff was serving as a junior diplomat in London. The war with Germany broke out, and for Russia lasted until the truce with Germany in 1917, followed by the Russian revolution, followed by the civil war until 1922. There were the North armies and the South armies. The Bolshevik Red Armies battled the White Armies supported by forces from several countries intent on squelching the new communist government. There were millions of soldiers and millions of casualties.

Soon after the war with Germany began in 1914 Dimitri found work in the Foreign Office in London as a translator. His Majesty's Government was strongly opposed to all socialistic and communist ideologies. It did not want a bereft Dimitri getting mixed up with strident socialists, or any other wrong kind of people. He was useful for England now, and with his family connections in Russia, in time he might become considerably more useful. Dimitri's pay was enough to live secure from poverty, not enough to allow him to make any notable contributions to any radical organizations.

After the 1917 armistice Dimitri decided that he wouldn't go back to Russia until the civil war ended, until he knew who was running the country, until it was safe. Besides, he had another reason. He had an affair with a young Jewish woman with blue eyes and reddish brown hair. They had a child, a girl. She had blue eyes and reddish brown hair. In 1922 the Union of Soviet Socialist Republics was formed, it needed experienced diplomats, and Dimitri returned to Moscow with his wife and daughter, Anna. Anna became the mother of five more Marloff children. Since then several Marloff girls have been named Anna, and like Elena, have had blue eyes and reddish brown hair.

CHAPTER 7

Before leaving the Academy Elena received her assignment to the Ministry of Foreign Affairs and a date to report a month later. She drank a cup of tea with the Rector and thanked everyone on the faculty. She signed a sheath of papers and drew an allowance to cover her expenses in Moscow until she received her first paycheck.

Pyotr and Alex were commissioned first lieutenants and assigned to an army base seventy kilometers outside Moscow. Their assignment to the foreign service was deferred. Not cancelled, indefinitely deferred. They rented an apartment near a bus line that started in central Moscow, went near their apartment and passed the army base. There was a twenty minute ride to work, an hour and a half to Moscow for the weekend. Their computer repair business ended. Now they had what they considered generous salaries and housing allowances, and they were being introduced to space science projects being worked on by seasoned space engineers. They had fascinating work and money in their pockets. *Indefinitely deferred* suggested long deferred, perhaps years, but had no final meaning. They did not consider complaining.

Elena moved out of the family home, rented a modest apartment close to a Metro stop, put her advance in her Bank of Moscow checking account, obtained electric, gas, telephone and internet service, and then shopped for two new outfits. Balancing her funds and her purpose to be properly dressed for the foreign service, yet portray a certain individuality, at an upscale store she settled on white blouses, colorful scarfs, two black suits with knee length skirts, one outfit businesslike, the other more stylish could also be worn to a party.

For her first workday she was instructed to go to the Ministry of Foreign Affairs building for an introductory meeting with a member of the staff. A few minutes before nine o'clock, with a colliding mixture of expectation and trepidation, she entered the formidable landmark building of the Ministry of Foreign Affairs at 32 Smolenskaya Sennaya Square in Central Moscow. The twenty-seven-story building had a grand marble entrance, dark marble on the floor, light marble on the walls and beyond the imposing entrance hundreds of offices and meeting rooms. It also had an imposing spire on top. The twenty meter spire, according to the architect, Vladimir Gelfreich, was the result of showing Premier Joseph Stalin the design. Stalin looked at the plans for the massive, and hugely expensive project, and using his pen drew a spire on the top. And so it became a Moscow landmark.

Elena entered and satisfied the guards that she had an appointment about her employment in the foreign service. She was shown to an interview room where the Marloff name brought forth friendly smiles and she was politely escorted by a guard to the bank of elevators. She remembered that Uncle Lev had told her there was no elevator from the lobby to the twenty sixth floor where he had his office. She had been told about his grand office as a girl, had thought about it many times at the Academy, but had never seen it. For now, so close, yet still so far.

Sonia Lyadov was waiting for her at the sixth floor reception desk. She gave her a warm smile and said, "So Elena, we happily meet again. It seems so long since your wedding."

"Yes, it does."

"Your uncle is not here. He is traveling. He is on an Asia mission. Today he is in Beijing. So, for him, for me, welcome."

"Thank you. So kind."

"Come with me, we will go to better chairs in a comfortable room." When they were settled Sonia continued, "And first, before anything else, our congratulations again on your wedding. We are so very happy for both you and Pyotr."

"You are so very kind. Thank you."

"As soon as your uncle returns he wants to meet with you and Pyotr again. Pyotr is so handsome, so intelligent. We are so happy for both of you.."

"Thank you."

"So when he returns, perhaps a week, he wants to meet you and Pyotr again at his house. He will arrange his schedule, you will arrange your schedule, Pyotr will arrange his schedule. So you will talk to Pyotr."

"I will tell him. We will be happy to come."

"Definitely, a marriage like yours absolutely requires joyful family time together." Turning more serious she continued, "Elena, I should repeat what your uncle has likely already told you. For your personal life you can wear your wedding ring and be Elena Suvorova. Now you are here, and for your official work you can use your maiden name. For your own career interests, and for the good of the service, your uncle is suggesting that you make your career as Elena Marloff. In the foreign service women keeping their maiden name is not unusual. You will explain to Pyotr."

"Yes, I will."

"Let me say a few more things. For now, Pyotr as a lieutenant has a position that is far enough away that it would not be practical for you to be living together. In summer, with good driving conditions, it is well over an hour. In winter, almost impossible. Weekends, holidays, special occasions, you will be together, of course."

"I understand. We both understand. He has found his own place with a friend, another new lieutenant. It is near their work."

"For now, you can both manage your finances?"

"Pyotr has a good salary and a housing allowance. We will manage."

"So now that you are independent you are living on you own?"

"Yes, it was time for that."

"Of course. How are you getting settled? Have you found suitable housing, good modern housing at a fair rent?"

"I looked around, I talked to a real estate agent about apartments and rents, and what I have is suitable, and the rent is in line. I am near a Metro stop, so I don't need a car. I will get by."

"Moscow is expensive, and you have all sorts of expenses

getting settled. Deposits for rent, gas, electricity, telephone. You must have internet. Pyotr must have internet and telephone. And so you will stay in touch. It is not only for you, it is for the good of the service. So an advance until your first check at the end of the month will be proper."

"Thank you. I have some savings. I will get by."

"Elena, you have been two years at the Academy. There you only needed Academy clothes. You never needed a taxi. You never had to go to a good restaurant with a colleague for lunch or dinner. Here you are a professional and you need good clothes. You cannot dress like a clerk. You must have spare money. You cannot act like you're short of money. *You must always look and act professional.* You always offer to share the bill, and you always wear well pressed good clothes. Good quality and good fit. Never stained or rumpled. Never cheap gaudy jewelry. From your first day in the building you always respect yourself, and you always insist on respect from others. From everyone. Clothes are part of that, not the only part, but a part. It is showing respect for your uncle as well as yourself. So, Elena, with your savings you would manage to get by, but for your position here you need an advance."

"Very kind, but I wonder if that is the wrong way to start."

Sonia frowned and shook her head. *"Elena, your life has changed. You are here, and your life has changed.* You always need money in your purse and your bank account. You are coming from the Academy to the diplomatic service. An advance is the right way."

"I signed a lot of papers at the Academy, but I don't know what my salary is going to be. I understand that it may depend on the position I am put in."

"Your Academy work was professional grade. You will be assigned professional grade work. You will start a step above the foreign service entry level. An accounting clerk will contact you tomorrow about a month's advance."

"Thank you."

"So, enough about money. Now about your position. The first two weeks are orientation, forms to fill out for security clearances and meet the people who will be giving you assignments. You will learn about the work we do here in Moscow and around the world.

Foreign affairs, assisting Russian commercial interests, financial and travel arrangements for special situations. It all takes time."

"I understand."

"Your uncle has plans for you for the rest of your first year. When you show you are ready he will probably post you to the Seoul embassy. You will need to show that you know the Korean language, spoken and written, and Korean customs. To do that you will be part of a Korean language and culture course. You will have to show you can deal with embassy business. You will be given assignments that require understanding, analysis, and independent decisions. The complexity of the work, and the importance of your decisions, will depend on your progress. And you will have to show you can get along well with embassy staff. You will show that by how you get along with the executive staff and lower level staff here."

"That will be a full time first year."

"Elena, you are going into a man's world. It has been a tradition, especially at the highest positions. I have been in the foreign service for some twenty years. Before I came to work for your uncle I was in Warsaw, then Belgrade, then Madrid, then Brussels. At the Brussels embassy I had very substantial responsibilities. I did the work well, I was given responsibility for important work, but I could not get an appointment to a higher level position. Your uncle rescued me. He has helped many Academy graduates over the years, and many of them have risen to highly responsible offices. When something needs to be done they work together, and it gets done. Your uncle sees no need to help you here. He is going to let you take hold on your own without showing favoritism. You will do fine."

"Thank you, I understand."

"We will go up to the twelfth floor where you will be working, and I will introduce you there. They know that you are coming, and they expect that you will be signing in as Elena Marloff. Your uncle is confident that you are fully prepared and ready. They have security forms for you so they can get started on your security clearances. They have procedure manuals for you to bury yourself in. It will go on like that for a few weeks, but you will keep your sanity because you know that it will end, and besides, you will all the while be thinking of Pyotr coming for weekends, and that way you will survive. And, of course, you will be thinking about your future."

The same morning Pyotr and Alex also had papers to sign and learned that in a few weeks they should be granted high level security clearances. After that they would join a small group of space engineers working on satellite navigation. They were told that in the adjoining building, on the third floor, down the hall to the right of the elevator, desks with computers were waiting for them. Also waiting were a pile of manuals describing GLONASS, the Russian satellite navigation system. Their first assignment was to study GLONASS satellite electronics and the day by day operation of the system.

The same week Veronika reported to the Ministry of Agriculture and Food. If Elena's uncle had arranged to put her in Agriculture and Food, fine. She had developed more and more doubts about whether she was cut out for foreign travel and what she thought were the give and take troublesome parts of diplomacy. She had her undergraduate with honors degree in economics, the Academy strengthened her understanding of foreign trade, and she was well satisfied with her assignment to a ministry with enormous influence on Russia, its people, and many millions far beyond Russia's borders. Let the other Academy graduates who didn't go into the foreign service dive into the volatile fortunes of the oil and gas industry, the coal industry, the automobile and truck industry. Agriculture was not glamorous like atomic energy, it was not prestigious like banking, but agricultural production, and foreign trade in agricultural products, were vital to every part of Russia. Food and fiber production, processing, distribution, and payments always had been the bedrock of Russia's economy, like every other economy in the history of the world, and always would be. Where she was, she told herself, was a good place for a fledgling economist to start a career.

After a week of orientation and reassuring herself that she really was in the right job, Veronika had a telephone chat with Elena. They talked about Alex and Pyotr working together, living together, and sharing the rent. Also, about women presenting themselves as professionals, and they set a date for the four of them to get together. Afterwards Veronika shopped for two outfits for the office.

Elena soon knew that a diplomatic career fit her. She made friends with the staff. The staff gave her classified work. Interesting work. She discussed her work with the staff. She soon received higher level security clearances, was assigned more complex work, and started to work on her own, and with her pen make decisions on her own.

She shifted money and support positions allocated to this North Africa consulate to another African consulate. She signed her name and approved money for contracts to make building repairs at this consulate and denied additional funds for others. Her decisions could have been rejected or appealed, but weren't. Some of her decisions were confirming, or rejecting, the work of others at posts far away dealing firsthand with political instability, sometimes violence. She realized that with her pen she was changing people's lives. Some company far away will have its contract renewed, some company's contract will not continue. Employees will have to look for other jobs. At the embassy some staffers will get a one step promotion, others would be told to retire early. A complicated and troubling world unfurled before her and the power of her pen.

She felt herself changing as she wrapped herself in her increasingly important classified work for untold hours. She found an uncertain balance between always fitting in and sometimes remaining a step apart. She told herself that more than anything else she wanted a career as a diplomat, not a senior staffer, a career as a diplomat like Uncle Lev, a career with all the authority, the responsibility, and the soul searching that came with it.

Sonia called Elena exactly five months after she reported for work.

"Congratulations, you are now on permanent status."

"Thank you. I thought it would be after six months."

"There is a higher level project the staff wants you to get into, and they decided you should be moved to permanent status a month early. You will handle it, and you will receive a one step pay raise."

"I appreciate that."

"Your uncle also wants to congratulate you, and we are going to his office at three. I will come for you at two-thirty."

Sonia showed her pass to the elevator operator, and a minute later they stepped off onto the twenty-sixth floor reception area. She saw the red carpet and a guard dressed in a jacket and tie. She also saw a bouquet of flowers in a porcelain vase. All, she recognized, a message of power to all those who are privileged to pass into this world of high authority.

An attractive older woman smiled and asked Elena to sign the guest register. A few minutes later she answered the phone and nodded to Sonia who led the way down the hall filled with elaborately framed paintings of Russian royalty and ambassadors dressed in the formal attire of a past age. They stopped in front of a partly opened door and Elena heard her uncle cheerfully call, "Come in! Both of you, come in!"

The office was, as Elena expected, elegantly furnished. At one end near the mahogany desk a Persian carpet. On the desk two phones, one black, one red. At the other end arm chairs around a walnut table. Along the walls portraits of Pyotr the Great and Vladimir Lenin, and a bookcase filled with volumes of diplomatic affairs.

Uncle Marloff in his white shirt and striped tie thanked Sonia for bringing Elena upstairs. She smiled and said she would wait for her in the reception area. When the door closed he gave Elena a long hug, a kiss on the cheek, and motioned her to a chair by the table. He sat across from her and began cheerfully, "Has Sonia been looking after you like a good Russian mother hen?"

"I was never aware of anything like that."

"I suppose she told you that I did not interfere."

"The first day she told me you wouldn't."

"I didn't, but from time to time she had a chat with the staff and reported how well you were doing."

"I didn't know. Of course, with the way they piled the work on, I suspected."

"No matter how much, and what kind of work they gave you, she always reported that you were doing well in every way." He continued with a broad smile, "With your truly dedicated work I take it that you have decided to stay on. You have decided to join the family line and make the foreign service a career even though you know a little about the deadlines, sometimes frustrating people, sometimes midnight hours, and years away in strange places."

"My dear uncle, I have been looking forward to this for years. I have been looking forward to this ever since you started coming to the house to tell me about your travels and bring me little gifts. Do you remember that cotton dress you brought me from Egypt? I still have it."

"Certainly, and we talked about Egyptian cotton goods coming to Russia."

"And I remember that."

"So now," he continued with a more somber tone, "we need to talk about what you should do next. There is important work here at headquarters, and there is a world of interesting, engaging, and very important work outside. Our enthusiastic young people all want to go traveling. Right off, they want to see the whole world, thoroughly enjoy every bit of it, and do it all at government expense. Sonia told you."

"She did."

"They want to see the world, do great things for the world, for Russia and for humanity, and improve their careers. They soon learn that no matter how far away they are from Moscow, the important decisions are not made by the ambassadors around the world. Those decisions are hammered out here by our small group of senior staff officers. The offices you passed coming down the hall, they are the men and women I am talking about. We all believe in protecting Mother Russia from her historic enemies. We have all had many posts outside Russia. When we were young finding out about the world we could find young diplomats we could love beyond Russia, and we could make a sacred vow with him, or her, never to have another war. Yet wars came. Small wars, great wars."

"I think I understand."

"When you are older, and have lived much of your life outside Russia, you will understand in a way you can't now. Now you have to prove yourself before you can go traveling. Wherever you go you need to know the country's language, culture and history.

You need to know the country's treaties and agreements, how they treated them. An honored compact or a scrap of paper? You need to know the economy, politics, the army's role, all of that. That's why you needed the language, history, and culture programs you have been taking on top of the lower level work you have been doing. And, my dear Elena, from all reports doing very well."

"When I graduated from Pyotrsburg you called and invited me to lunch. You told me Pyotr and I had both been admitted to the Academy, and you told me not to get my heart set on Paris, London, or Washington. And then you ordered champagne and Napoleon cake."

"All to get ready for the Academy so that you could get ready to be here with me now. Sonia told you on your first day that I expected to post you to Seoul."

"She did. I have tried very hard to get ready."

"You tried and you succeeded well and quickly. Let's look at the larger area you will be getting into. There's China. China is a huge country with over a billion people, a huge economy, a military with nuclear weapons. Russia has a border along the Tumen River with both China and North Korea. The entire Korean Peninsula has only about 77 million people. North Korea has about twenty-five million, three million in Pyongyang. It has a small economy, but from a military standpoint it should not be underestimated. It has a substantial and well-equipped army. It also has an air force with Russian planes. The navy has surface ships and several modern submarines. It has an elaborate state of the art radar system all along its east coast. It may have short range and long range nuclear weapons that it can roll right up to the Chinese border and right up to the Tumen River Russian border. And it has volatile leaders in Pyongyang. They do not deny that they want to be able to fire nuclear tipped missiles from their mobile ground launchers and from their submarines. And so North Korea must be dealt with very carefully. South Korea has twice the population, about 50 million, with the same language, and the same historic culture. With Seoul at the center of everything it has a big high tech economy and a modern army, but it has no nuclear weapons. At least none that we know of. To stay separate from the North it must stay under the protection of the United States, Russia, and China."

"Strange bedfellows?"

"We have to work closely together to discourage the leaders in Pyongyang from provoking another civil war with Seoul."

"What do you think is going to happen between the North and the South?"

"Korea is a peninsula, so it is natural that it be one country. The Korean peninsula has been one country with one language and one culture for a thousand years, and while the wheel of history sometimes turns slowly, eventually the Korean peninsula will be reunited under one government. For centuries Korea has been invaded and dominated by China and more recently by Japan. The fifty years of brutal Japanese occupation is still fresh in the memory of both the North and South. The leaders of both the South and North know there will come a time when the North and South will need each other more than they need to look to outsiders to stay separate. Now there is forced separation along the demilitarized zone, and it seems likely to continue for years, perhaps even for decades, but historically, economically, and geographically, there is no good reason for the present separation, and in time North and South will reunite. By diplomacy, or by force, they will reunite. They will deal with China as a united country with nuclear weapons. It will be, as the Marxists used to say, the verdict of history."

"A temporary verdict? China has always dominated Korea. Will it intervene again?"

"Yes, eventually, China will invade, conquer and subjugate, history shows that, but not now. China has a significant Korean population. It doesn't want to stir up a problem with them. Every year China buys enormous tonnage of high quality North Korean coal in violation of United Nations sanctions imposed because of its nuclear program. China piles up cash reserves in case it must switch to more expensive distant suppliers such as Australia. China is satisfied to buy that coal at an affordable price from North Korea, and that revenue is a large part of the North Korean national income. Profitable exports, including steel, refined petroleum products, ferroalloys, electricity, cars, and vaccines, pay for imports, for everything new and modern around the country. Profitable foreign trade is the main reason for Pyongyang's high rise hotels and fine apartments, expensive cars, and fine restaurants for its small elite. For now, no one in Moscow, Beijing, or Pyongyang wants to be seriously concerned about China burning the coal that we are told is causing global warming."

"And Japan? No longer a threat to Korea?"

"Japan is becoming a land of older people doing well supplying the world with high end computer chips, automobiles, machine tools, and much more. Its skilled workers produce profitable exports while looking forward to retirement and living quiet lives on modest pensions. Japan can become an atomic power very quickly, in a long weekend the saying goes, and it has a small well equipped military. Military adventurism now would not mean a repeat of its World War II easy Asian conquests. It would mean the loss of its overseas markets for automobiles, electronics, and iron and steel, and with that loss massive unemployment. Also, Japan cannot defend its high technology factories against devastating missile strikes from afar. With China's formidable military looking for excuses to dominate all of Asia this is not a propitious time for Japan to take the initiative and intervene militarily anywhere in Asia. Instead, it will quietly produce its own atomic weapons and protect what it considers its core interests."

"What about North Korea becoming an atomic power? It probably can do that soon, it has set off explosions underground, but can it show it has an accurate missile to deliver an atomic warhead?"

"Very troubling. When that happens we will still want to trade with both North Korea and South Korea as friendly neighbors. Time does not stand still, and we will do what we can."

"Such as?"

"Russia has been close to Korea for well over a century. We have a certain amount of economic and military influence in the North Pacific area. Fokino, a few kilometers from Vladivostok, is the headquarters of the Pacific fleet. We also have Uglovoye airbase, also a few kilometers from Vladivostok. Vladivostok is only a couple of hours by air from Pyongyang and Seoul. We want better ties with their export industries. In South Korea there is STX in container ships and oil tankers, Hyundai in automobiles, Samsung in electronics and armaments. You have a lot to do in Seoul."

"I will do everything I can."

"And you will have a lot to do beyond Seoul. You know better than to expect that you will start off doing hands on diplomacy. You may be able to participate in a secondary role for months. Instead of doing chores inside the embassy you will become familiar with all our Southeast Asia trade promotion operations. You will visit our embassies and consulates in Singapore, Indonesia, Myanmar, Vietnam, Laos, and Australia. A week or so in each one. You will go to Vladivostok for trade conferences. Wherever you are you will have your cell phone and your credit card. You go to the restaurants and hotels diplomats go to. If you are with a friend, man or woman, and something bad happens you use your phone, you call for an ambulance, and you go to the hospital. If there is any question about paying you give you credit card. The next day you check on your friend. If it is serious, you visit him or her."

"About the friend? A man friend? A woman friend? That's a true story?"

"It happened over the years, men and women, several times. Twisted ankles, banged heads, broken fingers. For an old colleague, sadly, a heart attack. For your young and old friends, these things happen. They happen. You look after your friends, men and women, you keep in touch, and they look after you."

"I understand."

"Elena, you're too young to understand what that means. One of our senior men down the hall is thinking about retiring. When he was twenty-eight, he was posted to Paris. He fell in love with a lovely young Polish diplomat. They had an affair. They had wonderful jobs with good pay, he at the Russian embassy, she at the Polish embassy. They were tasting the sweets of Paris and the spice of Paris. Museums, art galleries, concerts, theater, risqué shows, good food and drink, good hotels. Outside Paris they went to Versailles, the Loire Valley, Rouen. Troyes, Bourgogne. They got to the point where they were thinking they would get married. She would change her citizenship from Polish to Russian. He wanted her, and she wanted him more than keeping her diplomat career. She told her parents she was serious about him. Her father was important in the Polish foreign service. He did not want a Russian diplomat in his Catholic Polish family. Neither did her mother. They wanted her to keep her diplomat job and marry a proper Catholic Pole. Her father had her yanked from sinful Paris and posted to more devout Catholic Rome… Life went on. They found other sweethearts. They married them. Life, and diplomacy careers, went on… Love, and memory, went on, too.

In a few years they were both in responsible positions where they could make their arrangements. They were together in Vienna, in London, and other major capitals. And between there were long visits… All part of roving diplomats' lives serving their countries."

They shared a long silence before Elena said softly, "You were in Paris when you were young."

"Elena, I have lived a full life. A roving Russian diplomat's life serving my country. She has lived a full life. A roving Polish diplomat's life serving her country. It could have been different. It could have been, but we soon learned life isn't always what we want it to be, and we must find our way."

"And Sonia?"

"Sonia and I have been together for many years. We haven't married because I cannot have her as my wife and have her work under me. I need her here with me, and she does not want to be put out under someone else. It could have been different, but she accepts what my life has been, I accept what her life has been, and it has worked well for us."

"Then, my dear uncle, I am so very happy for both of you."

"Thank you, Elena. I will tell her, and she will sincerely appreciate it. And she deserves it." After a silence he went on, "It will be another few months before you are posted to Seoul. Now you and Pyotr are together, then you will be separated, and you will have to work it out for yourselves what you do."

"Yes, we know it."

"We need to go on to more immediate and practical matters. You are going to have a session on professional responsibility, financial rules, security requirements, and quite important, personal relations. You are going to get some practical advice from a lady who deals with our people in the real world where people are fallible. They are good people who fail in different ways. They fail for themselves, and they fail for us. They become dangerous to themselves, and dangerous to us. This program was started some years ago when several of our people abroad found themselves in serious difficulty because they became involved with prostitutes who took their money, and also took money from others interested in blackmailing their clients. There were dismissals from the foreign service, and there was a suicide. Consider the session as an important part of your training. Maria Klishina will lead the discussion. There will be ten of you. You will get a notice."

"Can I raise a difficult issue?'

"What is it?"

"At the Academy we learned about Stalin's purges in the 1930's. He didn't trust the generals, the admirals, the civil servants, the diplomats. He got rid of many of them in terrible ways. He replaced them wholesale with incompetent people who were subservient to him."

"Elena, it was a terrible time for the whole country. For the miliary he got rid of most of the generals and all of the admirals. Evey last one."

"When the Germans invaded Russia in 1941, Russia, and the Russian people, paid the price."

"And you are asking what a patriotic Russian diplomat does if he, or she, must be an advocate for the government in such circumstances."

"Yes, It's troubling. You could be strongly opposed to what you are told to do, what you think is right."

"What do you do? You're asking a good question. It's not an easy answer. It's not black and white. You can resign. If you resign will someone much more in line take your place?"

"Probably."

"Elena, you remember the little talks we had at my house when you asked all sorts of questions. You were about 12, and you already read the encyclopedia, and played Bach and Schubert, and were taking ballet lessons. You said I should have been an ambassador instead of a diplomat. I told you that ambassadors are told what to say, and to do, and they run an embassy and use their influence following those orders. I said that a diplomat can have more freedom of action, and a diplomat at times may be able to help people who are in trouble because of what their government is doing to them. I told you I preferred being a diplomat. So, to answer your question, what should you do, I can only tell you that if we should have such a regime again it would be wise to resign."

Maria Klishina, a tall thin woman with glasses, wrinkles, and streaks of graying hair, looked over the eight young men and two young women sitting around the table. She introduced herself and told them with a smile that whatever warnings they may have heard about this part of their training, as far as she knew, no one had ever suffered any lasting damage from her talks about handling government money, official secrets, real sex in the real world, and saving a career by carefully searching for hidden miniature microphones and miniature cameras. Some, she added, had even told her confidentially that they had followed her advice, and they found it helpful.

"You all know each other from the Academy. You all understand you are part of a select team, and you want to be working diplomats for your country. You dream of being part of a team negotiating a treaty with diplomats of other great powers. You don't think about balancing embassy bank accounts that are going to be audited someday. You certainly don't think about being personally accountable for missing and misused embassy money. You don't think of being separated from a wife, husband, or partner. You should, you must, if you are ever to be part of a negotiating team at a table facing capable diplomats on the other side.

"You don't think about reporting security violations by acquaintances and dear friends, and on the personal side, engaging in casual sexual affairs when you have been away from your wife, husband, or partner for a year. Now we are going to think about all that."

She launched into the intricacies of dealing with embassy and consular bank accounts, continued with proper use, and misuse, of personal expense accounts, creating and keeping accurate detailed records, and ended the morning session with registry: obtaining permission to ask for registry files, signing out classified documents, using them only for the purpose permitted, keeping them in a secure place, and returning them on time in the same condition as they were checked out.

In the afternoon she started on marital difficulties arising out of husband, wife, and partner separations. It was, she said, one of the most continuing and most troubling problems for the military and also for the foreign service. It always has been, she said, is now, and as long as there are separated soldiers and separated diplomats, always will be.

"For those in the services who go off to distant lands, one long overseas posting after another, being separated from a wife, husband, or partner can be very difficult. It has always been that way. They go off and they become terribly lonely, and they want, they crave, companionship, satisfying sexual satisfaction, and it is all too easy for them to forget that those they left behind in big cities and small towns holding down jobs and caring for families are also terribly lonely, that they also crave companionship and satisfying sexual intimacy.

"We know that for both men and women, it is a normal part of being physically and psychologically normal, normal for those that go away, and just as normal for those left behind. It is normal for all of us, and it is normal that this natural desire for satisfying companionship and sexual intimacy continues over the years of service. With understanding, with acceptance, all can go well, but too often all does not go well. I have seen marriages come apart with terrible bitterness and careers destroyed. My experience tells me that for every one of you, it may not go well. Not for you, not for your wife, husband, or partner."

She paused, looked at the pained faces around the table, and continued, "So we need to think about the kinds of sexual affairs, and we need to get personal. We need to think about an affair by you when you are away for a year, or more, before you come back on leave, and an affair by the one you left behind alone. Listening to this isn't easy. All of you, every one of you, should be thinking I am normal, physically and psychologically healthy and normal, and I could end up in an affair. And when I am gone, when I am far away, could my good wife, or faithful husband, or dearest partner, get into a sexual affair?

"And so, you should ask, in an affair what could go wrong and ruin my career and my life? That is what we are all going to think about together, think about openly and honestly together. I am going to share with you some of what I have found to be helpful.

"Let's start. Usually, the affair is prompted by the man, the husband posted far away. Often the woman he wants is younger and involved with his work at a lower level. Senior diplomats and their younger assistants, other executives and their younger secretaries. There are little meaningful smiles. There are little gifts and nice restaurant dinners. There are thank you hugs and kisses. The sex starts. It goes on, it seems well for a year. He is sexually and psychologically invigorated. He boasts to her about how important his work is. Some of it is confidential, even very secret. She tells him much she loves him. He tells her he loves her, and he tells her more about his very important secret work. He blissfully assures himself that back in Moscow, or St. Pyotrsburg, or Sochi, or Novosibirsk, all is going well for his wife and children. Then, inevitably, the time comes when he is posted to another embassy or consulate. He must leave her. He tells her, he tries to break it gently, he doesn't want to go elsewhere but he has orders to leave at the end of the month. And he gets a shock. His new love, instead of thanking him for all he has meant to her, wants him to get a divorce and marry her. He tells her he is sorry, he can't. She insists. He tells her she must be reasonable for her own sake. She says she will tell his wife. He says he is sorry, but he has orders and what she demands is impossible. She writes to his wife about his bragging, his promises, real or imagined, and much more. Sometimes there are also pictures. The wife is bitter. Angry. She takes revenge. She goes to the authorities and says she is a loyal patriot, and so she must report that her husband has been telling vital secrets to his embassy mistress. She says she has proof that her deceiving husband is a dangerous lawbreaking scoundrel who must pay for his perfidious actions. She says she suffered a nervous breakdown. Her lawyer assures her she will get a quick divorce, child support, and half his pension.

"When you lose your marriage and half your worked-for promised pension you never make it up. You look hopefully for another marriage, a good marriage, and you find that every woman or man you want, always wants a loyal husband or wife with a good pension. Men with good sense think that way, women with good sense think that way.

"You are too early in your careers to be thinking of pensions. Now it is all about that first posting, and after that your first negotiation. When you are older, and your career is everything, if you have good sense, you will think a good deal about your pension. You all have good sense, that's why you are at our table. Keep your good sense about marriage and pensions until you retire and start drawing your pension. And whatever you do, don't be stupid and lose it after that.

"As bad as that is, too often it is much worse. His new love tells him she is pregnant with his child. Her contraceptive pills didn't work. He gently suggests an abortion. She refuses. She is adamant. He must choose between her and his unborn child and his wife and family. He tells her he must obey his orders to leave. She goes to the local authorities, and he is served with a court order not to leave the country without establishing an approved child support account with the country's Department of Family Welfare. If he cannot adequately fund the support account directly, or through an approved corporate bond, he is likely to be told to resign from the foreign service. The financial complications after that are endless. The personal complications after that are also very painful and endless.

"It doesn't have to be a letter with pictures to his wife from his mistress. One way or another, the wife finds out, and one way or another the marriage is wrecked, the career is ruined, and their marriage and lives are ruined.

"And something else that is very important, when there are children, young children, older more understanding children, they feel the pain, too. And it stays with them in their minds, and in their hearts, until they die."

Maria Klishina paused again. "It doesn't have to be that way, and it doesn't have to end that way. Overall, the couples having affairs that do best during the affair, and do best at the end, are both executives in the same embassy or consulate. So, executive Russian men with executive Russian women about the same age. German executive men with German executive women about the same age. Japanese executive men with Japanese executive women about the same age.

"Other couples having affairs do well when they are both from countries with similar histories and cultures. Danish executive men and Swedish executive women about the same age. English executive women and American executive men. Usually, the men are a little older, and a step or two higher in their careers. When the affair ends, permanently or temporarily, the couples in these better situations for the most part go their separate ways. They continue to do their good diplomatic work, often in different posts, and they successfully continue with their marriages. They continue, but for the family it is never quite the same.

"There are more very short sexual encounters than sexual affairs. There is the married embassy executive and his single somewhat younger admiring assistant. After a couple of years working closely together he is leaving for another post. He invites her to a farewell dinner. They will use his car. She thinks she knows why, but she smiles and agrees. They have cocktails, fine food, and marvelous wine. He picks up the check, takes her hand, and asks her if she has to go home tonight. She squeezes his hand. They go to a good hotel across town or the next town. Whether you are the executive, or the devoted assistant, you act in accordance with what your head and your emotions tell you to do. It is a night you will want to always happily remember. You do not even consider reporting.

"Many short flirtations and brief affairs in embassies and consulates end in heartbreak and bitterness without a divorce. During your posting you may have one of our older ladies complain to you about how her husband had an affair with that no good scheming woman in accounting, and that something should be done about it for the good of the service. Meaning that you should do something about it for the good of the service so that she can get even with him. Teach him a lesson, and ruin that vixen in accounting. When you have staff that you supervise you must listen to such complaints, but unless you sense a security risk, you don't have to get yourself involved. If the security threat seems at all real, you must report it. No exceptions. Nothing may be seriously wrong, a long career may be ruined, but you must report it. Two long careers may be ruined, but you must report it. If you don't your career may be ruined. On the other side, if you report everything that looks at all amiss it will soon get known, and you will find no one will talk to you.

"As I expected, I see you are all hanging your heads and looking discouraged. In practice it may not be that bad. We will take a break."

When everyone was back at the table Marina continued. "Now more specific direct advice. If you are married you need to talk with your wife or husband about how you are expected to behave during long separations. You can blame me for bringing the subject up but have an honest frank talk. You probably will need more than one. That is easy for me to say, easy advice for me to give, but it will be very hard for you to do. Whether you decide you want an agreement, whether you both reach an arrangement, that is up to both of you. Whether you both abide by that arrangement for a few months, or for many years, that is also up to both of you. I have the same advice for devoted long term partners.

"A word about prostitutes and the danger of using prostitutes. Prostitutes, women and men, all over the world are likely the biggest cause of security risk for diplomats. If you get involved with a prostitute you become vulnerable to blackmail, you become a security risk, and when it becomes known you may be dismissed from the service. Yet there has always been discretion in what has been reported, and there is still discretion about what you should report. It is accepted that married and single senior men diplomats, and senior women diplomats, may have open social relationships, and discreet sexual relationships, with respected men and women. It has always been that way for kings, nobles, high religious leaders, high generals, and senior diplomats.

"There is also a lighter side to being a successful diplomat. At the Academy you read in many books for many hours about the old history and present culture of many countries. You learned that Titian, Raphael, Veronese, and Bellini were all Italian painters, that the Concertgebouw is the symphony orchestra in Amsterdam, and that the National Gallery of Art in Washington rivals the Hermitage and Louvre in Paris. Now you should start going to orchestra concerts and museum exhibits in addition to popular entertainments. You should make time to do both. To become a fully respected diplomat you must embrace the humanities. Classical music, art, dance, literature. When you are in Italy go to the Uffizi gallery in Florence and see the Birth of Venus. The famous nude was painted in 1484 by Sandro Botticelli at the beginning of the Renaissance. Go see the Leonardo Vitruvian man in the Academia in Venice. When in London go to the faithfully restored old Globe for Shakespeare and the Barbican for twentieth century comedy and tragedy. That doesn't mean you can't ever take a quick look at the red light district in Amsterdam and Frankfurt, or Shanghai, Singapore, and Seoul.

"Come back at nine tomorrow. We will continue with a discussion on contraception, protection from venereal diseases, concern for hidden microphones, miniature cameras and recorders, and how to protect yourself from these nasty electronics. We will talk about how, when, and where to search for tiny hidden microphones, miniature recorders, cameras in hotel bedrooms and dining rooms, fancy yachts, expensive automobiles, and in the clothes of people who romance you and insist you can trust them to keep your relationship forever just for the two of you. There is a rule for dealing with someone who is new to you. It doesn't matter how much you really like him or adore her. You never trust him. You never trust her. Never. Always protect yourself and protect the country. We will go more into all that tomorrow. Now go find your sweethearts and friends and enjoy yourself until tomorrow."

In the morning there were no smiles around the table and Maria again began somberly.

"At the end yesterday I told you we will deal with venereal disease, transmission and protection, and I urged you to protect yourself, and protect the foreign service, from nasty miniature electronic devices. Protect yourself from the tiny recorder in the lining of the fine pants or hem of the pretty skirt your very nice new friend is wearing. According to the security manual, you must have him, or her, take off all of his, or her, clothes for you to carefully inspect. Not rummage through in a few minutes, but carefully examine inch by inch by firmly pressing on every flap and seam. You must minutely inspect not just the fly, shoulders, belt line, and cuffs. Coats and jackets, you must insist, go into another room with the door closed. Hats, shoes, and frilly underwear will have to go into a tightly closed dresser drawer. Pictures and mirrors on the wall have to be taken down so you can see if anything is under them. Ask yourself what could be hidden in the ceiling heating or air conditioning vents. If your new friend makes excuses, says that time is short, you are being too careful, it will take too long to take the place apart and put it back together, what do you do? Don't ask questions, don't argue, don't say goodbye. Just pick up your purse or wallet, put on your hat and coat, walk away, and never come back.

"The security manual says that if you get yourself in such a situation you need to report it. You won't. It is too embarrassing. If you do security will want to know in excruciating detail everything else that has ever happened in your personal life. No matter what the security manual says, there is always discretion. Unless thinking back there really was a security risk, you use your discretion.

"So, I have been talking about discretion. That is another way of saying mature good judgment, and it applies to everything you will do for the foreign service, and for yourself. I cannot teach good judgment. No one can. It is in you. Use it wisely. Don't risk your career for some misguided affair. Never hide what you think could be a real security risk.

You have been looking around our table at each other and making friends. Some of you may already be good friends. You understand we are at our table together because you are a select corps expected to give your lives to years of faithful service, and by doing so earn exceptional careers serving your country. Some of you as ambassadors, most of you as negotiating diplomats.

"I look forward to seeing every one of you become Russian ambassadors and diplomats. I look forward to seeing every one of you become honorable and honored Russian ambassadors and diplomats."

CHAPTER 8

After her year of diligent study focused on the Korean peninsula and Southeast Asia Elena showed that she had become sufficiently knowledgeable about the governments, economies, and cultures of the area and particularly South Korea and North Korea. She also demonstrated that she was acceptably fluent in contemporary written and spoken Korean. Sufficiently knowledgeable also about anything and everything in contemporary Korea to be posted to the Seoul embassy to work under the close supervision of Ambassador Ivan Kandinsky and his knowledgeable executive staff. Her close relationship to her distinguished uncle came with her.

With the help of the embassy staff she found an apartment in a good area of the sprawling city of nine million bustling people crowded together on a small fraction of Moscow's land area. She quickly learned about the expensive best food markets, the modern and very well stocked expensive shops, the excellent and expensive restaurants, and the parts of the city best to stay far away from. In a few months of concentrated effort on embassy work, and warming personal relations, she was accepted as part of the embassy executive staff.

She soon learned from Ambassador Kandinsky and the embassy files everything of importance the embassy was doing, including Russian trade promotion. That included, as Uncle Lev had told her, the executive staff trying to ingratiate themselves into the management offices of Hyundai, Samsung, and the other giants of South Korean industry.

In a few short months, where others had failed to reach the closely guarded executive offices, she succeeded. With smiles and light flattery she explained to industry officers that her efforts were for the mutual benefit of all enterprising South Korean firms wanting to do more business in Russia, and Russian companies wanting their business.

Elena managed an invitation to the reception for the newly appointed chief operating officer of one of the major electronic firms. After considering several outfits she dressed in a fashion she thought appropriate for a Moscow woman executive although, she realized, slightly provocative for a young Russian woman not wearing a wedding ring when smiling and mixing with highly respected executive Korean men.

She was in a company penthouse with middle aged men waiting for the new CEO to join them and present the company's promotion, production, and financial goals for the next year. All smiles, light banter, polite nervous laughter. Liquor and delicacies were passed on silver trays by young women dressed in 18th century Korean servant fashion.

The big man was announced. As he stepped through the door everyone in the room froze. The men looked down and bowed, the serving women with their trays held in front of them bowed even lower. No one moved, no one spoke as he walked to the front of the room. By tradition the royal personage may not be approached by anyone without permission. It is to maintain his dignity and protect him against any verbal indiscretion or physical harm. Tradition for everyone there except Elena. As soon as he ended his talk she stepped forward, introduced herself, offered to shake his hand, which with a smile and slight laughter, he did. They talked for a few minutes while the rest of the amazed guests stood still and watched. He thanked her for her good wishes, and then, showing that he knew Western ways, kissed her on the cheek and told her how much he admired her uncle. She smiled and thanked him for the compliment, and with that he waved to the welcoming committee and the party began.

After that Elena had smiling friends in other major company executive offices, and continuing to charm and dress by Moscow standards, she professionally promoted the trusted products and very reliable services of major Russian companies. Contracts purchasing Russian products and services were made. Contracts selling South Korean products and services to Russian firms were secured. Success led to success. She was escorted through giant shipyards, huge factories, small factories, all the makings of a country thriving by its profitable exports to Western markets. She was realistic, she knew that in good part her trade promotion efforts were successful because her uncle was His Excellency, Lev Marloff, who put in a helping word here and there. All for the good of Russian commerce and the foreign service. Still, the substantial contracts she successfully promoted worked for Russian companies and their Korean customers because as negotiated there were good values on both sides.

She devoted herself to her work with a will to succeed. To succeed for herself, for Uncle Lev, for her career. Ambassador Kandinsky recognized her ability, told her pleased uncle, and gave her increasing responsibilities. Through long hours she quickly grasped complex issues, sent precise reports to the ambassador, made quick decisions, and insisted that her orders to the staff be complied with.

The foreign diplomatic corps in Seoul had an organization, the Seoul Diplomats Club, that sponsored social gatherings at a hotel for its members, their guests, and invited Korean and other officials. There was always wine, liquor, and a buffet of light food. There was always music, usually couples dancing. There was always gossip and light flirting. The city, always seeking continuing good rapport with its foreign diplomats, always graciously picked up the tab.

Three months after taking up her post at the Seoul embassy Elena was invited to attend a SDC party at the thirty-story high penthouse of the Park Hyatt hotel. Rated Five Stars, with prices to match. Renowned elegant restaurants and small well stocked wood paneled bars. Knowledgeable and sophisticated concierge all day and all night. Deluxe rooms and suites feature spectacular night views from floor to ceiling windows. Amenities include workstation with worldwide communications, widescreen multi program television, bathroom with double deep soaking bathtubs, and rainfall showers. And, of course, fine robes and slippers.

Elena dressed fashionably. Soon after she arrived a few older women let her know that they had good contacts with officials in the South Korean government, and other governments, too, and they would happily share their good fortune with her. They also suggested that she could reciprocate. Elena smiled and nodded her understanding and agreement. Middle aged men took her hand, smiled, and told her she looked lovely and told her that if in any way they could be helpful with officials, or anyway otherwise, they would be most happy to do so. They added that she should never feel any obligation to reciprocate. Elena smiled and nodded her agreement.

There was only one man there she was attracted to. It was Rolf Ericsson. He was from the Swedish embassy, good looking in a chiseled Nordic way, and six years older. Like her, he was not wearing a wedding ring.

Rolf came over to Elena's table to get acquainted, chatted with her in good Russian with a Swedish accent. He was, he explained, like her, a junior diplomat and trade promotion officer. He fetched white wine, they talked, and he asked her to dance. They danced comfortably together. Not too close, not far apart. They came back to the table, slowly drank the wine and talked about their work, and then a little about their lives. The band played another ballad and couples danced. They didn't hear the music. They didn't notice the dancers. They were alone as they talked and slowly drank the white wine. They both knew they would meet again. It would be at a little out of the way restaurant where they would drink some white wine and talk about Russia and Sweden, about Moscow and Stockholm, about life in Seoul and Pyongyang, about anything and everything, and then more deeply about themselves. There would be a telephone call, it would be answered, there would be a conversation, and it would be arranged.

They met for lunch several times. Near her embassy, near his embassy, and with his car in the evening, further and further away. They talked about too crowded Seoul and getting along in the city with its newly minted millionaires and several billionaires living the good life with beautiful women in high rise elegant apartments, and a small but growing middle class. At later meetings Rolf showed his serious side, and they talked about the city's millions tethered to low paying factory jobs, and its half a million foreigners, many of them there illegally, barely surviving in the putrid slums. And they talked about the famous red light district with hundreds of young women serving thousands of well pleased residents and delighted tourists.

Their luncheon meetings became longer, more and more serious, and more personal. Elena asked Rolf if he knew about her Uncle Lev. He answered that he did. She told him about her family history of Russian diplomats, and he told her his extended family also had a history of diplomats, Swedish diplomats. She told him she had a degree from St. Pyotrsburg State University - history, economics, and languages. He told her he had a degree in economics from the Stockholm School of Economics, and his family, his uncle, had a tie to Finland, to the Ericsson electronics business in Helsinki. Not all that substantial, but in management. A significant tie. That seemed, he said, to have help him in his Sweden trade promotion work where a little more discount, and a little faster and cheaper delivery, can make the difference.

Soon there were long restaurant dinners and still more personal sharing. She liked the kind of books, movies, and music he liked. For the most part. Translation helped. For the most part he liked the kind of food, movies, books and music she liked. He didn't need translation. She told him she wondered what it would be like having an evening together, just relaxing, really relaxing and listening to music they both liked. He kissed her and answered it would be wonderful.

He told her more about his family. His father was a senior diplomat, his mother a classical musician, his two older sisters were both physicians. He told her that he had never been married, but that before being posted to Seoul he had a long romance with a girl in Stockholm. She was also in the Swedish foreign service, and when they were both posted out of Stockholm it ended. He also explained that he was a lieutenant in the Swedish navy reserve, and that when he was on active duty he wore his blue uniform with the royal crest and stripes on the selves.

She asked, did he have a photo? He did, a small one, and she asked him to give her a copy at their next meeting. He did with *For Elena RE* written with careful script on the back. She took it home and put it on a table where she would see Rolf in the morning and in the evening. At their next meeting she gave him a photo of herself with *For Rolf EM* written with careful script on the back. He put it in a box with his family photos. He looked at it on weekends, he didn't need to look at it every morning and every evening because Elena was always in his mind. She wasn't wearing a wedding ring. Had Elena had a romance that faded like his? Was she married and keeping her maiden name? Probably. Beautiful young women like Elena can have their pick of young handsome upcoming diplomats. They are pursued by the best and the brightest, and they are quickly caught. Talk to her about an affair? He couldn't bring himself to ask. The time to ask was coming, it would have to come, but not now, not yet.

Their meetings became open. They held hands and briefly kissed. Their friends noticed, and soon everyone in her embassy knew. For the ambassador, in their circle it was accepted. Nothing wrong. It wasn't his job to tell Lev Marloff.

With the help of a language program Elena started to learn Swedish. She started using a few Swedish phrases with him. With their first passionate embrace they stopped thinking about what they didn't both like and started thing about what their life together could be like. She thought about the name Mrs. Elena Ericksen. They both knew it was a romance that had to go beyond holding tight and kisses or end.

As Elena expected, Rolf asked to see her in the evening, and she let him come to her apartment. He brought wine, she put out cheese and crackers. She knew him, there was no need for anything fancy. They talked, they nibbled, and then she put on slow music and they danced. They talked, then danced again with Rolf holding her close against him. They nibbled, they sipped more wine. After another slow dance holding each other close, they shared a long tight embrace and goodnight kiss.

The next time, a week later, they again had wine, cheese, and crackers. No need for her to put out anything fancy. They drank the wine, they kissed, they danced very close. More wine, another kiss. Then another. Sitting on the couch next to her he gently pressed his left hand against her right breast and with his other hand around her shoulder drew her against him and asked her to go to bed with him. He told her he would be gentle, he was prepared, he would protect her. She kissed him, and then pulled back. She told him she was terribly fond of him, really, she was, she really was, but she couldn't do it. He was free... she wasn't. She didn't want to hurt him, she couldn't do it. She should have told him? If she had…? Could he understand? He bowed his head and said that he understood. When they said goodnight, they held each other close for a moment, but did not kiss.

After that in Seoul they were close friends who danced at SDC meetings at the Hyatt and met for long lunches at a café where they talked for a long time about everything except their lives. They were there to be with each other, even though it could never be the same again. World news, local news, shop talk, other romances, but not their own. The candle that had burned so brightly for both of them had been much dimmed, but it had not gone out. He told her that he was keeping her picture. She responded that she would keep his picture.

They both expected that they would be posted to Pyongyang in a few months, perhaps a little more for one, a little less for the other, and that they would want to see each other again. They were both diplomats, they had access to all the current embassy rosters, and once they were both there they would know. When they both had time to settle in there would be a telephone call, it would be answered, and it would be arranged. They would meet, they would talk, memories might find a way to speak, and the future would take care of itself.

Elena was back in Moscow at the end of her first year in Seoul. There was a week of personal leave, and two weeks of reports, briefings, and conferences. Who were moving up at the top of the South Korean government? Who was moving up in North Korea? And who were slipping? Where in the South and North were the best opportunities for Russian refined petroleum products, gas turbines, nitrogen fertilizer, timber.

There was time with Pyotr for one evening visit with Veronika and Alex, not nearly enough time to get beneath the surface of their lives, and not nearly enough time with Pyotr to make up for all the lost hours of being together and making love.

As for talking to her husband about a Maria Klishina open marriage arrangement, she thought about it, she thought seriously about what she could say. In the end how could she talk to her husband about her having an affair, about both of them having affairs? She couldn't.

Pyotr told Elena that he was satisfied working with Alex on space engineering projects instead of delving into the foreign service communication systems. Those worldwide systems were complex, they had special cryptology for different work and different conditions around the globe, but they were not at all comparable to what he and Alex were into. Some of it was classified, and it was all far too complicated to talk about. As for talking to her about a marriage arrangement for him, for her, how could he even suggest it? He couldn't.

For Pyotr there was another reason he couldn't talk about having an affair. The usual reason. It was Alyona Boyarskaya. She had been a Pyotrsburg university student with Pyotr, also near the top of their electrical engineering class. Nothing serious, just some mild flirting. At the university they had worked together several times on computer projects, and for the two years that he was at the Academy in Moscow she remained in Pyotrsburg to earn her advanced degree in mathematics. Now Alyona was part of the team of space engineers at the army base. Most of the time Alyona worked by herself on satellite maneuvers using Riemannian four-dimension geometry, but sometimes they were together. She told him with a smile that they were happily back together.

Alyona was different from Elena. Like Pyotr, she was born, raised, and educated in a small city far from Moscow. She had a scholarship to the Pyotrsburg university elite science program because a science teacher at her gymnasium recognized her ability and became her benefactor. Elena was beautiful, outgoing, always making new friends. Alyona was brilliant, somewhat pretty, and she lived comfortably within a small circle of close friends. For the satellite program she would work alone over a difficult maneuver problem for days, even weeks, before she produced her results. Whether they were used or not she knew that was the way for recognition and promotion. It was also the way to work again with the friendly fellow she had smiled at back in Pyotrsburg, who always smiled back, but it seemed was not interested in more. At least not then.

Elena could not have been a success as an engineer, and Alyona could not have been a success as a diplomat. What they had in common was high intelligence, a passion for excellence combined with a high sense of self-worth. For Alyona it drew to her a certain type of highly intellectual introspective young man like Pyotr. She was not much interested in most of them, and she showed it. Her romances didn't progress beyond good night tight embraces and long kisses.

With Pyotr she showed an interest and with Elena away he responded to her advances. Pyotr wore his wedding ring and told Alyona his wife was in the foreign service, at an embassy in Seoul, South Korea, but more and more she allowed herself to show him her warm personal and sexual side. She could hardly believe she was doing it, but still, more and more, she did.

After several months Pyotr and Alyona were intimate, and they acknowledged that they wanted, and needed, each other for more than the sex itself. Alyona wanted more than the shivering thrill of a sexual romance. She wanted love, true sincere love, and with that deep craving she gave herself sexually to Pyotr and soon bound him to her.

Alex left the apartment he shared with Pyotr so Pyotr and Alyona could have it to themselves. For both of them it was living a working dream during the day, and a heady dream at night in bed. As they cuddled together and their emotions responded she whispered in his ear that they were dancing among the stars and flying around the Moon. He answered that they were cavorting in space, and he was bringing the wine and roses for them to enjoy and to share. And considering the secret space work they were both doing during the day there was a measure of truth to what they lovingly told each other at night while making passionate love. For both of them, with their continuing rapture, part of reality lost meaning. Elena was far away, she was time zones away, they were both important to the space program, and at work they were always discreet. The practical army knew they were not the only couple at the base living like them. There were several. Why disturb their important work, why interfere with any of them.

When Elena came to Moscow on leave after her year in Seoul they separated. Alyona left the apartment the same day Pyotr told her Elena was coming back on a three week leave. She took with her everything she had brought. Clothes, toiletries, photographs, records, laptop computer, paper clips.

Three weeks later when Elena left Moscow again Alyona insisted that Pyotr had to choose, agree to a divorce and marry her, or she would not come back, she would never come back. For her there was nothing to talk about, any other way was out of the question.

He told her that she was right to ask for what she wanted, she was right to insist he had to answer, but he was not able to give her the answer she wanted. He told her he really cared for her but he couldn't divorce his wife and marry her.

The next day Alyona asked for a transfer to another base several hundred kilometers away that was also doing space work. There would be no loss to the unfinished work she was doing, she could continue it there. The army was practical, her mathematics work was not tied to any particular base. She was reassigned to the new position at the end of the month.

For Pyotr it was bittersweet, sadness mixed with relief. He missed Alyona. He missed her coming home with him after work, shopping for food together, and fixing dinner. He missed cleaning up with her after dinner. He missed her alone in the evening. He missed her getting in bed at night. He missed her in bed whispering in his ear. He missed the sex she gave him. He missed her waking up and getting out of bed in the morning. He missed Alyona but, thankfully, there was no need to confess anything to Elena.

Pyotr asked Alex to return to the apartment, but Alex told him it was better that he didn't. For Alex there was no need to tell Veronika she had been right about Pyotr and Alyona all along.

CHAPTER 9

A week before the end of her leave in Moscow Uncle Lev called Elena and asked her to come visit him in his office. Walking down the hall of portraits she was thinking that she had been away from Pyotr for a year, she had to get ready for what could be a difficult year, most probably in Pyongyang, and it would be another year away from Pyotr. Uncle Lev wanted her to come visit, she thought, to wish her well, explain who she would be working under, about trade promotion, but she wondered what else he would tell her about her work in that land bordering Russia boasting about developing atomic bombs and intercontinental rockets.

Uncle Lev was in a somber mood. He began by telling her she had done very well under Ivan Kandinsky because Seoul had opportunities for success that she saw and exploited with help from Moscow. And she did well because South Korea wanted good relations with Russia and was economically and politically stable. Pyongyang, he continued, was a far different post. It was more difficult in many ways, including all aspects of trade promotion with Russian firms. North Korea, he said, was both economically and politically unstable.

He went on that all of the Middle East was politically unstable, including Iraq and Iran. Iran, he said, was continuing to fund Hezbollah, its proxy army in Lebanon, and in Gaza, Hamas, whose charter calls for Palestinians to lead in the destruction of the State of Israel. It was costing Iran a small fortune, he said, year after year.

Elena asked, "Are you concerned that there will be open warfare between Israel and the Palestinians, that Iran will more openly get into it?"

"I think that may be coming. Not now, in a year or two, and we may be pulled in."

"You are painting a very bleak picture of the Middle East," she said.

"There are days, Elena, when I am afraid I am going to wake up in the middle of the night because the red phone is ringing and ringing. I will stumble over to the phone, pick it up, and I will be told diplomacy is failing and we are on the verge of another World War, this time with atomic weapons, big and small, loaded on short range and long range missiles."

"Really, that bad?"

"There are days when I am afraid the red phone will ring and I will be told diplomacy has ended, that an army with hundreds of tanks and thousands of aircraft has crossed our border, we are already in another World War, and to prevent a massive knockout nuclear attack on us, we are ready to launch our nuclear weapons at scores of targets."

"It's the nuclear first attack, and nuclear retaliation, that is so scaring you?"

"It is more than that. It is more than Iran lavishly supporting Hezbollah in Lebanon, and Hamas in Gaza, to support an Islamic crusade against Israel. It is the whole Middle East being drawn in. It is the rest of the world being drawn into an Islamic war on Israel with atomic weapons being used."

"You can't worry that way about the Middle East, and the rest of the unstable world, and sleep at night with your red phone ready to ring."

"There are too many countries already with atomic bombs, big ones and tactical little ones, and missiles to carry them. In time there will be many more countries with atomic weapons. Some will have autocratic leaders with great ambitions to glorify themselves and expand their country's frontiers. There will be determined enemies looking to revenge past wrongs. Diplomacy will fail, so there will be a World War with atomic weapons."

"That's not going to happen any time soon."

"Half the discouraged worried minds up here think there will be an atomic war."

"And the other half?"

"The other half? They like to think Hiroshima and Nagasaki taught the whole world a terribly bitter lesson, and atomic weapons will never be used again. They believe atomic weapons may be threatened, but they will never be used again because of the utter destruction of entire cities and the horrific number of corpses. You know, mutual assured destruction. One starts, and in a few hours all the others are going to be drawn in. The cities will be targets and they will be destroyed."

"My dear uncle, I am more hopeful. No belligerent supreme leader, no arrogant president, no determined prime minister is insane that way."

"Unfortunately, Elena, sooner or later there may be some who are." He paused. "Enough about red phones, we have to go on to your day by day business in Pyongyang."

"Definitely Pyongyang?"

"As you expected after your year in Seoul."

"I did, I'm ready."

"There is something else. It is important, it is complicated."

"Oh?"

"I will get to it, but first things first. The Pyongyang embassy is the right place for you and for the service. You will serve under Grigory Sukhinin. Grigory is a well-seasoned good ambassador. We are both concerned, deeply concerned, about North Korea's atomic program, its missile program, and the danger of nuclear proliferation if Pyongyang under Kim Jong Un sells its uranium, plutonium, and missile technology to other countries."

"Of course. I understand."

"Grigory has been running the Pyongyang embassy for a long time, four years. He took over from Andrei Karpov. Grigory is competent, he handles his people well, but it has been difficult for him just as it was for Karpov. Kim's people want to know about everything we are doing. They want to restrict what we can be doing. We try to talk with them and they put us off. Finally, we reach some agreements, and a little later they change their mind on what they agreed to and start badgering us about something else. It's maddening but not all that serious."

"It sounds serious."

"They know they need us. We get along. You will get along."

"With Kim's reputation, secret, belligerent, I rather expected you might tell me something like that."

"Grigory knows that I am sending you to work directly under him for important matters. With him and under him. Under him as a Deputy Ambassador."

"Thank you. For Pyongyang the Deputy Ambassador title should be very helpful."

"Elena, it is more than a title. You will have two important responsibilities. You will be part of the embassy executive staff, and you will take over as our next prime Southeast Asia trade representative."

"Southeast Asia?"

"By Southeast Asia I mean not just North Korea, but all of Southeast Asia. There are several opportunities we want you to develop. You will be traveling frequently, from Australia to Seoul, and monthly conferences at Vladivostok where you will meet with senior Moscow trade promotion officers who will be looking over your work, discussing prospective deals, and generally helping you when they can."

"I'm used to working independently on trade. That could be uncomfortable for me and for them from time to time."

"They are getting old. Treat them well and you will work it out. Set up a monthly Vladivostok meeting schedule. Use the Lotte Hotel. It is comfortable, and it has a big indoor pool if you want to relax and stay an extra day."

"So, I can expect important assignments very soon after I get to Pyongyang?"

"Very likely, but Grigory will give you time to settle in. Pyongyang will take time. With your stipend you will have enough money for good food and good housing. The social and business contacts you made in the South will not be forthcoming in Pyongyang. Still, even in the North, with all its street police, secret police, and legions of informers, people are people, and you may make some Korean friends. And you will have friends from the embassy and from the other embassies. As in Seoul, don't do anything that might get you in trouble. Even if you need help, never suggest, offer, or give a bribe to anyone. Never offer a little money to anyone to do you a little favor."

"I understand."

"As for your treatment at the embassy, Grigory will support you. Expect resentment about your executive position, especially from the other women. I am confident that, as in Seoul, you will soon win them over."

"I expect it, and I will try."

"Inside the building, and outside, with your friends you can continue to be social. Don't hold back in dealing with the government officials and business people. It will be more difficult in Pyongyang, sometimes maddening, because even when you are frustrated you must always be very polite in dealing with them."

"I will try."

"Enough about dealing with Korean officials and business people and staying out of jail. Now I have to get into a special situation that has come up. We are always concerned that Kim Jong Un may partner with Iran to help Iran get nuclear weapons to go on Iranian missiles. The DPRK has sold missile technology to Iran, and it has weapons grade uranium and plutonium that it probably will sell to Iran for the right price. Tell me immediately if you pick up anything new about the North Korean nuclear program or missile technology. Not just more of the continuing scary fluff on television and in the newspapers. Not just another underground nuclear test. We carefully monitor all their news but call me about anything that could be new and different."

"I will, but that doesn't seem likely."

"Actually, Elena, it is quite possible."

"Really?"

"It's complicated. For you to understand, I have to start with the railroad."

"The railroad?"

"Yes, the railroad. The Trans-Siberian railroad line ends at Vladivostok. It has an extension South to the Tumen River bridge where it hooks up with the North Korea rail line, Korean State Railway, that runs down the peninsula, crosses the demilitarized zone, and continues down past Seoul to Busan. The South Korean part of the line, KORAIL, is modern, it even has a streamlined highspeed train from Seoul to Busan. The North Korean economy depends on the railroad more than the South, but the railroad is also important to every part of the South. Soon after you get into the embassy work Grigory will get you involved with the program for improving the North Korean part of the railroad and get you into the embassy files on the very expensive very long term improvement project. Take a whole day to study the files. The engineering part, the projected cost. The people who are pushing the project. What you learn will soon be important to you."

"How so?"

"There is this fellow, this railroad official, we are interested in. His name is Ban Chul. Until recently he was a DPRK diplomat we dealt with, and now, instead, he has a minor, but for us a potentially important position with the railroad."

"What has this Ban Chul got to do with me?"

"Several months ago the Ministry of Transportation arranged with the embassy a five day all expenses paid conducted tour of the transportation system. They assigned Ban Chul to conduct the tour. The Ministry told us he is an officer in the train scheduling department and that he would provide literature and explain the importance of the rail and bus integrated transportation system. We assigned one of our experienced staff ladies to make the trip with him. Ban Chul gave her a pile of useful information. All the women's necessities during the day were acceptable. All the hotels and restaurants were first class. We expressed our appreciation for the tour and for Ban Chul's explanation of the electrified rail system showing the need for an upgrade to European standards. Then there was another tour with another experienced staff lady. Again, Ban Chul explained the railroad's needs, how the bus system tied in, showed her around, and paid for everything. Again, we expressed our appreciation, and we showed continuing interest in railroad upgrade projects. More powerful locomotives, improved first and second class passenger cars, more sturdy freight cars, improving the electric power reliability."

"No money now, maybe later?"

"Right."

"When we announced that you were going to be posted to Pyongyang the Ministry let us know that they would be pleased if you would be made available to take a third tour in a month or so, that is, before winter sets in. Ban Chul will probably be the guide again. They know you are my niece, and they must hope that you will make a favorable report that will get back to me."

"I expect that I will have to study the files for days because I don't know anything about fixing railroads."

"Much of the Korean peninsula rail system was built under the Japanese occupation before the Second World War by what amounted to slave labor. With Russian help after the war it was much improved and most of it was electrified in the North. After your tour with Ban Chul you will know a great deal about fixing the North Korean railroad. They want us to loan them a few billion rubles that they will never pay back, or they will pay back in their own currency at their official exchange rate. They would, of course, prefer grants to loans. They say, with some justification, that modernizing the railroad is as much for our benefit as theirs."

"So, I am going to tour North Korea with this deposed diplomat, Ban Chul?"

"They want you, so it's likely. Our good staff ladies both reported that he speaks fluent Russian, is very likeable, gave out lots of information about kilometers of track to be upgraded, number of new electric locomotives needed, cost of widening tunnels, value of the mining and fishing industries being served, and so on, but as they expected, he said nothing about any military capabilities or any sensitive political matters. They both reported that he made no unwanted advances, was always courteous, but that is not the whole story."

"Oh?"

"It seems they both liked him very much."

"So?"

"It seems they both liked him so much that they are deeply concerned about his personal safety if he is kicked out of his position with the railroad."

"Is that any part of our business?"

"They both understand it's not any part of our official business to get involved with what may happen to him."

"And unofficially?"

"Unofficially, his work is very much our concern."

"And my concern?"

"Yes."

"What did we think of Ban Chul as a diplomat? Dealing with people? In negotiations?"

"Our people liked him. They considered him quite friendly, quite personable. They also considered him very skillful in negotiations and extraordinarily knowledgeable about a wide range of political and economic issues. He was middle level, but he was negotiating about matters that we would expect to have been reserved for seniors, especially import tariffs and franchise taxes on foreign firms doing business in the country. In negotiations with us he was always knowledgeable, skillful, and honorable. He could be flexible or stubborn, but when he gave his word, and we relied on it, he didn't change his position. As far as we know he has not been charged with any civil or criminal offense, but something serious may be hanging over his head and worrying him."

"Such as?"

"We don't know."

"Why is all this about a former diplomat so important for you, and important for me?"

"Ban Chul is in train scheduling. The military uses the trains, and so he may have access to worthwhile information he could give up to you on your tour."

"Such as?"

"Such as confirming our intelligence of a coming rail shipment of weapons grade uranium and plutonium to Pyongyang, and then an airfreight shipment of the uranium and plutonium over Russia, Manchuria, Central Asia, and the Caspian Sea to Iran using an Air Koryo Ilyushin 76."

Elena, stunned, raised her hand. "Let me understand. Our intelligence is saying that North Korea is actually selling, or going to be selling, weapons grade uranium and plutonium to Iran, and is getting ready to have Air Koryo deliver it?"

"Yes."

"How reliable is our intelligence?"

"The intelligence we have comes from several reliable sources, but it is incomplete, useless, until we know with certainty there will be a shipment, and when and how it will be made. Ban Chul may know something about a railroad shipment of uranium and plutonium to an airport. Pyongyang or possibly some other North Korean airport the railroad also serves. He may not know now, but he may be able to find out. If he does, and tells you, we can act to stop the flight and he will have to get out of the country. He will be suspected of passing on information about the railroad shipment, and he will have to get out before he is arrested."

"Arrested for treason?"

"Yes. Even so, he may be willing to tell you what he knows in exchange for your help in getting out of the country and asylum in Russia, or elsewhere."

Elena was silent for a long time, nodded her understanding, and said, "You are thinking that with some persuasion… whatever that might be… he might be willing to risk his life talking to me?"

"Possibly."

"He might risk his life?"

"How can I answer you? He was a diplomat. He was always honorable. He must have terrible thoughts about what could happen to the world if Ayatollah Ali Khamenei getting his hands on atomic weapons…"

"Thoughts are not deeds."

"Elena, you also worry about Ayatollah Ali Khamenei getting his hands on atomic weapons. You both have a conscience, an inner sense of what is right and wrong. Elena, this is about atomic bombs, big ones and tactical small ones. Really, there is no such thing as a tactical small atomic bomb. You didn't ask for this, but here you are."

"He will have to get out of the country, and because I was with him, I was the one he would have passed the railroad information to, I will have to get out, too."

"Yes."

"He may be ready to save the world. To be honest, I don't know if I am ready to save the world."

"You may have to find out. During his two trips with our embassy ladies he said nothing about what happened to him or could happen to him. He never suggested he could tell what he knew. Or what he may be able to find out. That's understandable because they couldn't help him beyond a little money. You can, and he must know it. Speaking frankly, Elena, if he had been kicked out of our foreign service, and sent to work for our railroad, he would be very worried about what could come next. Anxious that he is being watched all day, worried all night."

"But nothing is arranged in Pyongyang for me now?"

"Not now. When you get settled in Pyongyang Grigory will arrange the tour for you with Ban Chul. It may not produce anything useful for us. If not, it will still be worthwhile for you because foreign diplomats must stay within the Pyongyang city limits unless there is written permission to go outside."

Elena was silent again for a long time. "The embassy will be getting the third tour for me with this Ban Chul, this former diplomat. That will be the *easy* part. Learning if he has, or can get, useful information, and *persuading* him to be helpful... I've never done anything like that..."

"Elena, this is more than important, this is a special situation. It is more important than just Iran and North Korea. If Mikhail Gorbachev were here he would say history is watching. Up here on this floor we are thinking about a scenario where Iran sees an opportunity to dominate the entire Islamic world. From North Africa to the Middle East, to the Persian Gulf. So, if Iran goes nuclear, in defense the Gulf countries, and possibly others, will rush to go nuclear and Kim Jong Un will have more uranium and plutonium customers."

After another silence she asked, "What should I expect to get involved with? What should I do?"

"He must know you are my niece, and that you can help him make a new life elsewhere. In Russia, and if he wants to, some other country. He was a working diplomat until a short time ago. He must still be proud of having been a diplomat. He must be full of proud memories. Your professional bond, if you encourage it, can become a personal bond, a strong personal bond, and a willingness to join you in doing what you both believe you must do. Must do in spite of danger, do what your bond and your conscience tell both of you to do."

"And if he asks me if I can help him?"

"You can tell him that you will try to help him, money for bribes and papers, asylum and a good job in Moscow if that is what he wants, but you cannot promise what may happen, what will happen."

"I will have to report."

"Yes."

"I will have to report, and you, or someone else, will act on what I tell you?"

"Yes. A task force will be formed, and it will act. One way or another, the Ilyushin will not reach Russia."

"It will be shot down?"

"Yes, if necessary."

After another silence she said, "And if I feel I am also getting myself in a dangerous situation?"

"Elena, if for any reason you feel that you are getting into a difficult position you give an excuse and come back to the embassy. You tell what you know, and an embassy car will drive you to Seoul airport and you fly to Vladivostok. Then home."

"Could there be more to this? Could I be walking into... some sort of a trap?"

"Ban Chul may be in trouble, in some way he probably is, but I don't believe there is a North Korean dark side to your trip, your official five day escorted tour."

"Why do you say that?"

"Because Kim needs to put big money into his railroad, and he wants our rubles and our expertise. He wants our money for other expensive things, too. Don't let yourself become paranoid, but if you sense that you are being secretly photographed, or recorded, go back to the embassy and get out of the country. There are flights from Seoul to Vladivostok every few hours."

"My dear uncle, what you seem to be telling me is that it is very important for me to get close to Ban Chul, then to go further and take some personal risks and encourage him in every way I have to so that he will tell me his secrets, if he has any, and at the same time to be very careful doing... whatever I need to do."

"Elena, when the time comes you will know what to say and what to do."

"With your experience can you give me anything a little more specific?"

"I don't really think so. People are different in many ways and situations are different in many ways. When the time comes to talk, and to listen, you will know."

"He will know, and I will know?"

"Yes. You will both know. Enough now about Ban Chul. You have to get ready to go to Pyongyang."

"What, if anything, can I tell Pyotr?"

"You can tell Pyotr that you are going on the tour with Ban

Chul, that you will have good separate hotel rooms every night, but that is all."

"I understand."

"And afterward you can tell him nothing except that you did a publicized official tour of the country and wrote a report about improving the railroad."

"If that's all he will read between the lines, the lines that are missing, and worry himself sick."

"You can tell him where you went, what you saw, what you did, and a little about what you are putting in your report about improving the North Korean railroad and how in time that might help bring millions of rubles to North Korea."

"He will write back and tell me it is all very well to help the North Korean railroad, to get rubles to Kim Jong Un, and I should never even think of taking another North Korean tour."

"That would be just fine."

CHAPTER 10

The separation from Pyotr had taken its toll, and by the time Mongolia was far behind, Siberia was below, and Vladivostok only another hour away, Elena admitted to herself that after her year in Seoul, after living apart for what seemed like ages, after dearly appreciating a Swedish diplomat friend, Pyotr had become something of a stranger. And now she was starting a lonely year, perhaps more, in Pyongyang. She had a suitcase full of memories of Seoul, a briefcase full of concerns for Pyongyang, and little space left over for Pyotr who could not possibly understand what she was going to be doing. She couldn't tell him, so how could he possibly understand. And Rolf Ericsson would likely be coming to Pyongyang, too.

She arrived in Pyongyang tired but determined to successfully take on all the new assignments of a new ambassador boss, and to be smiling and friendly while getting acquainted with all the staff - friendly yet requiring proper respect for her as the new Deputy Ambassador.

She took a room in a middle priced hotel recommended for new Pyongyang staffers. She unpacked, called the embassy to tell the ambassador she had arrived, and the next day started the process of settling in.

The hotel provided a get acquainted package - maps of the city showing the Metro stations, police stations, and the passport control office. The package also showed emergency medical facilities and the location and telephone numbers of taxi companies, several department stores and restaurants. More important for her, it listed the telephone numbers of banks, telephone, internet, electricity, and real estate companies.

It took two weeks to settle in. After a month she wrote Veronika.

Dear Veronika,

It was so good to visit with you and Alex while I was back in Moscow. All of us being together again was like old times.

Galina is such an adorable child. Also, what wonderful jobs both you and Alex have. It would be nice if you could have Alex at home all week but at least you don't have to go traveling far away from each other for long stretches.

At the Pyongyang embassy I will be working directly under the ambassador. And I have a fancy title, Deputy Ambassador.

One big difference here from Seoul is that the Americans still don't recognize the DPRK so there is no American embassy. The Swedish embassy acts in a limited way to provide American consular service. No regular diplomacy, but sometimes sensitive work for us and the Swedes.

Pyongyang is a half modern city, several square blocks of new high rise buildings, good tourist hotels, a thirty story twin tower luxury hotel, expensive cafes, and fine expensive shops. There must be big subsidies for the right business people and the top of the military.

In winter Pyongyang is cold. Some winter temperatures compare to Siberia but there are fewer strong storms and less snow. If you use the modern subway you can get around the city quickly. Like Seoul, there are also slums.

The people are friendly enough as long as you stay far away from politics. I have a small apartment in a good neighborhood, and a good grocery a block away. Also, there is a well-stocked pharmacy nearby that's popular with the diplomatic corps. The prices are much higher than Moscow in the good stores and the fine restaurants.

The diplomats here in Pyongyang have a social club, very much like the one in Seoul. There are far fewer diplomats here and so our club is much smaller. Instead of meeting at the top of the Seoul Hyatt here we meet at the top of the Koryo. Four stars. It is only for the very rich. As in Seoul the city wants good relations with the diplomats, and it picks up the bill.

Several of the diplomats from the Seoul embassies have rotated up here just as I have so I have some friends here that way.

Big news. I am going to go on a trip around the country. No date has been set but probably in a month or so.

It will be a five day tour put on by the Ministry of Transportation. It is all about convincing us to loan, or preferably give, North Korea several billion rubles over the next several years to modernize its railroad which connects at the border to an extension of our Trans-Siberian railroad. The railroad is also important to South Korea. Russian railroad engineers have been involved with the planning for a long time.

I will have a guide named Ban Chul. (In Korean names, the surname comes first.) He speaks Russian and this year he has escorted two other embassy women on tours, one at a time. I have been assured that he is competent, pleasant, and quite harmless.

Do write to me at the embassy. I have enclosed a brochure with the address.

Love, Elena

Dear Elena,

Thank you for your wonderful letter telling me about your traveling around the country. I've been traveling, too.

A month ago there came across my desk a routine memorandum about an upcoming negotiation in Cairo for Russian import of Egyptian cotton and cotton goods. Then I received a telephone call from an assistant for your uncle. She told me he needed an assistant from the Agriculture Ministry for the Cairo negotiation. Could I get myself free to accompany him? I have day care for Galina, and also a lovely woman I can call on, but happily my parents agreed to take care of her.

When I took the travel request up with my supervisor he told me that as soon as I got the details he would approve and provide funds for up to two weeks away. Longer if necessary. I understood that it was all settled, and I had just received a polite invitation from your uncle.

Now imagine this. A few days later Sonia Lyadov asked me to come visit your uncle at his office, at three o'clock in the afternoon the next day. She met me at the building entrance and had a pass ready for me, and we went up to one of the top floors, and then we waited in the reception area. Your uncle came out and greeted me with a big smile and a big hug. I remember that you told me that you had been up there - carpets, plush draperies, and all that. He walked down the hall with me. Just as you told me there were paintings of czars and their ambassadors going back to Napoleon and even before. It took us fifteen minutes or so to just get to his office because he explained who they were and what they did in Russian history. He said some of the portraits were on loan from the Hermitage.

When we got to his office he asked if I could get permission to accompany him to Cairo, and he gave me a pamphlet about the meeting – who would be there from Russia, from Egypt, from Pakistan, from India, and so on. We talked for half an hour about the importance of the conference. Such a knowledgeable man and so very warm. The best kind of Russian uncle.

When I got to Cairo he was already there, and he had booked rooms for us at the Ramses Hilton. With Agriculture and Food, I would never have dreamed of asking for a room there, but there I was, and I was able to listen and even participate in the conference. At the end of the conference he flew back to Moscow. He had me stay an extra day to get acquainted with others who were staying over. He said it was for the good of the foreign service.

I had a promotion. I have my own office and much more responsibility.

Uncle Lev, wonderful man, must have been my benefactor. Tell him that I am very grateful, and that I will try my best to live up to his expectations.

Alex and Pyotr are still working long days together at the army base on space projects like satellite orbits. The senior engineers tell them they are in the right place because space is the future for engineers. Alex explains on weekends, and now I sort of understand some basics, but that's all.

They are like two kids in a sandbox playing with their toys, except that their sandbox is in space with space time which he tells me is not the same as our time. I tell him we are here, and we come first. I also tell him to stay far away from the girls at the base who think these space men are some kind of new gods. You tell Pyotr the same thing. We girls have so little time with our men and we have to stick together.

Love, Veronika

CHAPTER 11

Habig typed out his travel and funding request, five pages, trimmed it to two, then to one, printed it out, rewrote it, printed it out, put in an envelope, put an URGENT tag on it, and just before eleven took the elevator to the top floor, walked down a row of well furnished offices and handed it to the secretary of his branch chief, Douglas Harley.

Priority Request for Approval of Foreign Travel and Funding.

A nuclear proliferation situation involving North Korea and Iran has developed that requires immediate attention and justifies my travel to Moscow to meet with Lev Marloff.

You are familiar with my reports on His Excellency Lev Marloff over several years. Now he is concerned that North Korea is getting ready to sell, or already has sold, and is about to deliver, a substantial amount of weapons grade uranium and weapons grade plutonium to Iran, with delivery by airfreight using Air Koryo.

The delivery flight will be from Pyongyang to Tabriz. Air Koryo has an Ilyushin 76 four engine jet that it can use for a night flight to Tabriz. Marloff wants to prevent the delivery. I do not know what he wants done to stop the delivery. Perhaps a warning not to try, possibly negotiations, if necessary, shoot down the plane.

Marloff may have information about payment by Iran, through a Swiss bank escrow.

His niece, Elena Marloff, also in the foreign service, is married to an Academy graduate who is an electrical engineer. He is at an army base working on space projects. Elena has just been posted to Pyongyang. No doubt by her uncle. She will be a Deputy Ambassador. Her first posting, a year ago, was to Seoul.

Ban Chul, a recently discharged DPRK Ministry of Foreign Affairs diplomat, is now working in Pyongyang in the Ministry of Transportation. He is an officer in the railroad scheduling department. He is going to take Elena on a five day tour of the national transit system. Two other women in the Russian embassy have toured with Ban Chul. Two separate tours. They may have become sympathetic to Ban Chul. Elena may become sympathetic to Ban Chul, and they may become confidants because Ban Chul as a recent diplomat with something hanging over his head must know that Elena is the niece of Lev Maloff and may be able to help him.

Because of his scheduling work for the railroad Ban Chul may know of railroad movement of uranium and plutonium destined for Iran. He may be willing to provide Elena with sensitive information in exchange for money to help him get out of the country and asylum in Russia.

The information I have developed is consistent with several cipher intercepts during the same time period.

I know Lev Marloff. He knows me. I will request an appointment. Without it I will not go. I will not commit us to support any course of action without express approval.

I will not go to North Korea, and I do not anticipate meeting or speaking to Elena Marloff or Ban Chul.

Enclosed is a photograph of Elena Marloff.

Funding needed is $25,000. On approval I will make my own travel and hotel arrangements.

At two o'clock Harley called Habig and told him to drop whatever he was doing and come upstairs to his office.

Picking up the travel request he began, "I've read it twice. This is all very interesting, but I am not convinced you need to go to Moscow and see Lev Marloff now. Take it apart for me, piece by piece, and put it all back together with a timeline."

Habig said, "I know I don't have all the pieces, not yet, so I don't have a firm timeline. What I do have, as I put it together, fits an important operation getting underway."

"What kind of operation?"

"The weapons grade uranium and weapons grade plutonium going from North Korea to Iran."

"From what you have put together, do you really think that's realistic?"

"Yes. As you know, I've been following Lev Marloff for a long time. Ban Chul is new to me. He's young, somewhere around his late thirties, early forties, and he has been an active DPRK diplomat for several years. He was apparently always well regarded by us, and others. For some reason, or reasons, he was kicked out of their foreign service."

"You don't know why."

"I don't know why. I've been thinking of several possible reasons, continuing serious policy disputes with seniors, unwanted advances to women, but I don't know why. When I learned that Ban Chul was demoted to the Ministry of Transportation, and that he had been giving escorted tours on the rail system to women in the Russian embassy, and that now Lev Marloff was sending his niece to Pyongyang, I became interested, then concerned, because Elena may be getting involved with Ban Chul for a tour of the country, and Kim Jong Un keeps boasting about his atomic bombs and his missile capabilities. Grigory Sukhinin is the Russian ambassador in Pyongyang."

"So?"

"The national rail system is very important to the Army for the atomic and missile programs. And the Ministry of Transportation asked Sukhinin to send Elena Marloff for a third tour. He is sending Elena, most probably it will be with Ban Chul. The trip could be soon."

"How soon?"

"I would think maybe a month. They wouldn't have a tour of the country in the winter, but I don't have anything definite on the timing."

"Are you thinking that Ban Chul may tell Elena about atomic stuff in a bugged hotel room, making her vulnerable to arrest on espionage charges, and this could be a Kim trap of some sort for us?"

"No, very unlikely as to any espionage charges, and definitely not a trap. Why would Kim even think of doing that to a Russian Depuy Ambassador? Why would Sukhinin consider sending Elena if he suspected the tour around the country with Ban Chul could somehow be a trap?"

Harley scowled. "Habig, you may be on to something important, but what you have now isn't enough for a trip to Moscow."

"It's *very* important."

"What you have is that in the Pyongyang embassy Elena Marloff will be a Deputy Ambassador. The tour with Ban Chul will be part of her official duties. Ban Chul may have, or can get, information about a rail shipment of uranium and plutonium. He should know Elena will be able to help him get out of the country to asylum in Russia. Maybe, because there may be an escrow in Switzerland, something may be planned about flying uranium and plutonium from Pyongyang to Tabriz. Some of this, or even all of this, may have been intentionally leaked to you. For now, what you have is not enough for a trip to Moscow."

"I do not think anything I developed was intentionally leaked to me, and I have no reason to think any of the signal intelligence was intentionally leaked. What I do have all fits together for an operation to send weapons grade uranium and weapons grade plutonium from Pyongyang to Tabriz. I do know it is for a lot of money, equivalent to about to about four hundred million dollars. I do know that the Ministry of Transportation trusts Ban Chul enough to ask Sukhinin to have Elena go on the tour with Ban Chul. What I have is not complete, far from it, but what I do have all fits together."

Harley shook his head. "Pyongyang isn't that stupid. If this recently demoted Ban Chul has that kind of railroad information, or could get it from the train schedules, why would the Ministry of Transportation ask Sukhinin to send Elena on a five day tour with him?"

"The answer is because Kim wants big Russian money for the railroad and the Ministry of Transportation is not thinking about Ban Chul telling Elena railroad secrets."

"Not thinking about uranium and plutonium moving on the railroad and keeping it secret? They're stupid?"

"Moving uranium and plutonium is a complicated operation. It can't be kept secret."

"In North Korea? Why not?"

"They're putting a special train together and putting it into the schedule. All the people who work with the scheduling can see that. A lot of other people who aren't involved with scheduling will see and understand what's happening. They need containers, maybe steel drums in extra secure crates. People will ask why the railroad is carrying half a dozen steel drums? They need a bunch of armed guards standing around while loading the shipment on the train. They need to unload with armed guards at a freight yard, probably the Pyongyang railroad freight yard. Then the army has to move the shipment by truck with the armed guards from the freight yard to the airport freight yard where they also need armed guards around the delivery. There is nothing that can be kept secret about getting the stuff to the airport and getting it loaded on the Ilyushin."

"The Army, not the railroad, will be buying the steel drums and putting them into the crates?"

"Probably."

"What's Elena's story?"

"She went into the foreign service with honors from the Academy. She did regular diplomat work and trade promotion for a year in Seoul. She did very well in trade promotion because of her uncle, and he may have put a finger on the scale from time to time, and she had a way with Korean men in positions to push contracts to Russian companies."

"And Lev Marloff is in a position to get the Russian companies to sign on the dotted line even though the contracts have nothing to do with the railroad?"

"If he makes a telephone call to the right person and suggests a little discount for the good of the Russian economy, I would think so."

"This former diplomat, Ban Chul, is now somehow involved with the entire national railroad scheduling?"

"Right. That's what he does."

"What makes you think that just from working with from the

train schedules he is in a position to know what it is that is going to move, and beyond that, what is going to be sent to Iran, or be sent somewhere else?"

"He should know where the military facility storage locations are, and except for two storage facilities, one for uranium and one for plutonium, there probably are no special trains with guards going there. The special trains with armed guards suggests uranium and plutonium are being stored in these two facilities. He wouldn't know that a shipment from these facilities is going to end up in Iran, but several radio and cable intercepts between Pyongyang and Tehran strongly point to a sale and airfreight delivery to Tabriz. In North Korea that has to start with the railroad schedule and involve the Air Koryo Ilyushin as the only practical way for any North Korean uranium and plutonium going to Iran."

"There is no other way these days to get uranium and plutonium from Pyongyang, North Korea, to Tabriz, Iran?"

"There are ships with twenty four hour guards. That can't be kept secret. The long sea voyage would mean chartering a ship, a very expensive proposition for a good ship, and the ship could take several weeks even in the best weather."

"What else?"

"There are trucks with several twenty-four hour guards. The trucks would be subject to inspection at every border. If you are Kim you can't allow inspection of your radioactive cargo. Ships or trucks with guards both seems unlikely."

"Ban Chul is not trusted?"

"Probably not by their foreign service."

"And, quite possibly, not trusted with important sensitive work by the transport department?"

"I don't think so,"

"Why would the railroad take a chance on a new man, a lawyer who knows nothing about running a railroad, and put him in what could be a sensitive position?"

"Scheduling isn't all that sensitive. Still, that is a very good question."

"And you don't have a good answer."

"Right here in Washington one hand doesn't know, or care, what the other hand is doing. The DPRK bureaucracy is a lot smaller, but it is also full of stove pipes."

"That's your guesswork."

"It is more than guesswork. The diplomatic service decides to get rid of this fellow. Maybe he doesn't always follow the party line. He is a bit of a rebel. He could become a problem. Kick him out, gone, good riddance. Who cares where he lands. He has lost his diplomatic passport, he cannot leave the country, so who cares. On the other hand, the railroad wants Russian money, billions of rubles, and so it wants this former diplomat who speaks highbrow Russian for these escort trips on the railroad with the sophisticated Russian embassy ladies. They want him to be social, like a diplomat, and they want him to be impressive, to have some status. So, they put him in a job in scheduling right next to an old pro who will keep a sharp eye on him and make sure he doesn't mess up the system. And if he is thinking he may be in trouble, he is thinking he is being watched, that's all to the good because he will be careful about everything he does and everything he tells the Russian embassy ladies on these tours."

"That's not a good answer."

"It is not a good answer, but it probably is the real answer."

"That's all?"

"If Kim gets a few billion rubles not all of it is going to go into his railroad. He wants his locomotives to go faster, and he also wants his new missiles to go faster and further. Whatever his motives, he is not out to use Ban Chul in railroad scheduling to irritate Russia."

"That assumes we know what is going on at Kim's level. This could be a set up."

"Unlikely, I don't see one."

"I can see one. At work a well dressed lady pulls Chul aside and tells him she wants to talk to him privately. He knows he has no choice. He tells her to come to his apartment. There she tells him she has connections with the Ministry of Foreign Affairs. She tells him he was an exceptional diplomat, and he represented the country well. He is still valuable. He might be restored to his former position under a different supervisor. After a year he might be posted to Warsaw. After that a promotion and Paris or London. Would he volunteer to do a service, an important patriotic service? He hesitates. She tells him the most unfortunate question mark over his family could be erased. He bows his head and nods. She tells him she will come back tomorrow night with a friend who may be able to help him. At work the next day he thinks someone is watching his every move, every gesture. On the way home he buys a bottle of expensive liquor. When she returns with her friend he smiles and pours full glasses. The friend raises his glass and proposes a toast to Supreme Leader Kim Jong Un. He tells stories of diplomats honored, and diplomats deposed, by the Supreme Leader. Another toast to the Supreme Leader. Ban Chul proposes a toast to the Supreme Leader. The friend smiles and tells him what he has in mind for him to get Elena to talk about something going on at the embassy."

"If you are Kim, you don't bite the hand that feeds you."

"I said unlikely, but since when has that stopped Kim?"

"He wants stacks of rubles, and the Russian army is right across the Tumen Rive bridge."

"What more do you have about Elena Marloff?"

"Her picture tells me she is very bright, very appealing in a Russian way."

"Do you have other pictures?"

"I have several photos of her. Official and unofficial. I can make copies for you."

"Is Ban Chul married?"

"Possibly. No record I can find either way."

"Girlfriend? Boyfriend?"

"Probably girlfriend. Nothing I have been able to find suggests otherwise."

"You think Elena and Ban Chul may become confidants?"

"I would think so."

"Why?"

"They will be together for five days. She is a diplomat. He is a former diplomat in trouble. She thinks he may know secrets her uncle should know about. He thinks that for telling her his secrets she can reward him, get him asylum in Russia and the start of a new life. For both of them, this is about uranium and plutonium being carried over Russia by another country's freight airplane, and it is about atomic bombs being put together in Iran. There will be a war scare, and this can end up being life and death for millions. They are insignificant, and they do the right things for dear Korea and for Mother Russia, and everyone else, and for themselves."

"They become lovers?"

"I think so. For one night, their last night after a bottle of wine, after talking like good diplomats about saving the world from disaster, I would think so."

"Can he get out of the country?"

"With a bribe to a truck driver he might get across the DMZ to South Korea. Or he can get forged papers and try to go to Russia on the railroad. He could also think about how to get across the Tumen River to Russia."

"Habig, on their becoming lovers, I'm not with you. For both Elena and Chul, it is one thing for them to want to save the world from catastrophe, and another thing for them to risk their lives to do it. It is one thing for Elena to admire Chul for being willing to risk his life. She is married to an electrical engineer. Ban Chul will be a very good traveling companion, but it's another thing after just five days for her to sleep with him."

"This is about weapons grade uranium and weapons grade plutonium. This is about atomic bombs, big ones and little ones, tactical ones. That is what they are both thinking about, anguishing about. They are thinking about uranium for Hiroshima, plutonium for Nagasaki. Not in the abstract. We say Hiroshima and Nagasaki in conversation, and it just goes by. We have heard about them so many times we are numb to the reality of them. They are thinking, and they are saying to each other, *Hiroshima* and *Nagasaki*, and they are seeing the unbelievably brilliant flash, feeling the furnace hot scorching heat, seeing the horrendous results. All around charred human corpses, terribly burned surviving animals. In their room they will have only each other. They will need to comfort each other. They will want to hold each other. And then they will sexually want each other."

Harley said, "Habig, we're not directly involved and there is not going to be another Hiroshima and another Nagasaki tomorrow morning. You are obsessed with this because Elena is a Russian beauty."

"We are not directly involved now, but overall this is very important for us."

"Why would Lev Marloff talk to you?"

"He knows me."

"Secure telephones to Moscow still work."

"Too sensitive. Too important."

"He has his own intelligence. Why doesn't he already know most everything you want to talk about?"

"If that is what he thinks, if he thinks it is not important, I won't get an appointment."

Harley rubbed his chin and said, "That's a good point. How would you go?"

"Same as last time. American information official with an office in the Washington area. I will fly an American airline to Heathrow and Aeroflot to Sheremetyevo. Economy class, of course, whenever possible."

"Habig. If this goes wrong, it could be the end of you. You're sure you want to do this?"

"Yes. I'm sure."

"I'll talk to the Director. Wait here."

Harley returned an hour later, tossed the travel request on his desk and said, "He read it and he looked at Elena's picture. We talked about it. He is considering letting you have your trip if you have an appointment."

"Right."

"You can't commit us to do anything."

"Right. No commitment of any kind."

"I told him about Elena and Chul thinking about saving the world from atomic catastrophe, needing each other, and becoming lovers. He is worried that you are fantasizing about getting involved with Elena."

"I won't get involved with Elena. I won't talk to Elena. I won't get anywhere near Elena."

"And if you do, you won't tell me."

"I won't tell you because it won't happen."

"He wants you to have a session with Dr. Wilcox. He's away, but he is going to come back tomorrow to see you."

"Right. Dr. Wilcox tomorrow."

"Don't hold anything back. If you do you could lose your security clearances."

Dr. Eli Wilcox, chief of psychiatric services, sat across his desk from Habig at 10:15 the next morning. A page of scribbled notes was on his desk.

"Habig, this isn't routine," he began seriously. "This session is being pushed on me by Elliot. He told me to be thorough, take all the time we need, so don't play games with me."

"Eli, I never play games with you."

Dr. Wilcox frowned and scanned through his notes. "You still have your high security clearance?"

"Yes."

"You still gather information from foreign sources using your Pegasus software?"

"Yes."

"You review classified reports involving areas of your special interest?"?

"Yes, they are sent to me."

"You have assigned target areas, but by and large from your experience you decide where to probe and what to report?"

"Yes, my experience and my judgment are everything."

"You decide what to report?"

"I report every month. I report everything I've done that resulted in something I think is worth reporting. If I want to go into an unassigned area, I say so, and I explain."

"You usually get your way?"

"I have the long experience, and the insight that comes with experience. The Director and the Deputy Director usually, but not always, respect that."

Dr. Wilcox scanned his notes for several minutes. "I've been told you want a fist full of money to travel around the world, first to Moscow to see a Minister of Foreign Affairs, some title like that, and then perhaps to Pyongyang, North Korea, so you can meet, talk with, and maybe try to romance his very pretty niece who is worried about uranium and plutonium going to be shipped by an airplane out of North Korea to Iran. Is there anything real to any of that talking and romancing?"

"Not quite."

"Not quite what?"

"I can't tell you."

"I don't want secrets. I don't want details. Just give me the framework."

"That's an order?"

"It is a suggestion for you to take seriously so you can still be employed here tomorrow."

"I hear you. Lev Marloff is a Russian Deputy Minister of Foreign Affairs. I know him. I want to go to Moscow to talk to him about a complicated situation that involves North Korea. I am asking for an appointment. No appointment, I don't go. His niece, Elena, is going to be a Deputy Ambassador in Pyongyang. I am not going to Pyongyang, unless Marloff asks me to."

"That is possible?"

"That is possible, but unlikely."

"Do other people here, or elsewhere, know what you want to get into with Marloff?"

"I don't know, and if I did, I couldn't tell you."

"Habig, you are playing games."

"Eli, I am not playing games. I have never played games with you."

"Why do you need to travel to Russia to talk to this Deputy Minister of Foreign Affairs.? Why not get together on a secure phone?"

"I can't go any further into why I need to talk with Lev Marloff."

Dr. Wilcox scanned through his notes again. "You will have an appointment? A definite hour and day?"

"I will ask to be fit in his schedule between this day and that day. I can't tell you what I will do when I meet him."

"I don't want to know what you are going to do. I do want to know what you are thinking."

"Thinking and doing go together. It is all uncertain. What I am going to talk about, what I am going to do, it is all very complicated, uncertain, but necessary."

"Tell me something more. Fill in some details."

"That's an order?"

"I will give my opinion to Director Elliot. At the end it will say whether in my opinion you are psychologically fit to travel to Russia for what would seem to be very complicated work requiring good judgment."

"That amounts to an order."

"You can take it that way. Just tell me the framework."

"Lev Marloff deals with high level intelligence. He is not an intelligence officer, he is above that, but like intelligence officers around the world, he has to be concerned about a possible sale of weapons grade uranium and plutonium by North Korea to Iran. An imminent sale, and airfreight delivery."

"Airfreight?"

"Yes. Airfreight with a cargo of both weapons grade uranium and weapons grade plutonium from North Korea going across Russia and half a dozen other countries and the Caspian Sea to Northern Iran, all of which raises all sorts of problems for us, for Russia, and the other countries."

"About the niece, Elena. You have more photos of Elena?"

"Yes. I've accumulated them from her college days till now."

"Why did you do that?"

"She is going to be a Deputy Ambassador in Pyongyang, and they must share information about North Korea. She interested me, and she is beautiful."

"What else are you thinking about Elena?"

"She is interesting because she will be a very young Deputy Ambassador in North Korea, a country with atomic bombs. She is bright and ambitious. She can be charming, and for me, she is beautiful."

"Very beautiful?'

"Yes."

"Do you have a fantasy about her?"

"Yes."

"Do you have a sexual fantasy about her?"

"Yes, but I do not expect to ever meet her."

"If you could meet her, if you could have time with her, where would you want it to be?"

"I couldn't afford it."

"Suppose you had the money."

"I've always wanted a week at a first class resort in Hawaii."

"With a beautiful young woman like Elena?"

"Yes."

"What else is on your mind about Elena?"

"Eli, have you heard about the poet Petrarch in early Renaissance Italy, 14th century, near Turin, an introspective monk at the court loving his Laura from afar, and writing sublime poems about her beauty, her face and hair moving with the breeze. His writing is still taught in college literature classes today."

"I know Petrarch, the type and the poet. You're no Petrarch. You're no monk, and you are no poet."

"Eli, twenty years ago you started at the bottom, and I started in a cubicle. Now you are the chief of psychiatry with a secretary and a fine office, and I am still alone in a postage stamp cubicle. I suppose it's an honor year after year for me to keep coming back to you."

"Enough of that. What else are you thinking about Elena?"

"Elena is highly intelligent, very sociable, and she is beautiful. I would like to meet her."

"And?"

"And talk with her about her life. I have no plans to do that. I certainly will never have her for a week in Hawaii."

"Is Elena married?"

"Yes. Pyotr is an engineer, a space engineer, at an army base near Moscow."

"Is Elena sexually attractive to you?"

Habig reached into his shirt pocket, pulled out Elena's university graduation picture, and slid it across the desk. "This is from her St. Petersburg graduation about three years ago."

Wilcox studied the photo then looked across at Habig and nodded twice. "Very pretty, very pretty, and I would think a very warm Russian personality. Do you think about Elena during the day?"

"Yes. Sometimes. When I wake up in the morning."

"At night, do you dream about Elena?"

"Yes. Sometimes."

"Are the dreams important to you?"

"Yes. Always."

"Tell me about your dreams about Elena."

Speaking slowly, Habig began, "There are two types, very different the way they start, but they end the same. Not really the same, yet the same."

"Tell me."

"There is a storm. Wind and rain. I am on a train in Europe. First class compartment. Alone. I am traveling on a diplomatic passport from some European country. It is late at night, after midnight, the train is late as it pulls into Paris. The Gare du Nord. At the taxi rank I toss my bag in the first cab, climb in and tell the driver L'Avenue Bourbonnais. Number twenty-eight. I am acting like a foreign diplomat. The driver winds through Paris a long time and arrives at a house in the Seventh Arrondissement. I have the door key. I let myself in and I climb the stairs to the second floor. A light is on in the bedroom. There is a window with a closed curtain facing on the street. A bottle of champagne and two glasses are waiting. She hears me coming and calls out to me. She is very pretty. She is wearing a little white nightgown. Nothing underneath. She is Elena, I am sure of it. She asks me first in French, and then in English, where I have been, what I have been doing, if I have done what she asked me to do. I kiss her, and I tell her I have done what she wanted me to do, and it is done. I have killed him, her husband, Pyotr, so we can be together. She takes both my hands, kisses me, takes off the nightgown, and leads me to the bed. She wants me, and I satisfy her. I wake up early in the morning. Outside it is still storming, lightning, thunder, rain is drumming on the roof. We kiss, and I dress and leave. I know I may never be able to come back to the house."

"You are sure that Pyotr was her husband?"

"I killed her husband."

"Why?"

"I killed him so I can have sex with her. And after that she won't turn me away, and I can have her again. That's all there is about the dream."

"And the second dream?"

"I am in a small room in a great palace somewhere in Europe. Again, there is a storm outside. Thunder and lightning. This young woman comes in. She smiles and says I look like an officer who should have a royal title. I feel like one. She is wearing a long thin white dress, pure white, with nothing underneath. She tells me that if I will do something that must be done, she will be mine. I think that I know what it is. I understand that for doing it she will give me her kisses and her body. She tells me what to do. I leave the palace and start to climb up an ancient stone tower. It is a very high tower, and as I go up it becomes harder to climb. I stop and rest, and then I start climbing again. It gets still harder to climb and I have to stop and rest again. I start again, and this time I reach the top. I see a guard standing at attention by the door of a small room. I kill the guard. The guard I kill is Pyotr. I go inside the room. Inside is a marble table, and on the table is a box made of a special kind of stone. The box is just a few centimeters square. Inside the box is a special kind of pearl. It is lustrous, and it is very hot. It is so hot it gives off a blue glow. I know the burning hot pearl is radioactive. I bring the box with the burning hot pearl to her. The box with the burning hot pearl is a nuclear reactor that turns uranium into plutonium. I tell her what I have done. She tells me I have done a great thing that had to be done. She rewards me with kisses and her body. She tells me I can come back and I can have her again. I dress and leave. I know I may never be able to come back to the palace."

"Have you been thinking about how you would kill Pyotr?"

"I would never kill Pyotr. I would never do that."

"Have you been thinking about having someone do it for you?"

"It would break her heart."

"Suppose that in Russia you were introduced to Pyotr. How would you feel? What would you do?"

"That will never happen."

"Suppose her uncle arranged for you to meet Pyotr."

"I would meet him. I would look in his face, firmly grip his hand, and tell him he is a very lucky man. I would not kill him. It would break her heart."

They shared a long silence. "Why did you tell me about your dreams?"

"You asked. You wanted to know."

"Why did you tell me?"

"Eli, why do old Catholic men confess to their old priests?"

The psychiatrist leaned over and said, "Various reasons. Religious practices, cultural customs, guilt. Habig, with you, it is Elena Marloff. You have her in the morning, you have her all day in your work, and you have her in your dreams. You say you will never have Elena., In your way, you do have her. She is very important to you, and you are afraid of losing her."

"I don't have Elena, I probably will never have her, never, so I can't lose her."

"You are afraid you will."

"I would never do that."

"You love Elena in your way. It is deep within you, and with some encouragement from her, you could become willing to kill her husband."

"I wouldn't kill him. I wouldn't do anything to hurt him. It would break her heart."

"If she held you tight against her, passionately kissed you, asked you to kill him, and promised to reward you with her kisses and her body, you could. You know you could."

After a silence Habig said, "If she held me... and asked me the right way..."

"You have Elena, you want Elena, and you are afraid you are going to lose her. You insist you can't lose her. Inside, you know better. In your dreams you have her. There is rain, thunder and lightning, you have her. You leave her knowing you can't come back to her."

"Yes."

"Is there something that may happen to her? Is there something violent that may happen to her?"

Habib was silent and Wilcox asked again, "Is there something that may happen to her? Is there something violent that may happen to her?"

"Yes."

"What is it?"

"She is in danger. She may be killed."

"Are you involved in any way?"

"Yes. Yes and no. Not directly."

"Indirectly?"

"I can't make any of the decisions, I can't make any of the decisions that would change anything. I tell our senior people what I know. I tell them what I think other people know. Or they could know. That's all."

Wilcox leaned forward again. "Habig, you believe that in a meaningful way you are involved. You are afraid to admit that in some way you may somehow be responsible for the results. Tell me what is going on."

"What do you mean?"

"Tell me where you fit in. Tell me where you could make a difference in the results. Tell me how you have been thinking about all of that."

Habig told his story. For half an hour, without interruption, with increasing emotion, he told what he knew about an Air Koryo charter night flight from North Korea to Iran using an Ilyushin 76 carrying weapons grade uranium and weapons grade plutonium to Tabriz. That the Ilyushin would be shot down over the ocean. That the wrong plane, the one Elena might be on flying to a meeting in Vladivostok, might be shot down by mistake. That he understood that the Ilyushin must be stopped by whatever means necessary, it could not be allowed to reach Iran. That to protect Elena, to protect all the passengers and the crew, he wanted the pilot warned not to continue, warned by several bursts of tracer fire in front of the plane, if necessary several more bursts, so that the pilot would turn back.

"What if the plane doesn't turn back?"

Habig closed his eyes, looked down, and shook his head. "I don't have the words to tell you."

After a silence Wilcox said, "I understand. Is there anything else I should know?"

"No."

"Do you remember the drill from last time?"

"Yes, and the time before, and before that."

"If we went through it together again, would any of the answers change?"

"No. You don't change, I don't change. Standard questions, standard answers."

Dr. Wilcox scribbled a few notes, sat back and said, "You'll pass."

Habig went back to his cubicle. As he sat down in front of his computer and the monitor blank screen he felt alternately elated and depressed. Elated, because he was a step closer to boarding a plane for Heathrow and then Sheremetyevo International. A step closer to a reserved Moscow hotel room. A step closer to His Excellency, Lev Marloff. And a possible step closer to Elena. Depressed, because he had babbled to Dr. Wilcox about his private dreams with Elena. Not all the intimate details, not her combed out hair, light scented perfume like cinnamon, her soft eyes and lips, her smooth curved body, her response to his touch. Depressed in a different way because a possible step towards her was not enough, and it would never be enough. He didn't need Wilcox to tell him he yearned for what he knew he could not have, that he knew he would never spend a week with her at a Hawaii resort. Not one of the crowded Honolulu tourist hotels, but a first class resort like the Kahala where millionaires, presidents, and kings stayed. A private balcony with chairs a few feet apart looking out to Diamond Head and the blue ocean to the horizon. He again imagined Elena with her blouse open sitting in a pose like an actress letting him look at her, letting him watch her face as passing clouds changed the light and gusts of wind blew strands of hair across her cheek. She would smile at him, they would kiss, and then they would go inside, kiss again, and undress. Eli Wilcox, he thought, listening to him could not help but imagine that soft erotic sense of Elena, too.

Scowling, CIA Director Howard Elliot shoved Dr. Wilcox's report across his desk to his deputy, Douglas Harley. "Wilcox gave me his review on Habig. I told him to be thorough and he is giving me a course on psychiatry theory and practice. It's all about personal motivation, personal involvement, and being competent while acting under short and long term stress. He starts with two pages of his jargon about highly intelligent, highly imaginative, complex profiles acting under different kinds, different lengths, and different amounts of stress. At the end he says Habig has been under considerable long term stress, in addition he is now under short term stress, he continues to be moderately eccentric, but he is as fit for important and sensitive duty as he ever was."

"Sounds like Wilcox."

"He might as well have added in plain language that I should let Habig go see Lev Marloff."

"Did you really expect anything different?"

"Not really."

"So?"

"If I send Habig to Moscow I'm responsible for what he does in Moscow."

"You can give him orders as to what he can do, and what he can't do. If you think it is the right thing to send him to Moscow to see Lev Marloff, you do it. You're not responsible for what you can't control. You're not responsible for what Kim Jong Un does with his weapons grade uranium and plutonium. You're not responsible for what Iran buys from North Korea, and what the Russians do, or don't do."

"I may not be responsible, but I'm sure the one who will take the blame if this Kim and Khamenei business goes wrong."

"Howard, this is different, but in terms of atomic proliferation it isn't all that different, and you get paid for taking the blame."

"Thanks for reminding me."

"It seems to me that Habig made a good case for going to talk to Markov if Markov gives him an appointment, and Wilcox cleared him to go."

"So let him go?"

Harley shrugged. "If Lev Marloff is thinking the same way Habig is thinking, and so Habig gets an appointment, I don't see any great harm in letting him go for a few days with instructions not to commit us to anything."

"What if somehow he gets the chance to go see Elena Marloff? If he is manages to be alone with her, after an hour or two with a big hug and a passionate kiss or two, he could blissfully agree to most anything."

"He wants to keep his job. He won't commit us to anything. And we know Lev Marloff. He would never ask Habig to commit us, and he would never take anything Habig said as a commitment by us. He will never mention Elena. He is not going to give Habig the chance to go meet her."

"Even if he asks?"

"Especially, if he asks."

"What do you think about twenty-five?" Elliot asked.

"Ten should be enough."

The Director nodded.

Harley said, "More important, what about Secretary Carter and Secretary Kerry? This Ilyushin business heavily involves both Defense and State. Isn't it time to bring both of them in?"

"What do you think?"

"I think it's time to bring in Ash Carter, and if we do, we have to bring in John Kerry. It will complicate things for us, that's sure, but it's time, and sooner or later we have to do it."

"Stalling won't make it easier. Call Carter. Tell him it is about

Iran and North Korea, that we can't go into it enough on the phone, and we want to give him a full briefing when he can clear his calendar. He's not going to be happy, but he will calm down in a few minutes."

"And Kerry?"

"Call him and set up a meeting for us, tonight if possible. A couple of hours. Office or home, wherever he wants. Whenever he is free."

"We can only give him a couple of hours, and then we have to get back and finish our Russian work for tomorrow."

"Right."

"What can I tell Kerry?"

"Same as Carter. It is about Iran and North Korea, we can't go into it in any detail on the phone, we want to give him a briefing, and we will bring along some documents."

"We better not bring any documents. Too many things can go wrong driving around Washington at night."

"Right."

"I probably won't reach Kerry this afternoon or tonight."

"If you can't reach Kerry then call Steve Lessing. If you can't get Steve, then Warren Rush. Steve will give you an earful, but he'll calm down. Same with Warren."

CHAPTER 12

Harley tried but could not reach Kerry or Lessing. In the late afternoon he reached Assistant Secretary of State Warren Rush. After twenty minutes on the phone, Rush stopped him. "Doug, I hear you... my house at eight... I will listen. I won't decide anything tonight, but I will listen. I'll ask Jeff Levy to come."

"It would be better for everyone if we kept this tight. Howard, me, and you."

"Doug, I'm not going into this tonight alone. It is too important. I want Jeff."

"You can handle it."

"It's full of legal knots. I want Jeff."

"You win. We'll see you and Jeff Levy about eight."

Air Force Staff Judge Advocate, Major General Jeffrey Levy and Assistant Secretary of State Warren Rush tangled with related legal and diplomatic issues over twenty years while working their way up in State Department and Pentagon rank and responsibility. Jeffrey Levy, the Pentagon recognized expert on international law, also advised Secretaries of Defense and wrote pointed legal opinions for Presidents. Rush wrote short orders and long reports with uncertain conclusions for Secretaries of State.

When difficult decisions involving both the Pentagon and State had to be made Levy and Rush had frank discussions, sometimes verging on arguments, at Rush's home, more like an expensively renovated mansion along Rock Creek a couple of miles upstream from the Kennedy Center. Rush inherited the house and a small fortune from his father who inherited the house from a long line of diplomat grandfathers. Edith, his perfect wife and hostess, also the beneficiary of a substantial inheritance, quite knowledgeable about Washington extramarital romances, and a dabbler in original art, mostly English landscapes, was always busy upstairs for sensitive meetings. The temperature controlled wine cellar was always well stocked with fine wines from prized vineyards around the world.

Levy arrived near seven thirty. Rush warmly shook his hand, gave him a glass of wine and said, "Thanks for coming, and my apologies to Phyllis for ruining your evening."

"You said that Elliot and Harley are coming to talk about Kim and Khamenei getting together. She understands."

"Howard and Doug should be here about eight. Meanwhile, we can have a glass of Cru Beaujolais and talk about Kim and Khamenei shaking hands."

Levy took a first sip, then a second, raised his glass, smiled and said, "Very smooth, lovely color, fine nose, and chilled just right. Warren, I can almost see the rolling hillside vineyards and the charming villages."

Rush smiled, picked up his glass, took a sip, then another, raised his glass and nodded his appreciation.

Levy asked, "What's so hot tonight about Kim and Khamenei wanting to come together?"

"Doug called me on our secure line. He said they are convinced that North Korea is getting ready to sell weapons grade uranium and weapons grade plutonium to Iran and in a week or so deliver them by airfreight to Tabriz."

"Weapons grade?"

"Yes, weapons grade."

"Airfreight? Can't be traditional airfreight. Can't be, even if it is not weapons grade."

"Doug said they think Kim will use Air Koryo's freight plane, an Ilyushin 76. Fly it as though it was commercial airfreight, from Pyongyang to Iran. Probably fly at night from Pyongyang to Tabriz."

"Why Tabriz?"

"Tabriz has a lot of history, but now it is a modern industrial city in the North, capital of a province, with a population of about one and half million. It probably has some company able to deal with nuclear materials."

"That wouldn't surprise me."

"Harley said that flying from Pyongyang to Tabriz means flying seven or eight thousand miles across Russia, Mongolia, and Central Asia. The Russians won't want to let the plane get near Russia, much less fly across Russia."

"You are certainly right about that."

"From what Doug told me I take it CIA is cooking up some plans for stopping the flight in its first hour or so. Some place where it flies over the ocean. Shoot it down, with or without the Russians, before it gets very far, before it gets out of North Korea, before it gets near any part of Russia."

Levy nodded thoughtfully and said, "Warren, this North Korea uranium and plutonium sale isn't a new idea. Kim has a stockpile of weapons grade uranium and weapons grade plutonium. For several years he has boasted that North Korea has the ability to make atomic bombs from uranium and plutonium. And to prove it he sets off these underground tests. Does Kim need the money? North Korea's treasury isn't suddenly going bankrupt, so why sell now? What makes Elliot think this can be the real thing?"

"Doug says there is a lot they don't know, they may never know, but they do know there is a contract for sale and delivery to Tabriz, and there is a funded escrow in Switzerland. Equivalent to several hundred million dollars."

Thoughtfully, Levy nodded again. "That sounds to me like Elliot has been to the President, he has given him a briefing, and the President is not ready to sign on. He wants to see more detailed reliable intelligence, more detailed planning, and he wants nailed down full support from the Secretary of Defense and the Secretary of State. Barack Obama is a careful man, especially when it comes to foreign relations. From my experience that's the way he handles the heavy stuff we send over."

With a wry smile Rush said, "My office with the Secretary of State is a few blocks from the White House, the Pentagon is across the river in Arlington, but you are a lot closer to the White House than I will ever be."

"Warren, maybe sometimes, for some things. Air Koryo is the national state owned airline of North Korea. Air Koryo is Kim's airline. Intentionally shooting down Kim's freight plane, his big Ilyushin 76, is the next thing to declaring war on North Korea and on Kim personally. I would guess that the Director of the CIA is coming with Doug because he wants you to give the blessing of the Secretary of State to his plan to shoot down Kim's freight plane, probably in some way with the Russians."

"You are probably right. Tonight I am going to be careful. I will listen, ask questions, and stop there. They will tell me alarm bells are ringing at Langley, that the Russians will agree to the CIA plan, so on behalf of the Secretary of State, I need to bless their plan tonight, bless it whatever the plan with the Russian military turns out to be."

"You should be careful, but their side of this is that when Langley's red lights are flashing, and they believe they have to move fast, pushing the Secretary of State for approval is a part of their job."

"When they believe... *Here, use my pen, just sign on.* With or without the Russians signing on. Problems? We will figure out what to do when the time comes. Air freight at night, no problem. We'll go over there and shoot it down, or the Russians will shoot it down. Kim will throw a tantrum, he may even shoot off a couple of rockets. *Just sign on.*"

"Warren, calm down. In an emergency Elliot can go to the President and get approval for plans and operations without Ashton Carter and without John Kerry. He doesn't want to, but he knows that in a real emergency, like every head of the CIA before him, he can. He also knows that every time he calls the Chief of Staff and asks to speak to the President immediately, he has to have a very good reason. You don't want to be the reason. Secretary Kerry doesn't want to be the reason. You know that's the box you are in tonight."

"Perhaps so, but this isn't that kind of emergency. Not close. I am not going to agree to anything, and I intend to speak my mind. The President has to know, and he has to take the time and consider all the options, including State Department negotiations with Kim and Khamenei before he thinks about giving a go. If he approves negotiations, and they take a while to get results, it could be worth it."

With a worried look Levy said, "Warren, for Elliot and Harley to come here tonight, they must feel they have a very important and very dangerous situation to deal with, a situation involving atomic proliferation, and they somehow have to manage to deal with it successfully in a very short timeline."

"That's exactly what they will say tonight. That's the way they always are with me. Jeff, I'm sick of it. So is Lessing, and so is Kerry."

"I have a problem, too. Whatever the Ilyushin flight turns out to be, it will have to affect the Secretary of Defense, but I haven't heard anything about it from Carter even though there are obvious international law problems. It could be that Elliot hasn't come to see him. Calendar problems. It could be Elliot hasn't told Carter enough on the phone to satisfy him. Or, I would think just as likely, he hasn't said anything to me because there is some political pressure on him and he can't figure out what he should do about it. The point is that he doesn't like Elliot going around him, just as you don't, but he works it out calmly and quietly."

"Ashton Carter can do it that way because he had years as an academic, a Harvard University professor, and now he is the Secretary of Defense. Jeff, this is going to be the standard CIA poke in the State Department eye. They give you what they call a briefing, an hour or two, an outline of sorts, they don't answer most of your questions, they tell you to sign, you sign, and they are gone. You never find out what happens, or you find out what happened months later from the television news."

"If they are working with an emergency, no news may be the right way to go. In other situations delayed news reports may not be their fault. And there are some results you don't want to ever know about."

"I don't know if there really is an emergency the way I understand an emergency. Tonight I am representing the Secretary of State, and I want them to tell me everything they know. I want them to tell me everything they think they know. I want them to answer my questions in a way I can understand, and then let the State Department work the way it was designed by the Constitution to work."

Levy took a slow sip of his wine and said, "Sometimes, Warren, we really don't know just how the United States government is supposed to work. The nine justices of the Supreme Court often don't agree."

"That's why the Constitution puts executive authority on the President, and the officers he appoints and are confirmed by the Seante, the Secretary of State, Secretary of Defense, and the rest of his cabinet, all of whom are directly responsible to the President. Howard Elliot thinks the Director of the Central Intelligence Agency can act like he is the Secretary of State. He thinks that because he can personally confer with the Russians about intelligence, he can also confer with them about all sorts of other matters the Secretary of State is involved in, all while keeping it to himself. All while refusing to tell the Secretary of State what is going on. And then he can cut out the Secretary of State, and the Secretary of Defense, and he can take whatever action he wants on his own. Or at least he can go to the President on his own without telling the Secretary of State or the Secretary of Defense. Jeff, with a little negotiating the Secretary of State might be able to take care of this international airfreight business."

"Ashton Carter is a good Secretary of Defense. He has a good staff. John Kerry is a good Secretary of State. You are part of his good staff. They do not decide for the President. The President decides whether the Secretary of State should try to negotiate with Kim Jong Un."

"Negotiations are tough, they take time, but unless there is a real emergency, we should try. The Secretary of State should know everything that is going on. In a situation like this, the Secretary of State, not Elliot, should bring the complete package to the President with recommendations for his decision. Instead, Elliot goes to the President all by himself with his recommendations. You think he may have. That wouldn't surprise me. You say he does it all the time because the President wants him to. Jeff, I understand that sometimes it may have to work that way. I've been around long enough to understand that, but I don't like it in a situation like this where there may be time for negotiations."

Levy nodded and took another slow sip. "Did Doug say anything on the phone about the actual workings of any plan with the Russians?"

"There was something about shooting the plane down at night over the ocean. Shooting it down at a curve in the Korean coastline, a few miles out. There was something about a Hornet fighter from a small American aircraft carrier maybe fifty miles offshore, and a Russian backup fighter from an airbase near Vladivostok. Nothing definite. He said somebody will be talking to Admiral Mullin about the fighter on the carrier."

"Parking a carrier anywhere near the North Korean coast is asking for trouble."

"He said they realize that with the carrier there are all sorts of positioning and timing problems."

"For tonight, Warren, when push comes to shove, where are you?"

"Jeff, I can complain to you. It doesn't help me tonight."

"So where are you?"

"I'm in a bind. If Elliot can show me tonight that it is likely there will be an airfreight delivery to Iran very soon, a few days, a week, two weeks, if he can show me that for practical purposes there is no time for negotiating a way to stop it, I will have to advise the Secretary to sign on tomorrow. If I think there is time to negotiate, I'll advise the Secretary to call Howard Eliott and give him a piece of his mind."

Levy shook his head. "You don't want Kerry to do that. All negotiations with Kim, and all negotiations with Khamenei, are going to take a long time. As you said, State Department negotiations about uranium and plutonium are tough. They can take years."

"Always tough, sure, but not always a long time. The Russians have the same interests we do. I'm talking about joining with the Russians, and also other countries with the same interest we do, to put quick pressure on Kim to stop the flight, stop the whole idea of a sale to Iran, or a sale to any other country."

"Elliot's always practical. He probably has been thinking that negotiations with Kim won't work, even with other countries on our side pushing Kim, negotiations just won't work for us."

"If that is the way he is thinking he may be right. Until he shows his cards how can I know. Jeff, tonight I am listening. Tonight, I am not agreeing to anything, and you back me up."

Rush served full glasses at the dining room table. For five easy going friendly minutes, seemingly friendly, Elliot praised the Beaujolais, Rush explained the location of the Cru villages and praised the beauty of the northern Burgundy area. Harley smiled, agreed, and added that it reminded him of the vineyards and little towns north of San Francico, Calistoga, St. Helena. The light banter couldn't last.

Elliot looked at his watch and turned dead serious.

"Warren, we thank you for your hospitality, but we don't have much time. As Doug told you on the phone this afternoon, this is about the uranium and plutonium airfreight from Pyongyang to Tabriz using the Air Koryo Ilyushin 76. Doug could only sketch it on the phone. What I can tell you is that several intelligence sources are involved. We think our sources are reliable. Everything we have points the same way."

Rush said, "Everything is reliable? Everything makes good sense?"

"Yes, the intel is reliable, and everything we have points the same way. The Ilyushin will fly, we can't be certain when, probably in a week or two, starting from Pyongyang at night, refuel in Mongolia, and land in Tabriz in the afternoon the next day. There are three sets of issues for us: should we or the Russians be primary, how, and where, to shoot the Ilyushin down, and if we are primary getting full Russian support. We will be acting thousands of miles from our nearest base, and we must have full Russian support. We understand, and the President understands, that every part of this is difficult and risky business, and the President wants the Secretary of State and Secretary of Defense to sign on before he considers approving anything."

Rush said, "Of course he wants full support. He always does. The question is support for what."

"He wants to know the support for the operation and details on the operation. I have to get with Secretary Carter and explain what's happening with Kim and Khamenei. Like you, he will want a full briefing, and like you, he will have a lot of questions I can't answer. At this point in an operation that's the way it always is. Jeff, I'm glad you're here. If you have questions, go ahead and ask, because there are international law issues involved and the

President will want a supporting legal opinion from you because of your international law expertise."

General Levy said, "The President has a flock of experienced international law lawyers."

"No two of them can agree on anything, and they can take forever."

"If you are talking about long delays by the Office of Legal Counsel, it is because of the nature of what they are being asked to deal with."

"Jeff, he will want your opinion because of your fine reputation, your good work, your prestigious title, and, more important, because of the work you have done for him."

Rush frowned. "Jeff is here to listen. He is not here to talk about writing a legal opinion. I am waiting for the details of your plans going forward so that I can advise the Secretary of State in the morning."

Elliot put both hands flat on the table and leaned over. *"We don't know when this Ilyushin will fly but fly it will.* He paused, then continued without emotion, "Maybe at dusk with the new Moon, and fly dark. Not necessarily on a controlled route. Or maybe on a controlled route with lights on. Dark or light, it will fly. The next day it will be unloaded in Northern Iran with enough fissile stuff for several atomic bombs and dozens of tactical atomic bombs. Warren, I understand why you want to see more intelligence. As usual, the intelligence is incomplete, but everything we have, we have from several reliable sources, points the same way. We have good intelligence for a funded contract, escrow payments, and Tabriz delivery. At Langley we have to deal with that all becoming an overnight airfreight reality very soon."

Rush asked, "Is there more?"

"What do you want to know?"

"The money. If there is a deal, there has to be money. A lot of money. How about the money? There has to be an escrow. Is there a funded escrow?"

"There's a funded escrow with Credit Suisse."

"You are sure?"

"Our intel assures us that there is a fully funded escrow with Credit Suisse, so we are reasonably sure."

"What does that mean?"

"It means we have what we believe is good intelligence, and we are reasonably sure it is with Credit Suisse."

"Where?"

"Zurich."

"How much? How many Swiss francs?"

"I don't remember how many Swiss francs. It's the equivalent of four hundred million American dollars."

"What are the escrow terms? What are the obligations on both sides?"

"Half the money will move from Tehran to Pyongyang, bank to bank. The bird will fly, there will be a delivery, and the other half, less the escrow fee, will move to the Pyongyang bank. Both payments will be from an Iranian bank to the Swiss bank to a North Korean bank."

"About your bank intelligence, how certain are you about this Credit Suisse escrow? This fully funded escrow. What are your sources?"

"Warren, there is detailed information about the money transfers. The sending and receiving banks, dates, obligations, and amounts. I can't reveal the sources."

"Howard, I would guess that you believe your people found a way to penetrate the encrypted correspondence between all three banks."

"That's a reasonable assumption."

"And you also successfully decoded all the information from all three of them."

"That's also a reasonable assumption."

"I have doubts, very serious doubts, that you successfully penetrated Credit Suisse."

"You may be right."

"You may have fallen into a good intentioned intelligence mix up, or whatever name you want to put on it, by only penetrating the Iranian and North Korean banks."

"Unlikely, but possible."

"Suppose you were misled by the North Korean bank about the escrow, then what?"

"We were not misled."

"Suppose you were."

"Warren, if there were no escrow it would suggest to us that the Ilyushin will fly to Tabriz, but it will carry an innocent commercial cargo on the first of several flights to Tabriz, and on one of the later ones, we may not know which one, perhaps a few months from now, it will carry weapons grade uranium and weapons grade plutonium from Pyongyang to Tabriz. It will take off at dusk loaded and return empty."

"If there were no escrow, and North Korea agreed in negotiations to accept International Atomic Energy Agency inspection of the plane before every flight, then what?"

"It will never happen. It won't. Kim wouldn't accept it. On the Iranian side, we are confident Ayatollah Khamenei, and the army chief, wouldn't agree to it."

"How can you know?"

"We believe in history."

"It will never happen if you never try. For the Secretary of State, agreeing to IAEA inspections would mean that Kim is insisting on the right to have Air Koryo fly to Iran like every other commercial airfreight carrier. It would mean North Korea is making a statement that if Korean Air, with its headquarters in Seoul, can fly airfreight to Iran, so can Air Koryo from Pyongyang. We have to think first in terms of negotiations."

"Warren, I fully accept your views, your position. What you are suggesting may have diplomatic merit, I accept that, but negotiating with Kim and Khamanei at this time about international air freight rights is not necessarily the best way."

"And your way is not necessarily the right way."

General Levy said, "Let's lower the temperature. Howard, I take your point. From your position, I understand it. However, Warren's approach also makes sense. I am not speaking for the Secretary of Defense, I am speaking for myself when I tell you that the President should be told that, if possible, negotiations should be given a fair chance."

"We will certainly explain our position on negotiations in full to the President."

"Are the Russians already involved?" Rush asked.

"Yes. Korea is their backyard, they don't want uranium and plutonium being flown over their country, and they don't support having Iran becoming a nuclear power. It would upset the balance of power in the Middle East and Central Asia."

"Who is handling this for the Russians?"

"Warren, even if I knew, you can appreciate that I couldn't tell you."

Levy looked at Howard Elliot and said gravely, "Another big issue. You and your whole crew must have thought long and hard about what could happen if the plane is shot down over land instead of over the ocean."

"We have thought about it. Jeff, we have thought about it a lot, and we think the risks are worth it, serious as they are, considering the alternatives."

"So, tell us."

"If the Ilyushin goes down over land near the coast at night we would expect the crash site will be found from the air quickly in the early morning."

"Then what?"

"We would expect the people in the area would be ordered to stay where they are, and the area would be quarantined. A small search party would be quickly assembled and should arrive in a few hours. It should be able to reach the crash site and account for all the cargo by nightfall."

"North Korea has a lot of hills and mountains. Suppose there is a cloud cover so the crash site is not discovered from the air, and the plane goes down in hilly wooded terrain with the nearest road miles away. In that case the crash site would not be found and reached by the search party so quickly."

"Maybe not."

"With a small search party scrambled together searching in a remote area, probably not."

"If not by dark, with an organized bigger search party all the cargo should be found and secured within a few hours after daybreak the next morning."

"It might not work out that way. The missile blast might rupture some containers. The crash might rupture some containers. Some local people may get to the crash first and take off with some of the cargo."

"Jeff, over the ocean, over land, there are serious risks either way. The President will know what we think the risks are, and he will have to decide whether to go ahead."

"Just whether to go ahead?"

"He will decide whether to go ahead, and how."

"And how? What does that mean?"

"We will set out different ways, several approaches, and arguments for each one as we see them."

"What kind of approaches and arguments?"

"Jeff, you know I can't answer that, but in general it will be what we have been chewing over tonight with both of you. How do we know? What don't we know? What should be done? What are the risks?"

"Spell it out."

"I can't do that."

"Howard, it seems to me that the Secretary of State and Secretary of Defense have a right to know. Spell it out in general. As best you can."

"There is the intel part, how good and what is missing. There is the coordination with the Russians part. How solid is that? There is the operations part. Watching the Pyongyang airport for the Ilyushin to be loaded and take off. Relaying that to the Vladivostok airbase controllers. Tracking the Ilyushin to Wonsan and into the Vladivostok traffic stream. Relaying that to the Vladivostok airbase controllers to send orders to the attack aircraft."

"The tracking depends on the Russians?"

"Almost entirely. I can't go into that."

"A Russian controller in the Vladivostok airbase will give the order to attack?"

"Yes, in our view, it has to be that way."

"There could be an American officer giving his advice at the Russian's side?"

"Yes, but if you mean both agreeing on anything, we believe that would be a big mistake."

"So, what about us relying, or not relying, on the Russians?"

"Jeff, that's a big question. We will probably tell the President that we should not stand aside, that just relying on the Russians would be a mistake, and we should have the ability to work with the Russians as best we can as our plans develop and are put into action."

"The President may want an option. How about intercepting the flight, give a warning, and get it to turn back."

"He probably will ask about that."

"So, what are you going to tell him?"

"We haven't decided. Jeff, we don't have any reliable expertise on what to expect the Ilyushin crew would decide to do. We don't have any reliable expertise on anything like that."

"You must have some psychologists that study motivations of aircraft pilots in emergency situations."

"We do, but it seems none of them have ever had to think about our situation. We will probably want to talk to some of your Military Air Transport crews about how they would react to tracer fire in front of them at night from an unknown plane. The firing would be coming from a plane they can't see and a plane they can't follow to an airport unless it gets ahead of them and turns on blinking lights. Our present thinking, whatever that's worth, is that even if the attack plane fired a line of tracers in front of the plane, pulled ahead and turned on blinking lights, they would not change course. After a few minutes they would turn off all the plane's lights, maneuver sharply, and escape into the night. A backup fighter would not be able to find it."

"Then what?"

"There is no way I can answer that."

Rush asked, "What's this about an aircraft carrier? A Hornet attack from a carrier off the North Korean coast. Why get the United States Navy involved in any way?"

"We will support the Air Force getting involved as the first attack plane, or as backup to a Russian, but we will not support getting the Navy involved with an aircraft carrier. That is inviting an attack on the carrier by North Korean aircraft and submarines. This all goes back to who should be first, and relying, or not relying, on the Russians. The argument for the American fighter attack with a Russian backup is that this is a tricky night operation, probably a night attack, and requires American expertise to find and hit the right plane. The argument also is that the Russians might shoot down the wrong plane and let the Ilyushin escape. The Secretary of Defense does not want to be called to answer questions by a congressional subcommittee investigating the failure to stop delivery of weapons grade uranium and weapons grade plutonium to Iran. The Secretary of State does not want to be called to answer. The President does not want to answer. I do not want to be called. The questioning would come down to why did we let the Russians do the job? Because we trusted the Russians is not a good answer."

Rush said, "Suppose Pyongyang decided airfreight is too dangerous. They charter a small ship. You find out. Would you recommend sinking the ship?"

"We would support Admiral Mullin ordering the Navy to intercept the ship and turn it to a friendly port to be searched and seize the cargo."

General Levy said, "There may not be a friendly nearby port. What happens if there is an international maritime uproar and the port authority refuses to allow the search and seizure?"

"It would depend on the port and the crew. Greek port, Greek flag, and Greek crew? Hong Kong port, Panamanian flag with Vietnamese crew? Egyptian port, Portuguese flag, with Indian crew? The President would have to consult our allies and decide what to do."

"The President would ask the State Department, and he might also ask for your position."

"There will be lots of tough questions for the President to decide. For some of his questions we may not have an answer. Not a good answer. I should tell you I talked with Admiral Mullin. He is going to ask Secretary Carter to have Farah Habig brief the Joint Chiefs. You both know Habig, don't you?"

"Levy answered, "Yes, we both know Habig. Will he be speaking for himself, or for you?"

"For himself, within approved limits. I'll call Admiral Mullin and tell him that you can both have a copy of the transcript. I'm sorry we couldn't give you a better briefing. I'm sorry we couldn't reach more agreement for going forward. We have work to do, we have to leave."

Rush raised his hand and said, "One more question."

"Just one."

"About this aircraft carrier again. Finding the right plane on that route to attack at night. There are a lot of planes about the same size. They all have the same blinking lights. I think it's alternating blinking red and green wing lights, and a steady white taillight."

"I've been told several times that finding the right plane with absolute certainty at night is going to be a problem. They will be close together, one after another, going North and South on the same route, some of them off schedule a few minutes, and some an hour or more."

"It's a big problem."

"How does the United States Navy at night get its fighter with missiles to the right spot fifty or so miles off North Korea, and launch the fighter at just the right time for the pilot to find what he thinks is probably his right target and shoot his missiles at what he thinks is probably the right plane?"

"Warren, you're right, it's a big problem, and we will not support the Navy getting involved."

"It is more than a problem. What's going on?"

"I was told the Navy will find a way. Leave it to the Navy, the Navy will find a way. That's all I can tell you."

"Who told you?"

"A political figure. He was involved in starting this carrier and fighter attack business. It took on a life of its own. That's not very helpful, but we have work to do, we have to leave."

"Howard, I've listened to you," Rush said, "Now you listen to me. Don't jump into this. Leave time for negotiations. If the Iranians manage to put an atomic weapon together tomorrow morning the big picture won't change. They can't use it. They can't use it just as the English, French, Russians, Israelis, Chinese, Indians, Pakistanis, and North Koreans can't use it. The Ayatollah knows it. His army chief tells him that's the reality, and the people in the streets tell him the same thing. Negotiated coordinated economic sanctions have been the centerpiece of the JCPOA, and that could go on. That is why the Secretary of State should know a lot more of what is going on with the Ilyushin."

"Warren, you are right, but sometimes that is not possible. Sometimes the Secretary of Defense has to know, the President has to know, but the Secretary of State doesn't want to know. We're late, thank you again for your hospitality. We do appreciate it. We have to leave."

As the sound of the car faded away, Warren Rush picked up the bottle, looked gloomily at Levy and said, "For them, it's mostly full. For us, it's mostly empty. As I expected, that was a CIA poke in the State Department eye. That's what it was. Doug Harley didn't say a word, he didn't lift a finger, but it was a poke in the eye by both of them. First, Eliott says there is nothing more to tell me. Then he tells me I'm asking too many questions about things I shouldn't know about. And then he says after Habig briefs the Joint Chiefs we can both have a copy of the transcript."

"Warren, put the bottle down. I don't like their attitude either, but you better cut them some slack."

"Really?"

"Really. They have intelligence you don't have, you shouldn't have. They have sources you don't want to know about and I don't want to know about." He meant it.

"Henry, do you know something about this uranium and plutonium sale I don't? Do you know anything about the airfreight I don't?"

"It's new to me. The sale, the contract, the escrow, the airfreight delivery, all of this is new to me. Until tonight I knew nothing about any part of it."

"You do now. What are you thinking?"

"I have a feeling you're right about questioning their getting information about the escrow from Credit Suisse."

"Why?"

"Just what you were asking about. My guess is that they did not try to get inside the Credit Suisse elaborately protected information system because they were afraid they would be caught. If they did try to get inside, they couldn't. And maybe they didn't try because they have a well paid inside source for that kind of information."

"Right."

"And if they did somehow get in, they didn't get all the relevant information in the system, and they had problems reliably decoding all of it."

"Probably."

"And there is another reason. In the past they probably picked up Credit Suisse international messages and could not decrypt the highly sophisticated Credit Suisse encryption. They may have done better with the North Korean corresponding bank."

"This whole business isn't some sort of an intelligence mix up or a trap?"

"Some of the intelligence may be mixed up, but I very much doubt that any kind of trap was set for them by Kim himself, or any of his people. I also have a feeling they are already talking to Russian intelligence, sharing their information, and making plans. In a few hours it will be morning in Moscow. That's why they have to get back to their work tonight."

"Tomorrow I'll put together a brief for the Secretary. I am going to recommend that he ask for all the intelligence."

Levy shook his head. "Warren, you can get yourself so wrapped up in this you can't think straight. Elliot has good reasons for protecting sensitive intelligence."

"For Howard Elliot, everything is sensitive. The right way to deal with this is the State Department way. We pull in from everywhere all the information. Intelligence is more than one part of that. Intelligence is the bedrock. We put everything together. We send it with our analysis and recommendations to the President. We go see the President once or twice, or more, and he makes his decisions, and to the extent we can, we carry them out. It has been the proper State Department way for many years, though Republican and Democratic administrations. We haven't always done it that way, but it is the right way."

"Warren, for where you are now, I see two ways to go besides shooting down the Ilyushin."

"Just two?"

"There are negotiations, which we have been talking about, and there are warnings not to fly, which we haven't."

"I will recommend warnings. Before the flight, and after the flight starts. I will also recommend that the Secretary warn the President that the influential people that are pushing the carrier idea want the Ilyushin shot down to give Kim a lesson. They think it will make them look good. Some Russians may also want the plane shot down to give Kim a lesson, make them look tough, look good. I will spell out for the Secretary what the CIA is doing to us, and what I think are all the different ways to go."

"Warren, I would not do that. I would be careful not to pick a fight with Elliot and the CIA. You're annoyed. Don't turn this into an internal war."

"You really think I might do that?"

"Yes, I do."

129

"Jeff, I'm mighty annoyed, but I am not foolish. Thanks for coming. Regards to Phyllis."

"Give my best to Edith. And the next time I am here let's see her latest English landscape acquisition."

"She will be happy to show it. Lake Windermere in the morning sun. Oil on canvas. Young woman artist starting to make a name for herself in the English art world. Better yet, bring Phyllis over for dinner and you can both admire it. I am saving my German Riesling for such a happy meal with nothing about my work, nothing about your work."

"Good idea."

CHAPTER 13

Dressed in a long coat and wool scarf for Moscow cold weather and carrying a small zippered briefcase Habig walked through the massive doors at 32 Smolenskaya Sennaya Square, stopped at the reception counter and waited until an officer came over. He felt elated that he had managed to come to Moscow, and worried about whether, and how, he would be received by Marloff. He told himself had made his preparations as best he could. He did not have an appointment for any day and time, only an approximation. No doubt, if they met it would be in an interview room, and everything he said would be preserved on some hidden recorder, but, most important, he had started. He had come from the splendidly rebuilt Baltschug hotel across the Moscow River from the Kremlin, he was at the reception counter, he was starting, and whatever was ahead for him, so be it.

He said in Russian that he had a letter for His Excellency, Under Secretary Lev Marloff. The officer read it, took the letter to an older officer who read it and put his stamp and initials on the back. The younger officer returned and asked him to complete an identification form and Moscow contact form. He identified himself as Farah Habig, an American information official. He wrote a Washington street address and telephone number, and for Moscow a room number at the Baltschug Kempinski hotel. The officer read the information and said, "Sir, your communication to

His Excellency will be processed today. You may expect to be notified by telephone at your hotel within four days. If you return to meet His Excellency you may bring writing materials with you, but do not bring any electronic devices with you."

Late the next afternoon, after submitting to a pat down search, Habig met with Lev Marloff in a small office on the nineteenth floor. Marloff looked years older than he remembered him. Almost all gray hair, deeper wrinkles around the eyes, perhaps a bit shorter. Speaking Russian, Marloff welcomed him, served little cakes and. wine. Habig thanked his host for meeting with him. Marloff asked if his Baltschug accommodations were satisfactory. Habig replied the new Baltschug was equal in every way to any and all first class American hotels around Washington.

"My good old friend," Marloff continued, "It is a pleasure to see you again. And a pleasure to see you looking fit to deal with our Moscow weather."

"It is cold here now like December in Langley. Keeps you awake."

"You suggested on the telephone that you were most anxious to talk about North Korea and Iran soon becoming very close friends. I assumed you meant nuclear chums."

"Yes, nuclear friends, nuclear chums, nuclear troublemakers, too close, too soon."

"Nuclear troublemakers, indeed. We have an hour or so. Where do you want to start?"

For half an hour Habig told Marloff his concerns about what he believed about the expected North Korean sale and delivery of uranium and plutonium to Tabriz. The terms of the contract negotiated in Pyongyang over several months, the funded Credit Suisse escrow, the expected route of the Ilyushin 76 delivery flight to Tabriz. Marloff listened thoughtfully without interruption, then told him there was Russian intelligence along the lines he had been describing and followed with questions about the expected time of the Ilyushin's flight, its expected route over Russia, and the escrow payment terms. Habig answered that the intelligence he had was mostly what he considered reliable but everywhere incomplete. Marloff asked him to explain.

Habig answered, "All the information I believe reliable, points the same way. It is all generally consistent, but it is incomplete.

The rest of the intelligence is inconsistent. You may assume that others have information I do not, and some of it might be different. Some of it, more or less the same, can reasonably be interpreted differently."

Marloff waved his hand. "No need to apologize. That's always the situation with our intelligence about a very complex operation, and especially when it is about anything Kim may have decided to do."

"Not only is this important, it is also very complicated technically. Actually, in every way. It has parts that involve very difficult decisions on our side, and I thought it would be worthwhile for both of us to have a little talk and share views about what can and should be done."

Marloff nodded, and asked what he believed the American options were for dealing with the Ilyushin. Habig responded that he believed there were two possible approaches. First, immediately notify North Korea, informally, that no flight carrying uranium or plutonium would be allowed to reach its destination. Two, if the Ilyushin flies it should be given a warning soon after takeoff, and an opportunity to turn back - a line of tracer fire ahead of it, and if it did not turn back, it should be shot down, if possible, over the ocean north of Wonsan.

Marloff slowly nodded. "How much warning? If it flies at night, which seems likely, a second line of tracer fire in front of the plane? A third?"

"It will probably be at night, that's what my information points to, and I say a second line of tracer fire, and if needed a third because at night on a busy route there is a real risk the wrong plane might be destroyed."

Marloff said that in his opinion in this case it would be best if Russia dealt with the Ilyushin flight on its own, and the American military should not intervene in any way, or if it does, only with Russian coordination. Habig agreed.

After a pause for a sip of wine by both, Marloff asked Habig if he was still getting into proposals for international cooperation in space, in continued exploration, in technology, in joint habitation, in ownership and use of space minerals. Habig answered that he personally was devoted to all those grand ideas, but the specifics weren't being developed yet. At best, he might in time make a small contribution.

Marloff waved his arm again. "Don't apologize, my friend, small contributions can be important. We have some time, tell me where you think we should be headed in space policies and space politics." Habig talked for half an hour without interruption.

Marloff ended the meeting telling Habig that he had arranged a trip for him to talk with a colonel who is dealing with the Ilyushin flight to Iran, and he would be informed by a telephone call to his hotel room.

It was a slow taxi ride in late afternoon Moscow traffic, and an hour later Habig was back in his room at the Baltschug. He was tired, emotionally and multiple time zones tired. His whole body was very tired. He didn't want to look across the river at the walls and towers of the Kremlin and think of all the centuries of dark history that went with them. It was getting dark in Moscow; in a few hours it would be getting light in Langley. He lay down on the bed. Thinking about Marloff's informed questions he concluded that Russian intelligence may have penetrated his computer several times and mastered his encryption. Several times over the last year. He determined that the first thing he would do when he returned to his cubicle was run a full scan for unauthorized activity of any kind, and regardless of the results, add another layer of encryption.

An hour later the telephone rang. An army car would be at the hotel main entrance at nine to take him to an army base for an information meeting with Colonel Oleg Semyonov and return him to the hotel by six.

At nine Habig stood outside the hotel entrance holding his briefcase. A shining army car rolled up. The middle aged driver with sergeant's stripes on his sleeves came around and asked, "Sir, you are Honorable Farah Habig?"

"Yes."

"Sir, please to get in and fasten the seatbelt. We will drive to an army base about an hour and a half away. Depending on the traffic we should be there between ten thirty and eleven. I will drive to the headquarters building and show you the entrance to the building where you are expected."

"Thank you, sergeant."

"I will wait and drive you back to the hotel when you are ready to leave. With the heavy traffic returning to Moscow in the late afternoon it will probably take longer going back. If you must be back by six it would be better for us to leave at least half an hour early."

Habig climbed in and fastened the seatbelt. The driver closed the door, started the car, and without another word delivered him at high speed to the front entrance of the headquarters building on the army base. He came around and opened the rear door, waited at attention, and as his passenger got out, saluted, closed the door and drove away. Habig reminded himself that he must not under any circumstances commit Langley to anything. He tightened his grip on his briefcase and entered the building.

Colonel Oleg Semyonov, a sturdy compact man with keen blue eyes and gray streaked hair above his wire rimmed glasses welcomed Habig to his spare office with a smile and a firm handshake. He said that Marloff had called and explained that an old friend of his from Langley, Farah Habig, who speaks good Russian with a Washington accent, has come to Moscow because he is concerned about an Air Koryo Ilyushin 76. His concern is about the Ilyushin flying a load of weapons grade uranium and weapons grade plutonium from Pyongyang, North Korea, across Russia, Mongolia, and Central Asia to Tabriz, Iran.

"That's right, and thank you for letting me come. Lev Marloff just calls me Habig, and you can, too."

The colonel said, "So Habig, the plane, the radioactive cargo, the timing, the route, that is what you have come to talk about?"

"It is a big subject, and learning about Russian expertise, and how it might be used, that is why I came to Russia."

The colonel waved him to a chair. "He also told me you are a good and experienced man always looking for all the possibilities and details."

"Learning all the possibilities and the details, trying to understand them, and put them into a picture that makes sense to me, that is the first part of my work. The second part is explaining my picture to my supervisors and answering their questions to their satisfaction. Sometimes the second part can seem more difficult than the first part."

Colonel Semyonov nodded. "As it should be. He also said you

are an independent thinker, something of a political philosopher, concerned about nations competing with each other at great expense to plant their flags on the Moon so that someday soon their cosmonauts and astronauts in their spare time can enjoy whisky and vodka toasts in the dining room of a grand hotel on the Moon high ground."

Habig smiled and said, "I have an interest in the American space program and the Russian space program, the rush to put American and Russian colonies on the Moon, to put Russian and American families there."

"Families? Adults, young and old, babies in diapers, children, teenagers, do you believe that anything at all like that will ever be possible?"

"I believe cooperation would be much better than competition for both countries and for their astronauts and cosmonauts who sometime in the far future will produce and raise their children in space. I believe cooperation is essential for all the countries involving themselves at huge cost in space exploration and all claims to Moon sovereignty. However, I can't imagine an economic system that could sustain itself a week without massive continuing subsidies."

The colonel smiled. "Marloff is right. You do have vision about the future, and a good Russian heart. Is he also right about enjoying vodka?"

Habig smiled. "Yes, a small glass or two for the right toast, for the right occasion."

Turning serious the colonel said, "We have little time, only a few hours, and a lot to talk about, starting with the Air Koryo Ilyushin 76 flying across Siberia. The Ilyushin 76 is the right plane? Do you agree?"

"Yes, more exactly, navigating an Air Koryo Ilyushin 76 being used for airfreight delivery overnight of weapons grade uranium and weapons grade plutonium from Pyongyang over North Korea to near Vladivostok, then as I calculate it, across Siberia, Mongolia, Kazakhstan, Uzbekistan, Turkistan, and the Caspian Sea to Tabriz."

"With an Ilyushin 76 there would have to be a stop in Mongolia for refueling?"

"Yes, at least several hours bed rest for the flight crew, and also the guards, and time for the paperwork buying the fuel, and then refueling the plane."

"So, starting at night all this means it would be flying across Turkistan and then the Caspian Sea in daylight, and so considerably more total time than overnight?"

"Yes, over Turkistan and the Caspian Sea in daylight, and quite a while longer than overnight to Tabriz."

"Everything about this Ilyushin business turns out to be more complicated and takes longer. So, the question is, should this be solely a Russian responsibility or a joint responsibility with you Americans. That for me brings up big planning issues and an important operation with lots of gaps that have to be filled."

"I can appreciate that."

"So, to start, as best you can, fill me in about the attack plans being considered by your people."

"We believe it will be a night flight. One proposal, as I understand it, is to have two fighters find the Ilyushin along the coast north of Wonsan and make the attack there. Perhaps a few miles from shore. One American fighter with missiles, one Russian back up, or vice versa."

"There must be more parts to these proposals, these ideas, these plans."

"There are several more ideas, but they are not yet fully formed parts."

"What kind of parts?"

"At Langley we think that the Ilyushin will most likely fly at night. We don't have any assurance that the Korean planners have decided yet on flying day or night. Starting early in the morning and staying overnight at the airport in Mongolia would be much better for the aircrew."

"What else?"

"We can't predict if the Ilyushin will fly with exterior lights and its transponder connecting to air traffic controllers."

"For your thinking, should it?"

"It depends. Is it looking for secrecy, so flying without lights or operating transponder, or is it pretending in every way to be just another commercial airfreight flight."

"Any ideas as to which is more likely?"

"No, I go back and forth. In Pyongyang they may not have yet decided."

The colonel asked, "And do you agree that a night attack is far more dangerous in every way? More difficult to find the right plane and positively identify it, and far more dangerous for our pilot."

"In my opinion, any night attack is very dangerous. At night, even with lights and a working transponder, a night attack is dangerous. At night with planes going both ways on the same busy route how can the attack plane pilot be sure he attacks the Ilyushin instead of a previous plane or a following plane? If the pilot is watching the traffic going both ways and gets turned around, which is certainly possible at night, he could attack a plane going south instead of north. The backup pilot could follow and make the same mistake."

The Colonel nodded. "If there are no lights, and no connecting transponder, it's hide and seek. With lights and properly squawking transponder, it's how dare anyone even think of attacking and destroying it."

Habig asked, "To ensure it is the right plane being attacked, what does that require?"

"First, tell me what you are thinking."

"That requires, as I understand it, among other things, accurate minute by minute tracking of the right plane, and getting the right information to the attack fighter at the right time."

The colonel nodded again. "So, we have a full day. First, we will go into how to track the Ilyushin at night. Track the correct Ilyushin. Without accurate identification of the target aircraft, and precise continuing accurate tracking, nothing should even be considered, much less attempted. I have a book of instructions to go over with you. When we finish with it you will stow it in your case. You can carry it through the airport because it is not classified, just tried and proven stuff if correctly followed. Marloff suggested I give it to you so your Russia experts back in Virginia can assure themselves that we are competent, we know what to do. We don't always do it, but we know how."

The colonel stood up. "We've made a good start. We have a fine lunch with twenty officers in your honor. No vodka toasts today, just greetings, friendly handshakes, and good Russian food."

"Just as well there's no vodka. As I get older my experience has been that with a few vodka toasts I'm not talking good Russian, I'm not making sense, I'm done."

"You are safe here. You will meet my space happy engineers. They are good Russians. You will enjoy meeting them. And they will enjoy meeting you."

Habig said, "Sir, I thank you for your hospitality, and I am grateful for the tracking instructions. I will pass the book on to one of our experts who can pass it on to others."

"After lunch we can talk about what should be done."

At noon they broke for lunch at the officer's mess.

There were twenty officers: the colonel, two majors, six captains, and eleven lieutenants, four of them young women. Habig immediately recognized two lieutenants, Pyotr and Alex. He thought they looked just the way they did in Elena's pictures.

There was pink ham, steaming sausages, sauerkraut, boiled potatoes, bread, cheeses, coffee, and honey cake. The colonel told the officers with a grin that their guest was a visiting friend from America who speaks good Russian with an American accent, drinks vodka only for banquet toasts, and looks forward to the day when a lovely Russian cosmonaut and a handsome American astronaut make joyful love on an international space station and their full term baby is born there, and by international law gets space dual citizenship. All the officers smiled, welcomed him, and firmly shook his hand. Habig thought that one of the women might give him a kiss on the cheek. But with his limp he knew better.

When they returned to his office the colonel said, "We need to get back to what should be done about the Ilyushin. You are concerned about tracking an Air Koryo Ilyushin 76 with Air Koryo markings on the fuselage and tail."

"Right."

"Our intelligence is that most likely it will be flying at night from Pyongyang to Wonsan, and then join several other planes flying the route up the Korean peninsula coastline toward Vladivostok. Is that also your understanding?"

"That is also my understanding."

"The Ilyushin should be tracked from takeoff from Pyongyang

to a place where it will be over the ocean a hundred miles or so North of Wonsan where it should be attacked and destroyed. Is that also your understanding?"

"Yes, shot down over the ocean unless it is warned and turns back."

"A sensitive subject. Let's go into your feelings, your position, about a warning."

"My idea is that if it is a night attack the attack fighter would fire a long burst of tracer ammunition in front of the Ilyushin. Maybe two or three bursts of tracers. And repeat if necessary."

"Is that just your personal idea?"

"My view. My personal opinion."

"And a reasonable one, but there has to be more to it. Assume the Ilyushin is flying at night with blinking wing and tail lights, and it is under air traffic control. You track by radar as soon as you can, and you confirm the identity by tuning in to traffic control and the plane's transponder. You are tracking the plane successfully, but at night it may be the wrong plane you are tracking. The crucial part is using people who know what they are doing, who check and recheck, who keep the attack pilot informed all the way. At night, a busy route, one slip, and there can be a disaster. A hundred or two hundred civilians are killed. Perhaps also some military. High government officials are also killed. You agree?"

"Yes."

"So, let's start with the first steps. It's all in the book. Stop me any time if I am not clear." The colonel started explaining from the book the intricacies of night aircraft tracking. When he finished Habig put the tracking book in his briefcase, and asked, "Could the Ilyushin, instead of taking the controlled route to Tabriz chart a direct route, fly dark by night and avoid detection?"

"It could chart a shorter direct route, put on the needed extra fuel, start by night without lights, without transponder, but it would not arrive in Tabriz. Almost immediately, radar would recognize it as a stealth intruder."

"That means for you that it must be shot down?"

"Not in every situation, but very quickly any intruder is likely to have that result. We do not risk an attack by an intruder on what we do here."

"And in space?" Habig asked.

"In the future we will have the answer. For now, the answer is yes and no."

"What does that mean?"

"Habig, before lunch we were talking about a grand hotel on the Moon. So complicated. There probably will be national boundaries on the Moon, but that's not certain. If they are proclaimed it is reasonable to believe they will be defended."

"I told you my American personal views. I saw you listened carefully. You must have your own views."

"We Russians are part of the international community doing such marvelous things in space, mostly separately, some of it together with the United States, the European Union, China, and others."

"As Americans and Russians we both make more complicated plans based on each other's work."

"To some extent, yes."

"There are failures and successes. We explore, we plant our national flags, we celebrate, and we worry about who will own the Moon. Does planting our flag mean all the Moon is ours, or part of the Moon is ours?"

"Habig, I must tell that you that more and more each year it looks that way."

"And everybody crossing the border line without express permission is an intruder who can be shot?"

"Again, the present answer is yes and no. For now we are concerned about intruders flying across our national boundary lines here."

"Sir, I understand that, but I am wondering whether we are ever going to fight over intruders on the Moon. Will soldiers in spacesuits kill other soldiers in space suits for changing sacred border lines?"

"It could come to that."

"We can do better, can't we? There is the United Nations Outer Space Treaty that says no country can own the Moon, or any other celestial body, and the United States and Russia have both signed on along with many other countries."

"Habig, let me ask you a question. Can we have Americans and Russians peacefully living together on the Moon, or anywhere in space? Say perhaps fifty years from now."

"Someday, maybe more like a hundred years, or two hundred years from now, three hundred years from now, we could have a very small Moon colony with Americans and Russians living there. Peacefully, I hope."

"Habig, can you imagine having children there? Can you imagine having old and disabled people there with all their expensive medical, and other needs? Can you imagine some kind of workable joint government?"

"Sir, if it is only a hundred years or so from now, and the government can find a way to pay for it, I'm all for it. Cute little kids born with international space dual citizenship. I can hardly wait."

"I have to go to another more immediate matter. We are much concerned that someone with authority in Washington is arguing that to stop the Ilyushin you should go after the Ilyushin alone, keeping the Russians out. Pride and politics, or politics and pride, it doesn't matter. At Langley you know better, but it may be tempting for others in authority to think that without alerting the North Korean army, navy, and air force you can put a small aircraft carrier off North Korea, send in a fighter to fire a homing missile at the right plane, watch it explode, and sail away. That is not realistic."

"I can only speak for myself. That's not realistic."

"More than not realistic, it is stupid. Do you agree?"

"Personally, I agree."

"In my Russian mind any attack on the Ilyushin must be made by a Russian pilot following Russian orders from a Russian ground controller. A backup, an American backup, is not necessary, and would be very dangerous for both pilots. Do you agree?"

"We are together on that. Personally, I agree, but I cannot commit to anything for Langley."

"When you get back to Langley, I want you to tell your people to put themselves in our shoes. I want you to give them an example that will be truly meaningful to them."

"Such as?"

"If the Ilyushin were flying up the Pacific coastline at night from Mexico towards Los Angeles, you wouldn't let it get close to the United States border. You would track its flight and shoot it down without any warning, and you wouldn't want any Russians getting in your way."

"My trip report will say that you were very knowledgeable, and very helpful."

"Whether Lev Marloff was helpful, or I am helpful, will depend on what your people do. Be respectful of our ability and our determination to protect Russia. Also, tell them we will try not to kill innocent people."

"I will tell them we don't want another KAL 007."

"Good man. Take care with your case. I'll get your car and driver."

Back in his hotel room Habig was weary. He thought about taking a nap, an hour before dinner. Instead, he started writing his report. It did not go well, and after half an hour he stopped and took the tracking expertise book out of his briefcase and started reading. After half an hour he stopped and put the book back into the briefcase and zipped it close. He realized how little he understood while the colonel was explaining, and now again how little, how very little, he was understanding about successfully using radar readings and transponder signals to identify a particular aircraft out of many flying close together along a route.

He understood, painfully, that he knew almost nothing about navigating the attack aircraft at night to the right spot at the right time, maneuvering the plane, and locking in the right target before firing the homing missile.

He realized, even more painfully, that he was ignorant about much of the planning and completely ignorant about all the myriad details. Even so, putting Marloff and Semyonov together, he thought he was right. He was right that there was a negotiated contract for the sale and delivery of uranium and plutonium. He was right, this was not Kim Jong Un and Ali Khamenei getting together and playing intelligence games. He was right that there was funding for an escrow in Switzerland, almost certainly a substantial escrow. He was right that it would be airfreight instead of a ship, it would be an Air Koryo Ilyushin 76 flying from FNJ to ULN to TBZ. He was right that the plans being put together at Langley, and in the Pentagon and in Moscow, were for an attack along the East coast by a Russian fighter, with or without, an

American fighter backup. He was right about the danger of the Ilyushin being shot down over land and some of the cargo ending up in the hands of terrorists.

He was right to worry, to anguish, that Elena could be on the plane being destroyed by a missile.

At a late small dinner in the dining room his mind was racing. What should he put in his report and what should he leave out. Back in his room he continued writing until near midnight.

Elena's name nowhere appeared on what he put down line after line on the paper, but her image, and thoughts of her danger, of her mangled body at the bottom of the ocean, infused his every word, every stroke of his pen.

In the morning his mind was still fixed on the tracking book in his briefcase, what he had put on paper, and what he had left out. Semyonov had asked him if he agreed with this, and if he agreed with that, whether he agreed with almost everything, and he had answered that he agreed. Did he agree with Colonel Semyonov going back and forth about countries laying claim to the Moon? If he did, he didn't agree for the United States government, for the Secretary of Defense, for Langley. He agreed personally. Did it make a difference?

Could Harley or Elliot contend against strict orders he had committed Langley? Let them contend, they weren't going to cancel his security clearances and fire him.

Did he in any way show His Excellency, Lev Marloff, his obsession with Elena? Did he in any way show Semyonov his concern for Elena?

Did Pyotr understand for one moment he was thinking about his beautiful wife while he was looking in his face and shaking his hand?

It didn't matter, none of it mattered. He was useful. He was very useful. Nothing was going to happen to him. Nothing bad was going to happen.

He skipped breakfast and went back to bed. He couldn't sleep. He went back to worrying about committing Langley and justifying himself. He got out of bed and walked around the room. He worried about babbling his erotic dreams about Elena to Eli Wilcox. He got back in bed and pulled the covers around him. Without realizing it he fell asleep and had a dream.

Finally, he had the familiar same happy dream. A private balcony with chairs a few feet apart looking out to Diamond Head and the blue ocean to the horizon. Her blouse was open. She was sitting in a pose like an actress letting him look at her, letting him watch her face as passing clouds changed the light and gusts of wind blew strands of hair across her cheek. She smiled at him, they kissed, and then they went inside and undressed. She smiled at him. She put her arms around him and kissed him. She told him she loved him and he kissed her.

The dream faded and he slept fitfully until noon.

CHAPTER 14

September 28, 2016

The Pentagon E wing secure small conference room. Special meeting of the Joint Chiefs of Staff.

Present: Admiral Michael Mullin, Chairman; Major General Vincent Hennessy, Army; Major General William Turner, Air Force; Major General Graham Parker, Marine Corps; Major General Jeffrey Levy, Staff Judge Advocate, Air Force; Jason McNeill, White House; Howard Elliot and Farah Habig, Central Intelligence Agency.

Admiral Mullin went to the rostrum, thanked everyone for coming on short notice, and introduced Farah Habig as a veteran CIA analyst following North Korean atomic work, today speaking his own views about North Korea and Iran.

As Habig turned to face his audience his tight lips and bright eyes showed him determined to tell the complicated sale and delivery story, to tell the story, what he believed known, half known and unknown, his way.

"I appreciate this opportunity to report to you," he began. "I am authorized to explain what I believed to be known about a North Korean sale of weapons grade uranium and weapons grade plutonium to Iran, the means and terms of payment, and an imminent overnight delivery by air from Pyongyang to Tabriz. To some it might be considered one more delivery of valuable merchandise by airfreight.

"I have been closely following this operation as it has developed over several months but my intelligence, and my interpretation of that intelligence, like all intelligence, today can be valid and partly wrong, or entirely wrong, and more or less wrong tomorrow or next week. I cannot tell you everything I believe known and not known, certainly not in detail, that would take days. The issues I will cover will give you an overview and insight into the complexity of some parts. I am not authorized to answer any questions at this meeting.

"In my analysis of any information I obtain about a possible clandestine operation the first question is always the same. Is this inaccurate, false, information? Is this unintentionally false? Intentionally leaked, but false? Obtaining valid intelligence is crucial, but intelligence is not an end in itself. History shows that both Iran and North Korea are not above playing intelligence games, putting out targeted intelligence propaganda. In this North Korea and Iran situation I reject the game theory. Why invite attention, even possible armed attack, by putting on an elaborate stunt about Kim Jong Un helping the Iran Supreme Leader make some atomic bombs?

"This is not a game. This is part, only a small part, of nuclear proliferation, military and civilian. Atomic bombs, big and small, and nuclear powered power plants, big and small. Surrounding it there is the seven nation years old JCPOA negotiating history, and there is the immediate situation that must be dealt with directly and forcibly. How soon? Within a month, possibly within a week. The idea of a North Korean sale of nuclear material isn't new, but as far as I know, for the first time there is a signed and funded contract to sell and deliver weapons grade uranium and weapons grade plutonium. There is now a detailed sale, delivery, and payment contract with substantial money in escrow.

"The resumed JCPOA negotiations are bumping along, off and on again, going almost nowhere. There are now more than ten years of Iranian attempts to go nuclear. Why hasn't modern industrialized Iran succeeded when backward Muslim Pakistan and miserably poor but proud Hindu India have? Is it intentionally holding back? Afraid of foreign attack? Effective foreign sabotage? Too wound up in continuing expensive adventures elsewhere? To some extent, in my opinion, it is all the above. I see another reason. Resolving key issues would allow Iran to reclaim assets worth billions of dollars frozen abroad, but the leaders of its proxy wars would demand a big share and do away with one of Iran's big complaints.

"Why is North Korea selling, and how badly does Iran want, or need, North Korean uranium and plutonium now? The answer is Kim Jong Un needs money to keep up its sophisticated military, and Iran is putting up the big money to go nuclear at the expense of other military needs and important social programs.

"Iran's negotiators, led by its foreign minister, Mohammad Javad Zarif, staked out a hard barging position at the negotiations telling our negotiators that Iran has purchased enriched uranium from Argentina and bragged that with its underground well protected and sophisticated technology it can create weapons grade uranium and plutonium on its own. In negotiations over the years Iran has been both bragging, and threatening, showing off its rows of new more efficient centrifuges, agreeing to small concessions in exchange for larger ones, and then taking its concessions back.

"I am not challenging the Argentinian sale to Iran of enriched uranium from its enrichment plant, and possibly some plutonium from its reactors, but I doubt that Argentina has sold Iran any uranium or plutonium that was weapons grade. Again, only my personal opinion. In any event, in accordance with the final JCPOA agreement, Iran exported the bulk of its enriched uranium to Russia, severely restricted its own enrichment, and cut off its ability to produce weapons grade plutonium from its reactor. It agreed to, and did all this, to obtain sanctions relief.

"Iran found out the hard way how difficult, and how expensive, its atomic program is. Iran has decided that if is to be an atomic power it needs to import fissile uranium and plutonium. The military leadership of Iran has decided it is less expensive to buy from Kim Jong Un than mine uranium ore in its desert and through long and expensive underground processes convert the ore into weapons grade uranium and plutonium.

"The negotiations for the North Korean sale to Iran began about three months ago when an envoy from Tehran flew to Pyongyang. There were negotiations for over a month dealing with quantity, price, verification, and which party was responsible for delivery to

Tabriz. The price in Swiss francs is the equivalent of four hundred million American dollars. In my opinion Iran would not pay that amount unless the quantity and quality of weapons grade uranium and plutonium delivered was enough for several atomic bombs and many small tactical ones. Enough to let the world know that Iran has become an atomic power.

Tehran wanted payment on delivery and verification in Tabriz. Pyongyang wanted payment on delivery to an Iranian supplied airplane at the Pyongyang airport, or delivery to an Iranian supplied ship at Wonsan, a North Korean seaport near Pyongyang. The result was an escrow with Credit Suisse in Zurich. North Korea, within thirty days of receipt of payment of one half of the contract amount, undertakes to make airfreight delivery to the airport in Tabriz. Upon delivery in Tabriz the escrow pays North Korea the other half of the contract amount. If Iran is not satisfied with the quantity and quality of the delivery it may negotiate with North Korea. The escrow has no obligation regarding the success of any negotiations by the parties. The escrow has no continuing obligation, and no continuing responsibility.

"I believe that a shipment is almost ready. Three weeks ago I confirmed a payment by the Iranian foreign trade bank to Credit Suisse in Zurich in an amount equivalent to four hundred million dollars, and some two hours later payment by Credit Suisse of one half of that amount, minus the escrow fee, to the North Korean foreign trade bank in Pyongyang. The stated purpose of the Iranian payment to Credit Suisse, and the stated purpose of the payment by Credit Suisse to the North Korean bank, is identical. It is for the same numbered contract.

"Why did North Korea agree to undertake airfreight delivery to Iran? There are several other ways that North Korea could undertake the delivery. Consider an ocean freight commercial shipment. Start by concocting a plausible shipping manifest for the carrier. North Korea has an electric powered rail system. Its electrical equipment needs repair, and the shipping manifest could describe the shipment as railroad electrical equipment. Fix up a shipment of a dozen or so old electric generator parts. Put them in large sturdy containers on top of the fissile material. Delivery at the receiving port is to an established Iranian import company for final delivery to an electric motor manufacturing and repair business in Iran, not necessarily in Tabriz. Habig paused. You all see the problem. It is a childish fairytale. It doesn't make sense. It would cost far less to do the work at home, or close to home. With armed guards no shipping manifest story could make sense. A truck delivery with armed guards across Siberia, Mongolia, and Central Asia makes no sense.

"Why not charter a flight from an airfreight carrier of a friendly country? Again, with armed guards, it doesn't make commercial sense.

"The most practical plan is to use Air Koryo, the state owned national passenger and airfreight carrier. No shipping manifest needed, only a couple of armed guards. Air Koryo has an Ilyushin 76, a Russian four engine top wing jet designed for heavy equipment transport in Siberia. It is a sturdy long range bottom loading aircraft. Air Koryo flying to Iran, like any commercial airfreight carrier, will obtain overflight permission, and fly all the way under the directions of air traffic controllers. It must fly with exterior lights, and its identifying transponder properly keyed as directed along the route. It is what commercial airfreight carriers all do. Air Koryo already flies from Pyongyang to Ulaanbaatar, Mongolia, to Chinggis Khann International Airport, and Beijing Capital International. Air Koyo has experienced crews and the Ilyushin 76 has all the required communications equipment.

"The Ilyushin 76 does not have the range to fly nonstop from Pyongyang to Tabriz. Could the Ilyushin with extra fuel tanks fly without refueling in Mongolia, fly a onetime nonstop shorter route to Tabriz? To avoid being intercepted could it fly at night without lights and transponder? A tempting idea, secret, and hundreds of miles shorter, but day or night, it would almost immediately be detected by Russian and Chinese radar and recognized as a stealth intruder. It would never reach Tabriz, and Pyongyang would not get the second half of the escrow payment. So, with refueling available in Mongolia, Kim agreed to undertake what would resemble a commercial overnight airfreight delivery service to Tabriz.

"So much for Kim Jong Un. Now, what do *we* do? It is my understanding there is an active proposal that the Ilyushin should be attacked, shot down, and that should involve an American fighter with a Russian backup. In my opinion the United States military, by itself, cannot make a successful night aircraft attack along the North Korea coast. The United States is thousands of miles away. The Russians are close, something like five hundred miles to Vladivostok. We have no nearby base from which to make the attack. We have no nearby radar to identify the target aircraft to support an attack. The Russians have the Fokino naval base and the Uglovoye air base near Vladivostok.

"It is my opinion that an American plane and pilot should not be used. If the lead pilot, American or Russian, cannot be sure at night he is going to fire his homing missile at the right target. the second pilot, Russian or American, can't be sure either. Also, two planes without lights maneuvering into attack position together at night is dangerous. Even with all precautions taken, very dangerous. It is my opinion that if primary and secondary planes and pilots are used the Russian should be primary.

"If the attack does not take place the Ilyushin will follow its flight plan to Tabriz. It will start at night at Pyongyang with exterior lights and transponder properly keyed for identification and continuously operating. Under North Korean air traffic control it will follow the commercial flight route to Wonsan at the coast, then up the coastline to Vladivostok, then under Russian air traffic control fly across Russia, and later under Mongolian air traffic control to Ulaanbaatar. It will refuel at the Chinggis Khann International Airport, and after giving the air crew and guards time for a meal, personal needs, and some rest, continue under air traffic control of several countries to Tabriz. With the stop at Ulaanbaatar the Ilyushin should land in Tabriz in the early afternoon. So, we have an airfreight flight from FNJ to ULN to TBZ, and we would expect return by the same crew two or three days later by the same refueling route. TBZ to ULN to FNJ.

"There is also the possibility that the Ilyushin will be destroyed over land near the coast. The cargo would be in containers that probably would survive the crash intact. Unless the crash is in some mountains within a day all the containers would likely be found and secured by a brigade of searching North Korean soldiers. However, if any of the containers ended up in terrorist hands it could lead to all sorts of very serious mischief. For example, threatening to contaminate a lake or reservoir. A town's water supply. Or even doing it.

"There is a proposal to put an American aircraft carrier off the North Korean coast that would monitor the South Asia air traffic route and send in a fighter at night to attack the right plane at the right time. That is not practical. It could result in a wrong plane tragedy, and it could also result in another tragedy, a successful North Korean air and submarine attack on the carrier.

"This area already has a tragic history. KAL 007 was a scheduled Korean Air Lines flight from New York, via Anchorage, to Seoul. It was something over an hour to Seoul when a Russian fighter shot it down in September 1983. It was carrying 269 passengers and crew. Congressman Lawrence McDonald was a passenger. The plane was a Boeing 747-230B flying in daylight off course over the Kamchatka Peninsula. It was moving off land to the Sea of Japan towards North Korea when it was shot down by a Russian SU-15 Flagon interceptor firing a Kaliningrad R-8 missile. Russia at first denied any knowledge of the attack, but later admitted the attack and complained that KAL 007 was intentionally off course because it was on a photograph spying mission, and so, in the words of the Russian spokesman, the Flagon fighter pilot was ordered not to allow the target to escape.

"The Ilyushin 76 will be flying at night. The flight of the Air Koryo Ilyushin 76 will not be the same situation as KAL 007, but they could be remembered as tragedies together.

"Thank you all for your attention."

The Chairman of the Joint Chiefs of Staff returned to the rostrum and ended the special session. He walked out agreeing that one plane would be best, if two planes, the Russian should be primary.

Howard Elliot walked out confident that Habig did well.

Jason McNeill walked out with scribbled notes about loss of White House control of the operation.

Lieutenant General Jeffery Levy walked out with his legal opinion for the President half formed and half evading him.

Habig walked out hearing Elena screaming.

CHAPTER 15

Three days later, at 9:30 A.M. Admiral Michael Mullin finished his second reading of the Ilyushin 76 analysis by Captain Avery Randall, Commanding Officer of the USS Gerald Ford berthed at the Bremerton Naval Shipyard, and Captain Theodore Holquist, the Ford's Chief of Air Operations. The stocky Admiral took off his black rimmed reading glasses and peered at the skipper and CAO sitting uncomfortably in front of his desk. In their anguished faces, as with their bleak analysis in his hands, he saw a forecast of disaster.

The Admiral leaned forward and said, "Relax. There is no way I am are going to send the Ford, or any other carrier, to sit off North Korea or to cruise off North Korea. It won't be there. No American carrier, no American ship, will be there. A Russian speaking pilot will fly a Super Hornet over to the Uglovoye airbase. That will part way satisfy a certain eager Senator, and a few eager House colleagues, and others, but sending a Super Hornet with a Russian speaking pilot doesn't necessarily mean a Sukhoi and a Super Hornet will fly to an attack together at night. Also, it doesn't mean the Ilyushin won't be warned and turned back, or that it will be shot down without warning. The President will have to decide that. Avery, what more is there to say?"

"Sir, Ted and I support the mission, but if there is any way to avoid making this a joint American and Russian attack, we should.

It is too dangerous. Two high performance aircraft and two combat pilots from different countries with different first languages flying close together at night without lights searching for a target over the ocean, trying to coordinate, and then making the attack, that is *too dangerous.* The whole operation is risky, very risky, and with two fighters it is needlessly *too dangerous.*"

The Admiral replied somberly, "Avery, I understand. Ted, your turn."

"Sir, Avery runs the ship, I just fly the planes."

"If I have my way Avery won't sail any ship and you won't fly any plane."

"I am very glad to hear that."

"The trouble is that may not be what I am told to do. So go to it."

"Let me put the political arguments to one side, and push the people side, technical side, the radio communication problems for the two planes."

"Go ahead."

"On the technical side, two points. First, as we understand the plan, our American pilot confirms by radio to his companion Russian pilot that he has the right target, and the Russian pilot by radio is supposed to agree. Or the Russian finds the target, and the American pilot by radio confirms. That done, one of them by radio asks the base controller for orders and gets back orders, attack, or don't attack."

"I understand it has to be something like that."

"Whatever, none of this radio communication is going to be in the clear. All of it will be in code."

"Good point. Whose code?"

"If we send over a Russian speaking pilot it will be Russian code. Our fighter's radio link to the Uglovoye airbase controller several hundred miles away near Vladivostok is unreliable. The Russian fighters radio link is also unreliable."

The admiral said, "I understand."

"Sir, can you see the scar on my forehead?"

"I see it. For a naval aviator that usually is a badge of honor."

"I was seventeen years old driving my family's Chevrolet at night just outside Sebastopol, California. You know, north of San Francisco. Lots of Russians are there from way back. I spoke

English and some Russian, and my cute date spoke English and some Russian. I parked off a back road, we talked back and forth about doing this or that, you know, and later we were trying to find our way back to town in the dark. We were very happy and when she told me in Russian to turn left, I turned left, and when she told me in English to turn right, I turned right. We both thought we were doing beautifully. We came to a crossroad. I looked left, I didn't see any lights coming. I glanced right, I didn't see anything coming. I put the car in gear and started to cross. She saw a car speeding around the curve to the right. She yelled to me in English or Russian, I still don't know which, something like *Scoot Scoot*. I slammed on the brakes. My head hit the windshield. Four stitches. Her head hit the windshield. Three stitches. Something goes wrong at night at a black crossroad both cars manage to stop. If something goes wrong on a black night over the Korean coastline there is a tragedy. Our pilot is flying at night near a busy air route. There might be fifty planes in the air on that route. If they are bunched up there could be five or more planes an hour passing some point on the route. Like San Diego to San Francisco. The air traffic controllers around Wonsan and Vladivostok know the transponders squawking from each plane on the route, but our pilot doesn't, and probably his Uglovoye airbase controller doesn't."

"Could that be fixed?"

"I don't think so. Ordering our pilot to make the missile attack at night on the plane more or less on time for a particular point on the route is a tragedy waiting to happen."

"I hear you."

"Sir, my son is a naval aviator. I would not want him on any joint night mission like this."

Admiral Mullin looked at the two weary captains. "I hear you. You both put a lot into this and you made some good points. However, for now, I must assume the President will give me a go, and we have to be ready."

"Do we have a Russian speaking pilot?" Captain Randall asked.

"Commander Herzman has found a Russian speaking pilot. Steve is waiting for you next door."

Commander Steven Herzman, a balding tall thin man with

glasses like the admiral's greeted the carrier CO and Chief of Air Operations with a broad smile and firm handshakes. "Good morning, glad to meet both of you. The Admiral told me to take good care of you. I'm trying." He gave both of them a card with his telephone number and several other communication connections and motioned them to chairs by his desk.

"This idea of parking a carrier off North Korea is out for now, but Lieutenant Alan Rostov will get a Super Hornet to Elmendorf, and then to Russia. You will take care of him on the Ford for a week or so while Boeing puts two extra tanks on the Hornet. Find a quiet and private cabin for him with an internet hookup so he can download classified files. He may have to make some difficult spot decisions for us over there, and he is going to be reading classified background files for several days, and maybe some nights, to understand the plans, such as they are, and the military and civilians that may be involved. Directly or indirectly. Complicated planning, lots of people. From what I have been told it's all damn complicated and he is going to have to put it all together by himself."

"Meaning," Captain Randall said, "we don't look at the download files?"

"You help him if he asks for help, but don't get into any of it that's classified any more than you have to."

"I may have to bring in some teach savvy people."

"If you have to, you do it. I don't know too much about what tech may be involved, what will be classified, or how high, so I can't help you. You will have to use your judgement."

Captain Randall said, "With some tech help I should be able to give him a secure place with secure internet and communications on board the Ford."

"Good. We are on something of a tight schedule. I have both of you booked on United at 4:45 to Sea Tac. The motor pool will have a car and driver for you at 1:30. You should have time to go back to your hotel and get your bags but don't linger because in the afternoon it can be an hour or more to United check in."

The CAO said, "What's Lieutenant Rostov's story?"

"He is a 26 year old carrier pilot on the Eisenhower at San Diego. He speaks and reads Russian the way people in Northern California speak and read Russian. His CO tells me he likes people, and people like him. Girls like him because he is still not married. He has never fired a missile at an enemy target. Treat him right, and he should work out just fine."

"When will he get to Bremerton?"

"This afternoon he is flying from San Diego on Southwest. If he makes his connection in San Francisco he should arrive two hours ahead of you. He will be watching for you as you get off your United flight. I've reserved rooms for all of you at the Radison Hotel near the terminal. A shuttle will take you to the hotel. There will be a car and driver waiting for you at noon tomorrow."

Captain Randall said, "When does Rostov start his file reading?"

"He should be able to start his reading tomorrow afternoon. By then there should be internet downloads for him about the Vladivostok area, the Uglovoye airbase, and the Fokino naval base. He will have more about the mission and the people involved. That involves the idea that North Korea may be selling weapons grade uranium and plutonium to Iran and delivering it by Air Koryo airfreight. The sale, the delivery flight, everything is uncertain. There will be maps and charts about military and civilian air and sea traffic. There will be information on the North Korean army, navy, and air force, and the North Korean radar chain along the ocean from the DMZ up to the Russian border."

"That's a lot of radar and military assets to go through and absorb," Captain Holquist said.

"In the next couple of days there should also be downloads for him on North Korean government stuff and Pyongyang Russian embassy stuff. Who they are, what they do, who they associate with outside the embassy."

Captain Randall asked, "Who is putting all this together and sending it?"

"The Admiral's intelligence staff. They gather a lot of their stuff from the other intelligence services."

"I'm surprised that you can shake all that out of the other services."

"The Navy is under the Secretary of Defense. He reports to the President. All the intelligence services are under the Assistant Secretary of Defense for Intelligence and Security. The CIA also reports directly to the President and also briefs congressional intelligence committees. If we can't agree on what we should have the Admiral makes a call. If necessary, two."

"What about US markings for the plane?"

"The Hornet will keep its US markings. When it lands at Uglovoye it will go into a locked hanger. That much has been agreed on. Except when he's flying, Rostov will be in civilian clothes as a liaison to look at ways to make it safer for our aircraft to avoid trouble with Russian aircraft. See that he gets a physical exam and all the immunizations he needs for the Vladivostok area."

"He may not be allowed to get all of them at once." Randall said.

"He will survive. Leave him alone with his downloads for a few days, until he tells you has had enough, then get him civilian clothes for cold wet weather and anything else he thinks he might need. He will have a look at the Uglovoye airbase and the Fokino navy base. He will take the bus to Vladivostok, look over the on time and late arrivals of the evening flights, and stay at a hotel overnight. Get him Russian money. The Russian equivalent of five hundred dollars."

"He will be on his own in Vladivostok?"

"He should manage. Any more questions I can't answer the way you want me to."

The carrier skipper responded with a wry smile, "No, Admiral Mullin answered all our questions, you told us what to do, and Lieutenant Rostov will speak for himself."

"I'm sure he will. You have enough time for lunch. The officer's mess is on the floor below. When you get off the elevator follow the crowd. Good hot food and lots of strong coffee. If you run into an old chum, or an old flame, you'll have just enough time for a second cup. It's hurry up and wait, but sometimes with the Navy that's the way it has to be."

Randall said, "Just to be sure, the Ford is not going to Vladivostok, or North Korea, or anywhere else?"

"The Ford is probably not going anywhere. You take care of Rostov onboard, getting his shots and Russian money, and going around in Bremerton for his civilian clothes."

"What do we charge all this to?"

"I will arrange it. You will get orders."

"My finance officer is a nice guy, very polite, but he is not going to be satisfied with that. No orders, no money."

"Give him my phone number."

"I know him. He won't get himself into any part of this. You have to get him orders."

"I will take care of it."

"If Rostov has questions, or problems, who does he go to?"

"You take care of him."

"Security clearances?"

"Security clearances for all three of you are being upgraded. That takes some time. Unless there is some problem about his family background you should expect to get a notice of your upgraded status in a week or two."

"Meanwhile, how much do I tell Rostov?"

"You share with him everything you and Ted have been told. After he gets into the classified files he may want to ask questions to help him paint a picture of the flight of the Ilyushin 76 and where he fits in. If you think it might be helpful, talk with him."

"From what you're telling us, I gather we can be exposed to more classified material well beyond our present clearances for a couple of weeks, maybe a month."

"Don't worry about it."

"How long could Lieutenant Rostov be with us?"

"I expect it will be at least a week, probably longer, before he goes over to Whidbey Island for a briefing on flying the Hornet."

"And after that?"

"This is still being put together. I have a summary for you of the planning to date. Share it with Rostov when you get back to your ship. You will see it is incomplete. Don't worry about it because this a changing situation."

CHAPTER 16

Seven years earlier Alan Rostov, then 17 years old, wrote, and twice rewrote, a letter, then mailed it in the Sebastopol, California post office to his congressman's district office in San Francisco.

Dear Sir,

In May I will be graduating from Sebastopol High School. Last September I wrote you that I was beginning my senior year, and that after graduation I hoped to receive your nomination to attend the United States Naval Academy, and upon graduation become a Navy officer. You kindly replied to my letter encouraging me to write to you again when I graduated, include my academic records, recommendations from my school principal and faculty, explain why I wanted to go to the Academy, and how I was academically and physically prepared for the Academy.

I have always been interested in the ocean and ships. I have a small library about ships and celestial navigation used by explorers and historic naval battles. For my American history class, I have researched and written several papers about the increasing power and prestige of the American Navy since the Revolutionary War. Academically, I have taken all the courses in my high school's science curriculum, and I have the second highest grade average in the graduating class. I am also a member of the debate team, and I have been successful at several Northern California high school tournaments. In part this is because I do my own research and regularly follow national and international news in newspapers and public affairs magazines.

I am also a member of the school Russian speaking club. The members come from families, like mine, who came to America from Eastern Europe.

I am not on any sports team but when the weather allows I run several miles every Saturday and Sunday.

Enclosed is a copy of my grade record and letters of recommendation from the school principal, Mr. Ralph Warner and my debate coach, Mr. Anthony Margulis.

I have tried very hard to earn your nomination. I hope that I have earned it.

Sincerely,

Alan Rostov

Alan Rostov was nominated by his congressional representative for admission to the United States Naval Academy at Annapolis, Maryland. After a plebe summer he became a midshipman in the fall along with the thousand young men and women of the entering class. He accepted the routines and traditions of the venerable institution. He accustomed himself to the tight living conditions at huge Bancroft Hall. He quickly made friends with sons and daughters of families like his and offspring of captains and admirals. He devoted himself with a will to his courses and marched smartly in his brigade.

He wanted to be recognized as an outstanding midshipman. He enrolled in the aerospace program. As he submerged himself in quantum physics, molecular chemistry, high speed computers, and satellite orbits, he turned his fascination with ships to marveling at naval aviation, and in his senior year he joined the aviation squadron for flight ground school.

After being commissioned as a lieutenant (junior grade) he received orders to report to Pensacola, Florida, for flight training. Six months later he joined the fleet at Norfolk, Virginia as a novice carrier pilot.

Two years later, and a full lieutenant aboard his ship at the North Island Naval Air Station, San Diego, he received a late morning telephone call from a Commander Steven Herzman at the Pentagon.

"You are fully qualified as a carrier fighter pilot?"

"Yes. Fully qualified."

"And you speak and read Russian?"

"Yes, the way people in Northern California do."

"Well enough for an ordinary conversation in Russian and read and understand a Russian newspaper?"

"I think so."

"Are you familiar with Russian fighter aircraft?"

"Generally, yes."

"Would you understand a Russian aircraft navigation manual?"

"Not enough to fly with. I would need some help."

"Have you ever been to Vladivostok or North Korea?"

"No."

"Do you know anybody in the region?"

"No, but I may have a distant Russian relative in Vladivostok."

"Have you ever been to North Korea or Iran? Do you, know anyone there?"

"Never been, don't know anybody."

"Are your security clearances up to date?"

"Yes. As far as I know. For what I do now."

"Your CO tells me you are a history buff. American history and Russian history."

"I read a lot."

"Any special reason?"

"I have an uncle in the State Department. He gives me reading lists. He wants me to flip over, get in to the State Department at the bottom, take college language and history courses, and work myself up to be a diplomat. I haven't filed any transfer papers."

"Don't leave until I call you."

Late that afternoon, with only a foggy idea of what the North Korea and Iran fuss was about he hastened to a San Diego International airport departure gate for his Southwest flight to San Francisco with a connecting flight to Seattle Tacoma.

Shortly before midnight he went to scan the passengers coming off the United flight from Washington. There he met weary Captain Avery Randall and Captain Theodore Holquist. He told them he had no orders as to what to do next. Randall told him not to worry, some orders would show up in a few days. They collected their bags and took a shuttle bus to their airport hotel.

The next day after a late lunch on board the Ford, Captain Randall explained to Lieutenant Rostov what was happening.

"There is intelligence that North Korea is selling weapons grade uranium and weapons grade plutonium to Iran, and it intends to use an Air Koryo Ilyushin 76 for airfreight delivery flight. Much of what we should know, we don't know. For now, there is nothing for sure. Everything, including the flight route, is uncertain."

"So where do I, a carrier pilot, fit in?"

"The Russians may have to shoot down an Ilyushin 76 at night somewhere along the busy controlled route to Vladivostok. You can be part of that. They have an airbase near Vladivostok, also a naval base, and it is uncertain, what part the Russians will play and what part you may have in stopping the Ilyushin flight as soon as it takes off, or anywhere along the route to Iran. What I can tell you is that in a week or so you will fly a Super Hornet with extra fuel tanks to Anchorage, to Elmendorf, and then across to the Uglovoye air base."

"I could be firing a missile at night at a plane on a controlled traffic route?"

"You could, but I don't think that's likely. I think most probably you would be a far distant backup to a Russian fighter."

"Backup or not, I would have to have lots of training, flight preparation, and clear orders."

"For this mess you are asking a lot."

"Sir, I am not asking. With respect, Sir, I am telling you that without orders I cannot do anything. I certainly cannot fly."

"Your right, and if your orders are not here in a few days I will work on it."

"Thank you, Sir."

"For now, Captain Holquist and I have enough assurance from Admiral Mullin and his aide, Commander Herzman, for me to go on telling you what I have been told about what you may be getting into. And you have enough assurance from me that you can listen."

"Yes, Sir."

"You will spend several days here on board watching internet downloads of intelligence that probably will be about the North Korean plans, Russian intercept plans, and people that may be involved. Our people, North Korean people, and Russian people who may have a connection. I would think that after you get to Russia you may meet Russian officers and learn what the Russian plans really are, and where you may, or may not, fit in. When the operation is done you fly back to Elmendorf, and then to Whidbey Island."

"How much time will I have for training?"

"I don't know. You look over the Uglovoye airbase and the Fokino navy base nearby. You take a bus to Vladivostok and look over the evening flights. Are they coming and going on time, or are they bunched up in times of arrival and time of departure. Except when you are flying you will be in civilian clothes."

"I don't have any with me."

"Don't worry about it. You will go shopping here. You will

get clothes for cold wet weather. In Vladivostok if you are asked why you are there, your answer is that you are there to find the best ways for American and Russian aircraft to fly safely in that area."

"I will be flying a Super Hornet from Elmendorf across to Uglovoye?"

"Right. I'll see to getting the extra fuel tanks installed on it."

"I am not flying anywhere near Russia unless the Russians are expecting me."

"I understand, and somebody, somewhere, will work on your safe arrival at the Uglovoye airbase and taking good care of you and the Hornet afterwards. Without assurance on all that you are not going anywhere."

In a small cabin by himself over many long hours during the next week Lieutenant Alan Rostov tried to put together, jigsaw piece by jigsaw piece, an understanding of the expected night flight plan of an Air Koryo Ilyushin 76 with a cargo of fission grade uranium and plutonium that would fly from Pyongyang, North Korea, to Tabriz, Iran, and a return flight to Pyongyang. He read, and reread, on the screen before him short precise intelligence reports, and long rambling intelligence reports with different conclusions. He also read several translated North Korean documents covering some of the same materials reaching different conclusions. Other translated documents dealt with Ambassador Grigory Sukhinin and Elena at the Pyongyang embassy, and her monthly travel to Vladivostok for conferences with Moscow trade officials at the Lotte Hotel. There were official announcements of the Vladivostok trade conferences.

There were official photographs of His Excellency, Lev Marloff, in Moscow, Ambassador Ivan Kandinsky in Seoul. There was an official photograph of Ban Chul, a diplomat of the North Korean Ministry of Foreign Affairs. There were pictures of Ban Chul with Anna Volkova going into seafood processing plants and tractor plants, and also pictures of them going into and coming from restaurants and hotels. There were photos of Irina Orlova with Ban Chul going into and coming from restaurants and hotels..

There was a photo of an Air Koryo Ilyushin 76 at Pyongyang airport.

There were other pictures of Elena. Elena graduating from the

Academy. Elena with Ban Chul. Elena with Pyotr. Elena with Pyotr, Alex, and Veronica. Elena with Rolf Ericsson in Seoul. Elena with Rolf Ericsson in Pyongyang.

Lieutenant Alan Rostov studied Elena's pictures. He read, and reread, each analysis. He studied Elena's official picture with Ban Chul. He studied Rolf Ericsson's pictures with Elena. There came a time when he was sure he knew Elena. He was sure that she was sociable and intelligent, and she was very beautiful.

He made a list of the dates that Elena had hosted Vladivostok trade conferences at the Lotte Hotel ending with the upcoming conference. He thought she didn't realize it, but anyone interested in her work could know when her next trade conference at the Lotte Hotel would be. She didn't know it, but flying to Vladivostok she was in danger.

Lieutenant Alan Rostov, United States Navy, flew a Super Hornet jet fighter with two homing missiles and extra fuel from Puget Sound to Elmendorf Air Base, Anchorage, Alaska, refueled the plane, rested, confirmed his orders, and then overnight flew the Air Canada route across the Pacific Ocean to Vladivostok. 6348 miles, 10,216 kilometers.

At thirty thousand feet above the black ocean, the Hornet on autopilot, he had long hours to think. To think about his days looking at a monitor screen trying to make sense of public information, highly classified information, some verified, some partly verified, some acknowledged as speculation. Again, he pulled apart the jigsaw pieces in his mind and rearranged the pieces. He realized that he was still missing pieces of the reality he wanted to know, and to understand. Still, he accepted that the Air Koryo Ilyushin 76 flight was to be funded by a contract with Iran, that the Ilyushin would fly at night from Pyongyang with weapons grade uranium and weapons grade plutonium, and that its destination, after a refueling stop in Mongolia, was Iran's fourth largest city, Tabriz, and there was a company there that processed radioactive materials. He accepted that there would be an attack on the Ilyushin north of Wonsan at an area where it would fly for a short time over the ocean. He thought he knew, and understood, Lev Marloff and Grigory Sukhinin. They dealt with their government's risks, and their government's rewards. They were like all men with power in all governments. They dealt with people under them. They rewarded those who were extraordinarily competent and loyal, and when they considered it advisable, they risked and sacrificed them. Elena and Ban Chul, he thought, must both know they have become important in stopping the delivery of the weapons grade uranium and weapons grade plutonium to Iran. Beyond that, about Elena and Chul being close together, everything that could happen was uncertain, but understandable if it did..

An aircraft carrier pilot does not try to land on a carrier deck at night without the deck lights, and if the Uglovoye airbase did not turn on its landing approach light for him, Lieutenant Alan Rostov was going to land his Super Hornet at the Vladivostok International Airport, park his plane at the airfreight terminal, make a telephone call to the American embassy in Seoul, explain what had happened, and take a taxi to the Lotte Hotel.

Attack plan decisions at the Uglovoye airbase were made by Colonel Eldar Fedotov, a graduate of the Marshal Leonid Govorov Air Defense and Radio Engineering Academy. Colonel Fedotov had no problem finding a fighter pilot to fly with American pilot, Lieutenant Alan Rostov. Several were near fluent in English. He chose Flight Lieutenant Nicholas Levlenko, several years older than Rostov, and more experienced.

Levlenko told Rostov that he spoke English because his mother and father both spoke English. His mother was a retired professor in the economics department of the Far Eastern Federal University in Vladivostok, and his father was a retired Aeroflot pilot. When they lived in Moscow, he told him, his father flew Airbus and Boeing from Sheremetyevo to London Heathrow, New York Kennedy, Washington Dulles, and Los Angeles International. In order to fly in American airspace and communicate with American air traffic controllers and airport officials he had to read, write, and speak English well. So, he told Alan with a smile, English truly had become the international language. Aviation is international, and English made it so for air crews, and also police, taxi drivers, hotel receptionists, restaurant waiters, and young women making their living by serving men who spoke English.

Colonel Fedotov explained to the two pilots, and two Uglovoye air traffic controllers, the mission to shoot down the Ilyushin 76 at night north of Wonsan. For an hour he explained the mission radio communications from takeoff to attack to return landing. He described the attack area over the ocean north of Wonsan, how the pilots were to fly close together with the Russian the lead attack fighter, guidance communications with the controllers, attack firing approval, and the American backup role, if needed. He handed out notebooks, pens, instructions on aircraft night tracking, and told them to study for one hour, put aside what they had been reading, and for one hour explain the search, attack, and return procedures. Rostov to write in Russian, Levlenko in English. The controllers in English and Russian. He scanned through their efforts, frowned, told them they all had to do better, much better, and gave them an hour's break for lunch.

When they returned he handed out more detailed aircraft communications instructions, pilots with controllers, controllers with pilots, pilots with other pilots. Study for one hour, put aside, and write. Rostov in Russian, Levlenko in English. The controllers in English and Russian. He reviewed their work. He told Levlenko he had to improve. He told the controllers they had to improve. He told Rostov he was not sufficiently proficient in Russian military aviation, and unless he improved considerably, he might not fly. He might not fly with a Russian. He might not fly alone. He might not fly. At the appropriate time an appropriate message would be sent to a United States Navy commanding officer. Until ordered to do so, he told Rostov, do not leave the Vladivostok area.

The next day Alan Rostov in civilian clothes, and Russian money in his wallet, took the afternoon bus to Vladivostok. For the United States Navy he was there, as instructed, to look over the airport, the amount of passenger and freight traffic on the Southeast Asia route, note all late arrivals and departures in the late afternoon and early evening, have dinner, and sleep over at the Lotte hotel. For Alan Rostov, the Russian heritage man, he was also there because he had become fascinated with Deputy Ambassador Elena Marloff who he knew was scheduled to be at the Lotte Hotel for a monthly conference with other Russian regional trade officers and Moscow trade officials.

That evening in the hotel dining room he saw a table with what he thought must be the Russian trade officials. At the tables he saw Elena. There was no mistaking her. She was, he thought, as beautiful as her pictures as she sat at a table with four older men who seemed slightly drunk and enjoying being with their beautiful hostess. The table had been set for six. There was an empty chair across from Elena. From time to time he glanced at her through the empty space. He caught her eye and slightly nodded. She noticed, and slightly nodded.

When the party broke up Elena glanced knowingly at him and he watched her go toward the elevator with the men. He finished his meal, paid the bill, left a tip, and went to his room. Half an hour later, just after nine, he picked up the telephone. He told the hotel operator, in Russian, that he was staying at the hotel, room 314, and he would like to speak with Elena Marloff from the Pyongyang embassy. Would she kindly tell Miss Marloff that he was Alan Rostov, an American military officer, a United States Navy Lieutenant, on official business in Vladivostok. The operator relayed the message.

Alan knocked, Elena opened the door, smiled, and motioned him to come in and sit in an arm chair across from her. She smiled again and started in English, "Lieutenant Rostov, you were looking at me all during dinner, and so I have the feeling you may have something to tell me. The hotel operator told me you speak Russian. True?"

"I speak Russian the way an American from Northern California speaks Russian."

Turning to Russian she said, "You are a United States Navy officer. A lieutenant. You have come a long way. There must be a reason. Some sort of important reason. You knew when and where to find me. It could be there is a connection? Please, tell me, don't stand on ceremony."

"Thank you for allowing me to come to your room. Yes, I knew where and when to find you, and the reason I have come here, to your room, is because I have something important to tell you. You are a Deputy Ambassador at the Pyongyang embassy. That is part of the reason. I need to start that way... It is complicated, and it will take some time."

"Important matters take time. First, tell me about yourself, and more about why you are here."

"I am a United States Navy pilot. A fighter pilot. I flew here a few days ago. My plane is a fighter, a Super Hornet. It is at the Uglovoye airbase. It is in a locked hanger."

"So, you and your plane are on some kind of secret business, official secret business that can somehow for some reason involve a Russian Embassy Deputy Ambassador at Pyongyang?"

"I am in Russia on official business that officially involves military and airline traffic safety. And, unofficially, it also involves you. That's not quite right. It also involves you officially, unofficially… and personally."

She frowned. "Officially, and personally? Unofficial business, and personally?"

"Yes, both ways. I came to the hotel to meet you. I came because I believe you may, unknowingly, become involved in a situation that puts you in danger, puts you at serious risk… that could seriously affect your safety, actually cost you your life, and you should know about it. You should know about it, know exactly what it is, so you can protect yourself."

"Lieutenant, you are not a Russian officer with some kind of insider information, you are an American officer, but obviously you have very strong feelings about this. How is it that you speak Russian? Where are you from?"

"I am from near Sebastopol in Northern California. Fifty miles north of San Francisco. My family speaks Russian. They trace the family history back to immigration from Eastern Europe over a hundred years ago."

"Very interesting. Is this your first time in Russia?"

"Yes, first time. In a way I am coming home."

"So, welcome home. Where do you want to begin your concern, your warning? Whatever it is."

"I have to begin with a question."

"Alright."

"Do you know that the Russian government and the American government are both concerned about North Korea preparing to deal with Iran?"

"Deal with Iran about what?"

"About nuclear matters."

"What *kind* of nuclear matters?"

"Selling and delivering a substantial amount of weapons grade uranium and weapons grade plutonium... Can I assume you know about it?"

There was a long silence before she answered, "Assume that I do. Can I call you Alan?'

"Please, do."

"Alan, you can understand I am not sure how to treat you. No doubt you are authorized to come to Vladivostok and the hotel."

"I am."

"Are you authorized to come to my room in the evening?"

"I am authorized to come into Vladivostok from the airbase, to look over the airport traffic, see if the planes are arriving and leaving on time, and spend a night at the hotel. I am not authorized to come here to your room."

"So?"

"I am not authorized, but as long as I don't get in trouble with you..."

She smiled. "Alan, I'm not sure what that means for you... or what it means for me."

"Can I call you Elena?"

"Yes."

"Elena, there is more to this. Much more."

"So?"

"Some of it turns out to concern you, your personal safety, your life... and I am satisfied that I am doing the right thing. Right for you, and right for me. Believe me, if I had any doubts, I wouldn't be here in your room."

"You better explain."

"Because I read and speak Russian, and I fly a Hornet fighter, I was assigned to a highly classified possible operation in this area that could involves North Korea and Russia. For several days before coming here I studied classified reports about North Korea selling weapons grade uranium and weapons grade plutonium to Iran, and about an expected North Korean airfreight delivery to Iran. The timing is from a week to a month or so from now."

"Alan, I've been told about it. Of course, it is classified here, too, but for the embassy executive staff, not all that secret, at least the outlines of the sale and airfreight delivery are not all that secret. I may have read some of the same reports you did."

"The Russian reports, I would think so. Some other reports I read seem to me to be factually unlikely, and some of the analysis of your personal life seem at best doubtful."

"You believe there is a connection to me because I am with the embassy in Pyongyang?"

"Yes."

"So explain."

"The plane delivering the uranium and plutonium to Iran is an Air Koryo Ilyushin 76, a four engine bottom loading freight turbojet. It will be flying from Pyongyang to Wonsan and then north towards Vladivostok. It will not reach Russia. It will be intercepted. It may be warned and turned back, but if goes on it will be shot down. It will not be allowed to reach Russia."

"I will not be on that plane, so how does that involve my personal safety?"

"The Ilyushin will be flying at night, and another plane on the same busy route to Vladivostok, one that you could be on, could be shot down by mistake."

"I've been told about the Air Koryo flight to Iran. I have been told about the Ilyushin 76. I understand that it will not be allowed to reach Iran. It will not be allowed to reach the Russian border. As for my safety, the risk of shooting down the wrong plane at night, that seems real enough, but the risk that it would be a plane I'm on, that seems quite remote."

"It is not at all remote."

"From Australia to Vladivostok there are so many airlines and so many flights. There are morning flights, afternoon flights, evening flights."

"Elena, you are fooling yourself. You are fooling yourself because you don't want to believe you are putting yourself in real danger."

"Even if that is so, I can't stop flying to and from Vladivostok. My monthly meetings here in Vladivostok with my Moscow affiliates are an important part of my work. I fly at night so I will have a full day here."

"Elena, *you are in danger, real danger.*"

"Alan, you really do think so?"

"Yes. I studied the official announcements of your travel schedules. You have made yourself a target. You have made yourself a target, not intentionally, but you have. Your embassy has been putting out the place, dates and times of your monthly Vladivostok trade conferences. Like this one. That's good, maybe necessary, for your trade promotion work, but it's like publishing the dates and times of your plane tickets."

"I didn't realize..."

"You fly to Vladivostok at night. The Ilyushin may fly the same route close to the same time as your plane."

"May fly at the same time?"

"The Ilyushin may fly the same route, the same night, towards Vladivostok. By coincidence, or even intentionally."

"Intentionally?"

"Elena, I can speculate that a few hours before you fly a Koryo airfreight pilot will drop a hint that to protect the Ilyushin at night it will fly the same route at the same time as your flight. Your flight would be a protective screen for the Ilyushin. I say speculate, because after your flight lands at Vladivostok your screen for the Ilyushin would be gone."

"So?"

"To avoid being followed by Vladivostok radar and shot down over Siberia, the Ilyushin would have to turn off its lights and its transponder and continue without its lights and without its transponder operating. Even so, sooner or later it most likely would be found and shot down."

"I see... Who put this black scenario together?'

"I did. I did from the reports about you I have been reading and rereading. They are about the Ilyushin flight, and they are about you personally. More important, it could also be any number of North Korean intelligence officers who follow everything you say and do. They compile everything your embassy puts out about the Russian Ambassador, and everyone like you on the executive staff. For an intelligence officer following everything you do, the connection between the Ilyushin and your travel schedule should be obvious."

"So, these reports you have been reading, you are telling me they are about the Ilyushin flight, and they are more than that, they are also about me personally?"

"There are the technical reports about the Ilyushin long range capability, and there are the reports about you personally. Other highly technical reports are about the difficulty of tracking the right plane on the Vladivostok route at night. The reports are about how the planes on the route are expected to be tracked. And there are the reports about why the wrong plane may be attacked over the ocean. Or over land."

"Why the wrong plane?"

"Two reasons. Air traffic controllers map all the aircraft flying on the same route day and night. They do that by computers keeping track of radar responses and each plane's radio transmission of its assigned responder code. On the Southeast Asia flight corridor they are keeping track of dozens of planes. Others, without all that continuously changing information, can't accurately identify each of the planes at their continuously moving locations. The second reason is because at night all the attacking pilot sees is a stream of the same blinking wing and tail lights. Passenger planes and freight planes, the blinking lights are all the same."

"And the reports about me personally…"

"Elena, some of the reports are about you, and the people interested in you, and around you."

"You better tell me."

"There is a report about a CIA employee who has been following you and your uncle. He has been doing it for years. He has his personal collection of pictures of you. He is knowledgeable about Russian affairs, and he is going to Moscow to meet with your uncle."

"So my uncle must know him."

"Yes."

"Strange. Very strange."

"There are reports about you in Seoul and Pyongyang. Official type things, a lot about your embassy trade work, and as I said, also personal matters."

"Then you better tell me everything."

"Some of the reports are about how close you are to your Uncle Lev, how important he is to you, and how what happens to you might also affect him."

"It is common knowledge that my uncle and I have been close.

It has been common knowledge for years."

"There are pictures of you when you graduated from Pyotrsburg, and official pictures of you when you were posted to Seoul and Pyongyang. There is a picture of you with Pyotr, another with Alex and Veronika. Everybody waving and smiling."

"I see... Why would anyone collect...?"

"There are official photos of you and Ban Chul, the former diplomat now with the railroad, who will be escorting you on a tour of North Korea. There are photos of you in Seoul. At the Seoul embassy, with government officials, company executives, and at restaurants with friends, and with your Swedish diplomat friend... There are pictures of you kissing outside restaurants."

She scowled. "Does this Swedish diplomat friend of mine have a name?"

"His name is Rolf Ericsson."

"Is there more about this Rolf Ericsson?"

"Quite a bit."

"You better tell me."

"He is part of the executive staff at the Pyongyang Swedish embassy. Coming to Pyongyang from Seoul he had a promotion. He is in charge of trade promotion work. Like you."

"I don't understand. Why would anyone be interested in Rolf Ericsson in the Swedish embassy? In Seoul or Pyongyang? Because he does trade promotion work like me? There is absolutely *nothing personal* about trade promotions work."

"Part of the concern in these reports is that you and Rolf... are lovers."

"Even if that were so, who cares? Why?"

"The concern is that Rolf Ericsson may know sensitive information about North Korean businesses and he may learn from you something about the uranium and plutonium sale and the Ilyushin delivery. The arrangements for the sale, the arrangements for the delivery, whatever you want to call them, the contract terms, the way the payments are to be made. That he may know some of that through you, and that he will pass it all on to someone in Finland, someone, in Helsinki."

"Alan, that doesn't make any sense."

"It does make sense."

"How? Why Helsinki?"

"Because Rolf Ericsson from Stockholm Sweden has a family and financial connection to Ericsson electronics, the big electronics firm with headquarters in Helsinki, Finland."

"So what?"

"So the concern also is that Rolf Ericsson may be influencing you. Or you are influencing him. Or both ways."

"Influencing him to do *what*? Influencing me to do *what*?"

"That you would encourage, push, Rolf Ericsson to get into the offices of sellers and purchasers of high end electronics used in military equipment, including atomic related electronic devices."

"And so what if we were some ways able to help each other with textiles, petroleum, or electronics? Getting into executive's offices can give you insights into the company business, but it isn't like getting into the company secrets."

"I can only guess what the people who read these reports get out of them."

"It's all ridiculous. *Ridiculous*. How can anyone reasonably tie any North Korean contracts with Iran to ordinary Russian and Swedish trade promotion? And also to Rolf Ericsson and me? *Ridiculous*."

"Some analysts are paid to think about such things... and tie in government officials. Tie in government officials like you and Rolf Ericsson."

"Ridiculous."

"It seems to me from reading, and carefully rereading these reports, that they may be looking for connections between influential people, people like you in government, and Rolf Ericsson in government, who are close to each other, and who both can have business dealings with people involved with the sale of high end electronics, especially high end electronics that go into nuclear related devices, and many other things in modern warfare."

"I expect there are a lot of people in Seoul, Beijing, and Tehran who know the many reasons behind high end electronics sales, and also know about the North Korean uranium and plutonium, and the Ilyushin, and the payment for the contract... and about me."

"You are probably right."

"What else?"

"There are your Vladivostok trade conference dates here at the hotel. I knew them from your publicized schedule, and I hoped that I might see you at the hotel. And I started worrying about you."

"Worrying about me?"

"Yes."

"Have you told anyone else?"

"No. I haven't been asked about that."

"There's more?"

"Your Vladivostok travel is only one part. There are many parts... and many people."

"A particular person? Another person I know with a face and a name?"

"There is Ban Chul. You probably know his story, at least some of his story."

"The part about working on scheduling for the railroad, being a former diplomat, yes, to some extent, like many others, I know something about Ban Chul. There is a great deal about him I do not know."

"There is an official photo of you and Ban Chul together."

"Alan, it is an official photo. Nothing to write personal reports about."

"There are several reports by psychiatrists."

"*Psychiatrists?*"

"Yes.'

"You better tell me."

"The psychiatrists are speculating that you and Rolf will both be concerned that if the Ilyushin flight is not stopped the result will be Iran producing atomic bombs, and on the last night of your tour you and Ban Chul will realize you both want to do the right thing, save the world from Iran starting an atomic catastrophe, decide you both will do the right thing even though it means great danger for both of you... and on your last night together you become lovers."

"Ridiculous."

"The speculation is that he will give you information about the timing of the uranium and plutonium operation, moving the uranium and plutonium on the railroad to the airport. You will have to report it. As a result the Ilyushin will be attacked, shot down, and he will be the prime suspect for leaking the information about the railroad moving the uranium and plutonium, and so the timing for the flight. The speculation also is that you will try to help him get out of the country."

"How?"

"Money. Money for bribes. Money for forged papers. Money to live on after he gets out."

"And I will also have to get out?"

"You will get out of the country before him. There is also speculation you will plan to meet him in Russia later."

They shared a long silence. "You better tell me everything about Ban Chul."

"There are several reports. They are about his family, school, university, becoming a diplomat, his career, being pushed out of the foreign service to the railroad, and now his railroad scheduling work."

"Are there other reports about me?"

"There are. Several."

"Tell me."

"The reports are about your traveling with Ban Chul on the five day tour of the country. The reports are in detail about your five day schedule. Where you are scheduled to go, what you will see and do, together and separately, and your hotels every night. Pages and pages of the schedule detail."

"The people who put this together have nothing better to do? It is a *publicized official tour with an official guide.*"

"Do you want me to go into the schedule detail of which day for which factory, and which seafood processing plant, and which restaurant and each hotel room?"

"No... no."

"One report is different. It is a senior psychiatrist's evaluation of you and Ban Chul. He is the chief psychiatrist of the section where the other psychiatrists work, and where the fellow who collected your photos works. It is psychiatry jargon and personal stuff."

"You better tell me."

"He writes about the stress Ban Chul has been under at the railroad, worrying what could happen to him after the tour with you, and what he must be thinking of doing to help himself. He writes about the risks for both of you. Both of you being brought together by important secrets, and life and death risks that you both know about. Very dark. Very heavy."

"Life and death risks for both of us?"

"He thinks so. He thinks both of you will come to think so. He writes that you both may try and hide it, but you will both know it is real. Real because he will be suspect, and you having been with him, will also be suspect."

"What does this senior psychiatrist think of Ban Chul?"

"He gives Ban Chul a good report. A highly intelligent, highly articulate, and handsome man, emotions well integrated. A man with a conscience making a life and death decision."

"What does he write about me?"

"He also gives you a good report. A highly intelligent and beautiful young woman with a conscience making a life and death decision together with him."

"And after that?"

"On the last night of the tour the two of you will decide..."

"That's all?"

"Near the end he writes that he cannot agree with the analysis of the psychiatrists under him who believe it is very probable that you and Ban Chul will become lovers on your last night together. He says it is quite possible, but the inevitable sexual conclusion is not supported. What is important, he writes, is what you are willing to do to gain his confidence, and then his trust, and what you are willing to do when he is deciding whether to tell you his secrets and what he intends to do. He concludes that for both of you the process is too difficult to predict."

"What else?"

"He writes that you know you will have to make a decision and so you will have made plans to leave the country."

"And his plans to get out?"

"He writes that he won't tell you his plans beyond the obvious ways he could try. Better you don't know."

"What else?"

"He stops there, except for one final sentence. He wrote, 'In this situation it would be inconsistent with my professional ethics to speculate on Ban Chul's personal actions with Elena Marloff, or her personal actions with him.'"

A silence. "Thank you for telling me."

"Could you change your Vladivostok travel schedule? Give it out by telephone only to a few people, and fly on a different airline at a different time each trip?"

"If I change my travel schedule I would still have a schedule, just a new schedule I have to send out each month."

"Could you send someone else from time to time? Let it be known that someone else may fill in for you."

"It would be a signal that something is going wrong. I can't send someone else to take my risks. Anything else?"

"Elena, I don't have anything more to say. Tomorrow morning I'll take the bus back to the airbase."

"Back to the base, and to your plane."

"My plane is sitting in a locked hanger, and the chances are it will stay there until I fly it home."

"Alan, you are not sharing the whole story with me."

"I've told you everything I can."

"What if you are ordered to fly? What if you are ordered to fly your plane along with the Russian?"

"I will fly far behind."

"At night how could you know?"

"I will fly far enough behind that I would know."

"What if the Russian pilot tells you by radio that he has found the target?"

"I would radio back that I received his message and he can radio the base for instructions."

"He will radio the base for instructions? For orders?"

"He might."

"What if the Russian pilot fires his missile and it doesn't hit the plane. He fires another missile, and it also misses?"

"Elena, if I fly, unlikely, but if I fly, I will fire my missiles, and they will also miss the plane."

"Everyone above you would understand."

"Yes, they will understand."

"You know what that could mean for you, refusing to obey a lawful order. Dishonorable discharge. It would ruin your life."

"*Elena, heaven and earth could not make me gamble with your life.*"

They shared another long silence. "You flew across the ocean to save my life, you've met me, and after an hour together you are going to leave me."

"Elena, I flew across the ocean because I am a United States

Navy fighter pilot, and that is what I was ordered to do. Just as important, I flew across the ocean to meet you because I spent days reading about you and looking at your pictures. When I saw you in the dining room... I already knew you."

After a silence she stood up and he followed. "Coming to my room... it's all between us."

"It's all between us."

"What we talked about, it's all between us."

"It's all between us."

She looked into his face for a long time. "For coming across the ocean to be with good Russians and save my life, do I get to give Lieutenant Alan Rostov a hug and a kiss?"

"In another kind of world, Elena, in another kind of world where I wasn't here under United States Navy orders, and you weren't here as a Russian ambassador, I might ask to stay... and we would have wine, and we would talk a long time."

"Alan, this is the real world."

"Elena, this is the very real world, and so I must go and do what I have to do, and you have to go off with Ban Chul for five days... and do with him whatever you have to do."

"Yes, you're right, I have to do what I have to do. But you haven't answered. Do I get to give Lieutenant Alan Rostov a hug and a kiss?"

"You know the answer."

"So tell me."

A kiss, and a hug to remember."

Elena opened her arms. "Come here."

CHAPTER 17

Ambassador Grigory Sukhinin talked with Elena in his small austere office in the small austere Pyongyang embassy. It was small and austere because of the expense for a more elaborate building, and it was intended as a message to all that enter that Russian money does not flow easily.

Sukhinin asked Elena to speak freely and tell him if she had become comfortable working with the embassy staff, if she felt safe going about Pyongyang, if she was comfortable representing him in meetings with North Korean officials and all sorts of big and small business people. Elena responded that Pyongyang, with police everywhere, was a big adjustment from Seoul. It took some time, but she thought she was fitting in well. Now, quite well. All the officials politely accepted her, and all the business people were reserved and polite, even when she did not approve what they wanted. She told him she was ready for whatever new assignments he had for her.

"I've spoken with Uncle Lev a couple of times about your tour with Ban Chul. He was concerned about the continuing uncertain timing for your tour, and the uncertain timing of the Ilyushin flight."

"He is thinking the Ilyushin flight may come first?"

"Yes, and if that happens he is considering having us drop the Ban Chul tour. Right now he thinks that won't happen. It is too important for them, and fixing the tour dates any time before winter should be easy enough for them."

"So what's the problem?"

"Everything that has to get done before the Ilyushin can take off. They can have all sorts of problems we wouldn't know about."

"Such as?"

"They will need overflight approvals from half a dozen countries, and one or more of their air traffic controllers may not treat this supposedly ordinary airfreight charter like an ordinary airfreight charter. You don't use a big Ilyushin 76 for thousands of kilometers at tremendous cost for shipping a few dozen cartons of merchandise. One or more controllers may want to know if there are any armed guards on the plane, and what the plane is carrying that could be hazardous in an accident."

"There must be hundreds of commercial airfreight charters carrying all sorts of cargo."

"There are. All around the world."

"Aren't commercial approvals routine all around the world?"

"Yes, but this Air Koryo charter flight to Tabriz will not look to a seasoned practical air traffic controller like a commercial airfreight charter. Pyongyang to Tabriz is not at all usual."

"Maybe it is not all that unusual. Do we know if this is the very first Air Koryo charter to Iran?"

"Over the years there may have been a few commercial airfreight flights from prosperous Seoul to prosperous Tehran, and from Tehran to Seoul. Probably none from Pyongyang to Tabriz. I'm guessing. We have no information about any North Korean charter flights to any part of Iran, or from any part of Iran to any part of North Korea."

"And going back to the get ready timing problems for North Korea...?"

"Air traffic controllers can ask all sorts of questions, and if they smell a safety concern with the plane flying over their jurisdiction they can ask for detailed written answers. If they don't get what they consider acceptable answers they refuse to approve flying in their jurisdiction's airspace. That doesn't happen often for commercial flights, but this in no way is a commercial airfreight charter, and all the controllers will understand that. They have the authority to ask questions and refuse to grant approval. For practical purposes, there is no way to successfully appeal a refusal."

"Other problems?"

"The people setting up the flight here have to consider both the timing of the flight, and very important, maintaining secrecy at the airport from delivery of the cargo until takeoff. That's very difficult considering moving the uranium and plutonium by train to the Pyongyang rail yard, unloading there, then loading and securing the cargo on a truck, probably an army truck, to get it to a waiting plane with a waiting aircrew and armed guards. How can you keep all that secret? Do you clear everyone away from the unloading and loading areas for several hours? Also, there may be other flight shifting schedules for any number of reasons unknown to us in preparing to ship radioactive stuff and then doing it."

"I understand."

"For now, the tour seems to be on, probably in a week or two, and the question for us is what you are going to be doing for the tour five days and five nights."

"You mean what will I be doing with Ban Chul those five nights?"

"To be frank, that is part of it. Your uncle told you about the unsatisfactory reports by Anna Volkova and Irina Orlova. Both of them gave intentionally vague reports about how they got along with Ban Chul, about what they did with him."

"He told me about their reports. He did not tell me their names. He told me two of our reliable staff ladies took the tour with Ban Chul, that afterwards they made unsatisfactory reports, they were not being open about what they did with him, did with him personally, and how they felt about him."

"It goes deeper than that. Check out their reports from registry. In both of their reports there are a lot of statistics about the railroad, the passenger revenue and freight tonnage. The different needs and expenses for each of the rail area branches, the age and condition of the electric locomotives, passenger cars and freight cars, and the connections with the bus lines. That part of their reports is fine, all quite professional. There are sections on North Korean industry-seafood processing plants, automobile, tractor, and ferrous metals processing plants. All very good and professional. Both have a section on dealing with ordinary people. What they do, what their complaints are about the railroad and the connecting bus lines, but nothing personal about Ban Chul. Nothing. Anna has not been candid with me about what happened with him, about what happened *personally* between them. Irina also has not been candid with me about what happened *personally* with Ban Chul. I talked with them separately. They both told me the exact same story. He always was very helpful, and very polite. I asked if he ever suggested he might be helpful to us. The answer, by both of them was like from a script, the same script. He always was helpful and polite."

Elena nodded thoughtfully, then asked, "How much did Anna and Irena know about Ban Chul when you gave them their tour assignment, and they accepted it? What are you thinking they should they have known, or at least, suspected, after being with him and now are hiding from you?"

"I can't answer the second part. As for what they knew when they accepted the tour assignment, I asked Anna if she would be interested in doing the tour and writing a report for the joint railroad project. She said she knew about the railroad project. She said she had spent many hours going over the accounting for the railroad project, but she needed to know more. I told her to check out the Ban Chul file from registry. She came back two days later and said she had read the file, she was interested, but wanted to know more about the uranium and plutonium shipment. Was it real? I told her I thought the file was right about the uranium and plutonium shipment, and how Ban Chul fit into knowing about that. She came back the next day and said she had concerns, she had never done anything like this, it was as much about Ban Chul as the tour, and she wanted to do the tour with him, and that she would write a report that I could edit."

"And Irena?"

"Much the same. I told her to check out the Ban Chul file, read it, and then talk with Anna. She came back several days later and said she had concerns but she wanted to do the tour, and like Anna, she would write a report I could edit."

"It seems to me that you gave both of them a free hand in writing their reports, and in tacitly accepting that you would edit their reports you gave both of them protection."

"I suppose so. Irena was late turning in her report. On their last night she took a bad fall. Ban Chul took her to a hospital. She was off for a week before finishing her report."

"Is she all right now?"

"She seems fine."

"And their reports?"

"They both turned in professional reports about the North Korean rail system, how it affected the needs of the major seaports, how the railroad affected the country's imports and exports, mostly updates of government statistics we already had, but nothing valuable about Ban Chul. Nothing at all in any way *personal* about Ban Chul. They may be willing to tell you more about Ban Chul in one day at home than they are ever going to confide to me here."

"You believe they are protecting him?"

"I think so."

Elena nodded. "There are times when it is the right thing to do, and the Ambassador doesn't want to know. This could be one of those times?"

"I don't think so. The tours were five days. They were together all that time. They both could have become emotionally involved with him. Maybe more."

"Meaning?"

"For five days they were close together. They were traveling and sightseeing together. They were together for hours on trains. They were together for hours in restaurants, drinking wine, or whatever. After dinner, maybe a little tipsy, they were together in hotel rooms. Anna and Irina are both in their forties. They are not stiff with men. Their husbands are far away so they are lonely. When they want a hug and a kiss from a man, they tell him. If they get more now and then, I don't know anything about it. That's none of my business."

"From what I've heard, and seen in Seoul, that's not at all unusual."

"It's not."

"So?"

"Elena, you are a different kind of person from Anna, and you are a different person from Irina. Ban Chul will recognize that. Also. he must know that unlike Anna, and unlike Irina, you may be able to help him."

"Help him, if helps us?"

"Yes."

"Helps us with information about moving uranium and plutonium?"

"Yes."

"Helps us if he risks his life, if he becomes a traitor, and helps us?"

"Yes. To put it bluntly, yes."

"And to be practical, do you think he will be willing do anything that way?"

"I don't know. How could I know?" The ambassador closed his eyes and nodded twice before continuing. "Elena, this is about atom bomb. He must know what that means. For him, it means great risk, and also great opportunity. If he has, or can get, useful information from the railroad without getting arrested, and if he can get out of the country to asylum in Russia, and you encourage him to help us, and help himself, I think there is a good chance he will tell you what he knows."

"A good chance?"

"If sufficiently encouraged, a very good chance."

"What do we know about what he does at his railroad scheduling position?"

"Not much. The Ministry told us it involves routine scheduling of trains, passenger and freight. Routine, but important work. The system depends on it. If something is going wrong, he figures out why, and makes changes to fix it."

"That's his work. What can you tell me about Ban Chul personally?"

"About his private life, we know almost nothing. About his dismissal from his job with the foreign service, just what your uncle already told you. He could have shown too much independence. We really don't know why he left the diplomatic corps and went to the railroad, and we don't know what might be troubling him now. We can speculate about why he was dismissed, pushed out, kicked out. We can speculate for hours about what type of information he could get and give you. We don't know."

"What do we know?"

"What we do know is that this is one part of a bigger picture and we can make up all kinds of stories."

"Such as?"

"We can imagine this shipment to Iran is a Kim scheme. If we don't stop the Ilyushin flight it amounts to approval of more airfreight flights. If we do stop the flight, we shoot down the plane, Kim will charge it is because of a connivance with Seoul, and that justifies a reprisal."

"Reprisal? Like what?"

"Like sending rockets to blow up a South Korean electric power plant. Elena, we speculate, we worry, and we make up all sorts of catastrophe stories."

"So, we don't know about Ban Chul... but I may be able to find out what he will do for us?"

"If he is seriously thinking about what he should do, and you play your part well, yes."

"I am not a seducing actress, and I am not a spy."

"You will play your part as a professional diplomat, and as you see fit."

"What does that mean?

"You will do what you have to do. When you meet Ban Chul he is going to tell you that you will have your picture taken together. There will be a press release, and a piece in the newspapers about the coming tour for sponsoring friendly cooperation between Russia and North Korea. As with the other trips, when the time is set, there will be a radio and television announcement, and a piece in the newspapers."

"What do I do?"

"Smile, shake hands, and go along with all that we are great friends publicity."

"I will remember to smile."

"Your itinerary will go out to the police all along the way, so you should expect courteous behavior from them so long as you don't wander off into some restricted area and start taking pictures."

"I wouldn't do that."

"Never give or take anything to someone you don't know well and completely trust."

"I won't."

"For you it is a gift, an appreciation for some help. For the all too suspicious police, a gift by you to anyone for any reason is suspicious."

"About what?"

"It could be an illegal payment or a bribe. Anything you get back is suspect. Inside that trinket there could be a tiny film, or recording, or scrap of paper in code."

"I will be careful."

"If you are arrested as a spy and put in jail I will use diplomatic immunity to try to get you out. With arrests for suspicious activity and little more, I usually pay a small fine and that works . Sometimes they want a bigger fine and it takes a while to work it out. In any event, I will send you home. If it takes a while to get you out, it will not be good for you, and it will not be good for me."

"I hate jail cells. I will be very careful."

"Do what you can with Ban Chul, but be very careful. Be careful all the time."

Elena nodded. "Exactly what that means for five days and night with Ban Chul I don't know, but when I should be careful, I will be *very* careful."

"It means don't get caught on some miniature camera. It means don't get caught whispering by some hidden microphone hitched to a recorder."

"So, while I am being careful, how much... *suggesting*, how much *ingratiating*, do I have to do?"

"When the time comes, you'll know. Just be very careful at all times."

"You mean be careful how I go about making myself more desirable than just an ingratiating charming companion?"

"I didn't want to put it that way."

Elena met Anna Volkova the next evening in the living room of her small apartment filled with old furniture, Russian, French, and English books, and pictures of Russian authors and composers all around. After polite greetings Elena thanked Anna for letting her come and they sat on hard chairs facing each other with a low table between them. On the table was a magazine, *Foreign Affairs*. Elena smiled, pointed to the journal, and said, "Anna, you are a diplomat all day, a perfect housekeeper in the evening, and an academic at night."

"I work for the foreign service. I am part of the embassy support staff, not a diplomat. I know my place. Even so, I have substantial responsibilities, and like all of us, I am waiting for the posting to London or Washington."

"*Foreign Affairs* is in English. The erudite articles are by high ranking foreign service professionals. You are a professional. You read it as a professional. It's not there on your table to impress people."

"Reading English has its personal satisfaction, the articles are informative and interesting, and keeping informed may have its career benefits sooner or later."

Elena smiled again and said, "I'm with you. I am all for sooner than years later." Pointing to the bookshelves she added, "You have quite a library."

"Wherever I go, my books always go along with me. History, biography, and some classic fiction, too. I can do it because I don't have to pay the service for bringing them along. They are my lifeline to another kind of life."

"Anna, the reason I am here is that I am likely to have a tour with Ban Chul."

"I'm not surprised. When you came to the embassy as a Deputy Ambassador, I thought that would happen."

"The tour is like the one for you and Irina, all around the country, five days, all expenses paid. No date has been set, but I am here because the boss told me that I need to talk to you about your tour around the country with Ban Chul."

"It was an official tour. Why talk about my official tour here, instead of at work?"

"He is concerned about how you got along with Ban Chul. He said we need to talk freely, and it would be more comfortable here for both or us."

"And you are going to talk with Irina, too?"

"Yes. Both of you."

"Can you tell me why?"

"He feels both of you have not been candid with him about what happened. Not what could have happened, or might have happened, but what happened that is not in your reports. He wants me to go into that with both of you."

Anna frowned. "That assumes something happened with him.

Nothing happened with Ban Chul. There was absolutely *nothing* like that to report."

Elena nodded and continued, "Also, he wants me to get your advice on how I should treat Ban Chul, and how to take care of myself with him. Personal advice you would have no reason to put in your reports."

"Personal advice? I am not sure what you mean by personal advice."

"I mean practically, and professionally, what to do when I am with him, and what not to do when I am with him. I want your advice on how to treat him professionally, and, how should I put it, how to treat him as a man."

Anna scowled and stared at Elena. After a long pause she said, "*You are asking my advice about what to do with a man?*"

"Yes, with him as a man."

"What to do at a restaurant in the morning? What to do in a hotel room at night?"

"Yes."

"That depends on the man... and whatever the situation is."

"Anna, we are talking about being alone in a hotel room with one man, Ban Chul. We are talking about being alone in a hotel room at night with Ban Chul."

"I don't know what to tell you. I don't. I made a proper report of where we went every day, what we were allowed to see, what we were not allowed to see. I made it clear that he never made any improper advances, was always helpful and polite. Always. Irena also made a proper report."

Elena leaned forward. "Anna, this is not about a proper trip report, or not so proper trip report. You know that..."

"So, what is this about?"

Elena paused and raised her hand a few inches. "Anna, this is about what you think may happen to him, what will happen to him now that has brought you home, and you have said goodbye."

Anna stared at Elena again. "What do you mean? What is going to happen to him?"

"*May* happen. *Could* happen. *Will* happen."

"You don't know, or you don't want to tell me?"

"I do not know." Another pause. "Anna, before you started the tour with him you read his registry file."

"Yes, in the Registry small reading room."

"You read it very carefully."

"Yes. Most of the day. I wasn't allowed to make any notes. I didn't make any notes."

"Then the boss told you what he believed about Ban Chul and the railroad and the uranium and plutonium connection. From the registry file you knew that he was kicked out of the foreign service and sent to the railroad. By the last day of the tour, your last night with him after dinner in your hotel, you thought he might be in real trouble, and he might want to talk about leaving the country. You thought about what he knew, and with anguish you thought about what might happen to him when your tour with him ended and you thanked him and said goodbye at your door. You thought about all of that. And why not?"

Anna looked down with her hands clinched in front of her as they shared a long silence.

Elena continued, "You thought about what might happen to him. Anna, you understand. Of course, you did."

"I did not know what would happen to him. I more or less knew what could happen." After a long paise she said, "I have feelings, I'm human."

"You had terrible thoughts about what might happen to him. Would happen to him."

Anna looked up. "What might happen to him after we said goodbye? I told you. I have feelings, I'm human."

After a silence, Elena asked, "Why did you agree to take the tour? Knowing what you knew about Ban Chul, knowing you could beg off, why did you take the tour with him?"

"Why?"

"Yes, why?"

"Why? Because in my position it's not so easy to beg off. Because it wasn't more auditing claims and funds transfers. Because I had never held a registry file in my hands. Because I had never read a registry file. Because there was a picture of Ban Chul. Because I was going to be alone with a handsome diplomat. Because it was all terribly important... and I was flirting with danger. And I knew it. I felt it. Because after all these years of the same staff support work, I was being trusted."

"For years he was a real diplomat. He is handsome. He treated you well. He called you Anna, and of course, you called him Chul."

"I did. Of course, I did. That is what I was *supposed to do*. I understood that. It was the same with Irina."

"You know he probably is in trouble. You know what can happen to him."

"It's terrible… I don't want to think about it. I don't want to talk about it."

"By the last day you thought that far away from Pyongyang, far away from watching eyes and listening ears, he might confide in you about a railroad shipment of uranium and plutonium, and for doing that, he might ask for your help in getting out of the country. You understood."

"I understood, but for you to assume all that… is to assume a great deal. You are assuming we became very close."

"Anna, I am assuming you and Chul both thought a great deal depended on what you did together, and helping him was the right thing to do."

"I have feelings."

"You cared for him. You cared because you knew it was much more than the two of you. It was uranium and plutonium for atomic bombs being made somewhere beyond North Korea. It was all terribly mixed up, and you were flirting with danger for yourself that could become real. It would be understandable if you got very close to him."

"In my report I made it clear enough that nothing personal happened. I could have put in my report that he never talked about leaving the country, never suggested it, and that we were nowhere near intimate… Nowhere near passionate kisses, nowhere near intimate. I didn't think it was necessary."

"If Chul disappears you don't want to think that what you put in your report could have caused it. So, you just reported he was helpful and polite. That's all, helpful and polite."

"Elena, you said it's time to be open and honest. He didn't tell me any secrets and nothing personal happened. Nothing personal happened, and that is what my report says. I didn't need to use other words. As you said, this is not about my report. It is not about Irina's report. It is about my becoming a spy, acting like a spy, and reporting like a spy. Chul knows who you are, he knows who your uncle is. If he thinks you may be willing to help him, and if he trusts you, he may talk to you about secrets, if he has any, at the right time in the right place."

"If we are in a little room in an out of the way hotel, how do I get him to trust me?"

"There are two parts to that. The risk he takes, that's one part. The other part is the risks you take if you've turned yourself into a spy. You can be caught, arrested, put in a putrid cell, questioned for hours, questioned again for more and more hours until you sign a confession."

"True. How do I get him to trust me enough for him to tell me his secrets?"

"You really want that kind of advice?"

"Yes. Anna, and you know why."

"Yes, I know. I read the registry file very carefully. I asked for more, I was told more. and I listened carefully."

"And you put it all together."

"Of course, I put it together… No, that's not right."

"What do you mean?" Elna asked.

"I thought I understood what was going on. For an hour or so I did. Then the questions started. Missing people. Wrong places. Wrong times. Wrong reasons. Contradictions in the file from what I was told."

"Anna, nothing like this is straightforward and complete. Different people in different circumstances are reporting from different places at different times. You understood that."

"It is one thing to read and listen, another to try to put it together and actually be a part of what is going to happen."

"I understand."

"I know this is terribly important and I want to help, but I don't want to be used."

"You will have nothing more to do with Ban Chul."

"I am not going to have to add to my report?"

"No."

"I am not going to have to answer any questions?"

"No. Certainly not if we can be open and honest with each other. You have done everything you should have done, and I am not going to use you."

"You really want me to help you?"

"That's why we are together. How do I get him to trust me?"

"What do I have to do so that he will tell me his secrets?

"If he has secrets."

"Maybe he has and maybe he doesn't. Anna, you don't know, and I don't know. Help me."

"I don't know if I can, but I will tell you this much. If it is the same as my trip, and Irena's trip, the last night you will be in Sinuiju. We were both in a fancy new hotel. If Chul may be ready to confide anything to you, then you will be in an old out of the way little hotel. You share a bottle of wine in his room. Or your room. You take both his hands, hold them tight, look in his eyes, and ask him if there is some way you can help him. You tell him this is the last time you can talk about such things. If he has been thinking about telling you any secrets he will ask you what you will do and you will start talking. Or he may simply show you he is ready to talk. You will know what to do. You will do it because you know that tomorrow night it will all end and you will be missing him."

"You missed him?"

After a silence Anna said, "He is everything a woman wants in a man. He is Korean, but he acts like the best kind of Russian diplomat should act. If you give him an opening, or you give him a little push, he may tell you railroad information that involves military secrets. When he does it is because of you, and his life has changed forever. And your life has changed forever, because you must report. Something drastic connected to the uranium and plutonium will happen, and he will be suspected. If he has not quickly managed to get out of the country he will be arrested. Of course, he will be arrested... and interrogated in a jail... until he signs a confession. You will feel responsible. All you will ever know for certain is that Ban Chul no longer works for the railroad. During those days and nights, being so close to him all the time, you may come to care for him, care deeply for him. If you let yourself get that close you will want to help him... help him every way and any way you can."

"That's what happened to you?"

"After the first day, I liked him. After five days, I liked him a lot. I almost forgot he is Korean. From the way he looks, from the way he is built, I would guess there is a Russian on the family tree."

"Really?"

"Why not? We Russians have been in Korea for generations, since 1884. A small number at first, but Vladivostok didn't become a big city with only Russians. Over the years Primorsky Krai province has grown with Russians and Koreans to 600,000 people. In 1945, after Germany surrendered, Russia troops helped liberate Korea from the Japanese. It established Russia as a great power in the whole region."

"It did, and it still is."

"Before that, in the Korean Civil War, the Russian air force supported the North against the South. Koreans saw Russian warplanes and American warplanes in dog fights. And the people on the ground heard the planes and saw Russian aviators and American aviators parachuting to the ground. There were plenty of opportunities for the Russian fellows and Korean girls to mix it up. And in wartime there was a lot of it. It is common knowledge all over the country."

"I've heard some of those stories."

"Also, Chul thinks more like a Russian than a Korean. Once I asked him which Russian and American diplomats he admired most. He answered right off Yuli Kvitsinsky for Russia and Paul Nitze for America."

"The walk in the woods, 1982."

"When the intermediate range missile talks were stalemated at Geneva, they worked out an agreement for both sides limiting the type and number of intermediate range missiles. That made history, even though in the end, the agreement they proposed was not adopted. Chul thought that attempt to break the stalemate was a worthwhile goal for the United States and Russia."

"It was."

"Elena, that is one incident, but it tells you a lot about him."

"Yes, it does."

"I asked him about Henry Kissinger and his Vietnam peace talks. He knew all about Kissinger's Paris talks with Le Duc Tho. He even knew the dates, February 21 through April 4, 1970. Kissinger trying to save American interests, Le Duc Tho always politely listening and replying that the United States and its allies must get out of Korea. He remembers diplomats, their names, places, dates, and the good results, and the bad results, of their efforts. For me he is extraordinary. Truly, extraordinary."

"You have an amazing memory yourself."

"Elena, in North Korea there are rich people who live very well. All kinds of business people. All kinds of professional people. All sorts of senior military officers. High ranking government officials. They have the money, and they know where to go. The best stores, the best little elite shops, the best pharmacies, the best medical, dental, and other professional practices. Chul knows where to go. The Ministry is paying for everything for the tour, and he will treat you to the good life if you let him."

"Meaning?"

"Meaning drink his great French wine at fine restaurants, let yourself enjoy it. Maybe afterwards in your room drink a little more. Enjoy it. Stay away from politics, and don't ask too many questions about the government's position on this or that. If the time does come to talk about secrets, you will both know it. He will know it, and you will know it."

"Anna, for a man, and for a woman, there is more to the good life than fine restaurant with great wine and good hotels every night. You have to be close to each other. I've been told that you don't hold back, that when you are with a man and you want a hug, you tell him."

"Sometimes I get a hug and a kiss when we say goodnight. Or goodbye. Nothing wrong."

"Nothing wrong, but with Chul it was different. He was so very different. Anna, there would be nothing wrong if you were tempted to have one night with him, one night to remember forever."

"Was I tempted? Of course, I was tempted."

"And?"

"I'm a staffer. I couldn't do anything to help him, and I wasn't ready. So he wasn't ready."

"Even at the end when it was time to say goodbye?"

"At the end, when you get back to Pyongyang at night, and after the five wonderful days you say goodbye to Chul at your door, you will remember what you said, and didn't say, and what you did, and didn't, for the rest of your life. You will go inside, lock the door, turn on the lamp, go to the window, pull back the curtain, and watch the taillights of the taxi going away. You will close the curtain and worry about what is going to happen to him. When you are in bed in your dark room you will think of him, and you will miss him."

Elena met with Irina Orlova at her small apartment two evenings later. Irina welcomed her, offered a glass of wine. On one wall there was a library - world history, Russian, French, and Italian art, Russian, French, and English fiction and a shelf of classical CD's. Symphonies, concertos, operas. Bach, Beethoven, Brahms, Mozart, Grieg, Puccini, Vivaldi, Mussorgsky, Rimsky Korsakov, Borodin, Rachmaninov.

Elena thanked her for the wine, took a sip with her, pointed to the wall and said, "You have a nice library, and quite a library of classical CD's. I would guess one of the best in Pyongyang."

"Anna has her books, I have a few books and my music. We all need our havens from Pyongyang."

"Indeed, we do. You must have some favorite music for a winter evening."

"For a winter night it could be the Mozart Requiem and Rachmaninov's Second Piano Concerto."

"You know your classical music. Do you have a good CD player and good speakers?"

"For this little place they are adequate, and the new high quality players and speakers are much too expensive. It is kind of you to ask about my music, but you didn't come here for anything like that."

"No, I didn't."

"So, this is like your chat with Anna? This is about Ban Chul?"

"This is about your tour with Ban Chul. You know Anna very well. You know I talked with Anna about her tour with Ban Chul. About why she decided to go on the trip."

"She told me."

"And you? Why did you go?"

"Anna told me the first thing you wanted to know was why she took the tour with Ban Chul."

"And?"

"She told me she went on the tour with Ban Chul because she recognized it was important, and for the first time she felt that she was being trusted. On the practical side, she was asked to go, and if she didn't agree to go it might hurt her career. And if she did, it might help her career."

"Anything else?"

"And for her, it was going to be more than an adventure, more than five days of travel and fun with a handsome man who used to be a diplomat."

"Why did you take it on?"

"I did it for the same reasons Anna did. For the first time in my career instead of being told, I was asked. For the first time I was going to registry. For the first time I would read a registry file. For the first time I would be reading a registry file. For the first time, for the very first time, I was being allowed to be on the *inside*. I was being put on the *inside*, and on the inside everything about uranium and plutonium on the move is so terribly dangerous and exciting. A part of me wanted to just turn around and run away. It was once in a lifetime, with risks, and I went."

"You really thought there could be risks?"

"When you are on the inside in a situation like this, with a diplomat sent to the railroad, there are going to be risks. When you start you don't know what kind. Later, you find out. I'm not saying I was some sort of a heroine. I did everything I thought I should do. No more, no less."

"What did you think about the tour? About seeing the country with Ban Chul?"

"In one way for five days I was living the high life with a wonderful guy. Handsome, intelligent, full of life, strong, kind. Everything you always wanted in a man. On the other side, it wasn't carefree that way, it couldn't be."

"Why?"

"Because, more and more, talking with Chul I thought there was some possibility, maybe a good possibility, that I would get into secrets about North Korea selling uranium and plutonium to another country, and what was involved with that. What people? How? When? Where? I would ask him a question that wasn't routine and he would firmly steer me into something else. So, I was mixed up. With all that, by the third day, being with him was wonderful."

"Anna told me she felt the same way. He was wonderful. After five days close to him… she could have been tempted…"

"You mean was I tempted?"

"Yes."

"Towards the end, was I tempted in his room after finishing a bottle of great wine with him? Sure. I'm alone in this miserable country, freezing winter is coming on. I'm lonely, and for five full days this handsome, intelligent, warm man was there with me. Tempted? Why not?"

"Why not more than tempted?"

"Because it takes two. I couldn't do anything for him, because he was holding back, and because like Anna, I thought I knew pretty much what was going on with him and the shipment on the railroad and the airfreight. I thought he wasn't ever going to become a traitor for me, a grade nine office staffer, and I wasn't going to let myself become a spy. I wasn't going to live with what that could lead to."

"That's a warning for me?" Irina took another sip followed by Elena.

"Take it as a warning, and take it seriously."

"I take it seriously. Very seriously. Any advice for me?"

"Advice? All I can tell you is be careful about getting into anything sensitive. What his life is like now. What he wants to do with the rest of his life. You open the door and you are telling him he can trust you, and you will help him. Don't open the door one crack unless you are ready to feel responsible for what is going to happen to him."

Elena nodded twice. "You cared for him. You cared a lot. You still do."

"Yes. So does Anna. You will care, too. You think we are trained to be efficient, and polite, and respect authority, and to forget about emotions. We're human, so we care."

"Of course."

Irina went on emotionally, "Five days very close together, and at night a room apart, and you will care, too. On your last night together, no matter how mixed up you are about what is happening now, and what is going to come, you will care, too."

After a long silence Elena said softly, "Irina, you're upset. Something happened between you and Chul. If it should be just between us, that is what it will be, but whatever it was, I should know."

"Should you?"

"Yes."

"Do you really want to know that I let him run his hands all over my body? Do you really want to know that on the last night I let him get into my pants and open my bra? Do you want me to tell every bit of that into a tape recorder?"

"No, and none of that is going to be in any report. What happened?"

"Anna knows. He saved me. I was almost killed. He risked his life to save me."

"You better tell me."

"On the last night we were in a fancy modern hotel in Sinuiju. About seven thirty we walked to a restaurant across the street and around the corner. It was busy and we had to wait a long time for a table. We had a bottle of nice wine with dinner. He ordered some Korean dishes for me to try. We talked about the trip. And other things I'm not going to go into. A little after nine we left and started back to the hotel. There weren't any other people around. We were crossing the street and this car came out of nowhere going way too fast. It was headed right for us. I saw it coming, and I froze. Chul jumped in front of me and shoved me back. He shoved me very hard. I fell back and hit my back and head and I screamed in fright and pain. From what I could see the car went by so close it must have just missed him. I tried to get up. I couldn't. I thought my spine was broken. He came around and put his hands under my shoulders and pulled me back out of the street and up on the sidewalk. He ran his hands all over my body, he said something like no broken bones, don't feel any broken bones. He put his arms under me and pulled me up. He held me. He wrapped one arm tight around me and asked if I was all right to walk. I said I thought so if I held on to him, and he held me close all the way back to my room at the hotel. The back of my head hurt terribly. My whole back hurt terribly. When we got back to my room he took off my dirty jacket, loosened my dirty pants, lifted my blouse and unhooked my bra. He helped me take off my shoes and lie down on the bed and find a halfway comfortable position. There was a telephone in the room. He called some emergency number. He didn't get the response he wanted, and he called another number. Then another. When he put the phone down he told me to lie still and that an ambulance was on the way. They came, tied me on a stretcher, and half an hour later I was in a hospital where a doctor looked for broken bones and they took a lot of x-rays and did other things. A nurse gave me a jab in the arm and I went to sleep. In the morning a different doctor came in. He told me I had hairline fractures in two of my ribs, they would heal, the bruises on my skull and back would heal, and I needed pain medicine in the hospital until I returned to Pyongyang with Chul. Also, when I got home I needed to take a double dose of my Tylenol morning and night for several days. If I felt anything was going wrong, dizzy, blurred vision, trouble getting out of bed, to call for help, get someone to take me to a hospital immediately. He also said that all the ambulance and hospital charges were being taken care of. A nurse gave me another jab in the arm and I slept on and off all day and all night."

"It could have been much worse."

"I know. We both could have been killed. When we got back to the Pyongyang train station I was cold, in pain all over, shaking a little. Chul asked me if I wanted to go to the hospital. He said he would arrange it. I told him I wanted to go home. He asked if I was sure. I told him I wanted to go home. He got a taxi and helped me get in and we got home. He fixed some food for us and I took the Tylenol. He helped me undress and get into bed. He saw that I was shaking again and said he would stay a while and see how I was doing. I thought of telling him he could stay all night. I told him he didn't have to stay, to just leave a light on in the bathroom, and I could manage. He put my cellphone by the bed, called a taxi and left. Until I fell asleep I was thinking of him saving me in the street, caring for me. He called in the morning. I told him I could care for myself, not to call the embassy, I would do it. He called again in the evening and twice the next day."

"I didn't know anything about any of that. The boss just told me that you had a bad fall, went to the hospital, nothing about Chul saving you."

"I told him I had a bad fall, that Chul got me to the hospital, they kept me two nights, and told me to rest a few days. I wasn't going to tell him about how Chul cared for me."

"There was no need for that."

"Chul is a wonderful guy, and he may be in some terrible trouble."

"Why do you say that?

"The way he was kicked out of his job, he probably is. Now, with the railroad, he is in a position where he may be able to know a lot."

"He is in a position to know what?"

"You must know more about all that than I do."

"Possibly I do in a general way, but this is a situation where the details and the timing are very important."

"I sort of knew that when I started the first day with him, but I wasn't thinking that way. I know now."

"You know that the military can move uranium and plutonium on the railroad."

"I know now."

"Does Chul know where uranium and plutonium are stored near the railroad?"

"Maybe he does. I don't know."

"Does he know anything about when there could be a shipment on the railroad?"

"I don't know. I don't want to know. It's like Anna says, if you let yourself get too close to him you will learn too much, you will end up sleeping with him, you will report everything, and you may be sorry you did for the rest of your life."

CHAPTER 18

Pyongyang and North Korea were wearing on Elena. She was working in a new embassy with new people, several full of envy, the young newcomer with connections skipping over them, being given heavy responsibilities by the ambassador, and right off ordering people around. And demanding detailed on time reports. And completely taking over the contacts with key business people and all higher government officials.

She was asserting herself like an embassy executive, and the resentment was what she expected. It would take more time to be fully accepted. And there was the Ban Chul tour that could be coming up. Next week? Two weeks? Not until next month, or even longer? It was Ban Chul and his secrets, it was what they might do together, it was both of them escaping from the country, it was uranium and plutonium flying over Russia. It was to prevent atomic bombs being put together in Iran. And all that could mean. It was Pyongyang and North Korea, what was happening now, and what was likely coming. They were all mixed together, and they were wearing on Elena.

More and more as she dove into her assignments she was moody, irritable, inside the protecting embassy walls, and more so outside the guarded embassy doors. Seoul had been alive with opportunity in the safe embassy and had possibilities of promoting big trade deals outside. Seoul also had a raft of very large miserable factories producing all kinds of electronics, reliable automobiles, refined petroleum, and armaments for democracies and dictatorships. It had Its horrible slums, and notorious redlight district. But unlike Pyongyang, it also had its vibrant cosmopolitan side, ranging from the Seoul Philharmonic Orchestra to a world figure ice skating competition with South Korean skaters competing well. And dear Rolf Ericsson, dear Rolf, had been there in Seoul with her. So close... until it ended.

She learned from the Swedish embassy roster that he had been posted to Pyongyang, but he had not called her. She could understand why. A proud professional man, a seasoned diplomat, turned away from a glowing romance in Seoul, does not call the professional woman in Pyongyang who turned him away. She could have called the Swedish embassy and asked to speak to him, or leave a message for him, but she didn't because proud professional women do not shamelessly throw themselves at distinguished older professional men.

Pyongyang and North Korea brought thoughts of tragedy around every corner. The continuing militant news, atomic bomb tests underground, above ground intercontinental missile tests, constant propaganda everywhere. Patriotic informers everywhere watching and reporting everything in any way believed at all suspicious. And always, hanging over it all, was the coming five day tour with Ban Chul, and the role she was expected to play in a special situation where history was watching. Play a role something like a spy, a shameless seducing spy. Take the risks she was expected to take, whatever they actually were, because this was a special situation and history was watching.

She decided to go to the Friday evening diplomat party at the twin tower 42 stories tall Koryo hotel. As with the Hyatt in Seoul, 5 stars with prices to match. She would see some people she knew from her Seoul days. And Rolf might be there, be there looking for her, hoping she would come and would join her. She got ready, carefully considered the results in the bathroom mirror, decided she looked too formal, too professional, changed her blouse, and called a taxi.

A small band was playing old favorites, several couples were dancing, several were at the buffet carefully filling little plates, older people gossiped in little groups. After a few minutes she saw him sitting alone at a table, glanced at him, smiled politely, waved politely, saw him stand up, smile, politely wave back and bob his head. She walked on to greet friends and acquaintances from Seoul. . For half an hour there were smiling greetings, polite hugs, handshakes, a kiss on the cheek, chatter, light laughter, more chatter. She played her friendly diplomat part as they played theirs.

She sat down at an empty table and a few minutes later Rolf came over with wine, sat across from her and after an awkward silence said, "Elena, I've missed you. I've been watching your embassy personnel announcements. I saw the announcement that you were going to be posted to Pyongyang, and then that you were here with an impressive title, Deputy Ambassador, something like that. I hoped so much you would come tonight."

"Rolf, it's good to see you again... It has been a while."

"It seemed like... years. You look exactly the same. The same pretty serious face, same pretty little smile, same captivating blue eyes."

With the trace of a teasing smile she said, "Oh my. Very gallant, sir. Should I believe you?"

"Elena, you know me. You know I mean it."

"Should I believe your sweet words? You could have changed into someone I don't know. Someone with some little faults and a few little peculiarities."

"Elena, you know all my big faults and all my Swedish peculiarities."

She took his hand. "Little faults, Rolf, little faults, and a few unimportant Swedish peculiarities."

"I should wait an hour to ask, but can we leave and go to my place, or your place... To catch up."

Mischievously she said, "Leave right off? You don't want to tell me what has been happening in your life, your social life, what you have been doing to stay busy?"

He bowed his head.

"Why am I teasing you? Look at me. We'll leave."

He smiled. "My place? It's nice. Safe neighborhood."

"No, my place. My little apartment. It's livable, it's private. We'll leave in a little while. Let's dance first. I want... I want to live again, I want to come alive."

"What's wrong?" he asked seriously.

"Rolf, I've been in a dark funk… I want to dance, dance with you. I want to feel like my old self, feel alive being with you, and then we'll go to my place."

He held her close as they danced. They looked at each other. They didn't speak. In the taxi they didn't speak. They didn't need the words as they sat close together tightly holding hands. The words were there in the grip of their hands.

Elena locked the door, turned on the lamps, took him in her arms and kissed him. Then she led him to the kitchen, plopped him down at the table, leaned over, gave him another kiss, found a bottle of Pinot Grigio and a corkscrew, fetched two glasses and put out cheese and crackers.

"Rolf, I really wanted you to be there."

"Elena, at the party I wasn't just nursing my wine hoping you would come. I was waiting and remembering being with you in Seoul. I was remembering how we met at the Hyatt. I was remembering all the wonderful hours we were together. I was remembering… being close to you there. I remembered. They were sweet memories." He paused. "It was wonderful being with you… It was wonderful." He looked down at the table and said, "It ended. We don't want to go over that."

"No, we don't."

He took a sip of wine, and said seriously, "You said you were down, you were in a funk, a dark funk, you wanted to come alive. Something is bothering you."

She sat down at the table across from him. "Rolf, it is not about you."

"You're sure?"

"It's not about you in any way."

He looked at her and slowly shook his head. "So, something bad. Something happened, something is going to happen. Do you want to tell me?"

She took a sip of wine and said, "It is my work, something connected to work that has come up. Is coming up."

"Is coming up soon?"

"May come up soon."

"You better tell me."

"I am going to be traveling all around the country."

"Why? When?"

"A few weeks. Maybe a month or so for five days."

"You better start from the beginning and tell me what this is about."

"I am expecting to travel around the country for five days with a government guide. As you would expect, it is a carefully guided tour. This will be the third tour. An embassy woman went with him on the first tour. Another embassy woman went on the second tour. Like them, I am going to see how the railroad works, how it needs improving, how different improvements would affect different kinds of business and people's lives. I expect to talk mostly to business people. I will write the third report about what the railroad is doing for the country's business, and what the railroad needs to do better."

"So?"

"I will be going all around the country... There could be more to it."

"More to it? You will talk to business people, factory people, and some working people?"

"Yes."

"And anybody else? And do anything else?"

"I expect it will just be factories-automobiles, tractors, metals processing, and seafood processing plants."

"What's bothering you? You think you may be watched?"

"Yes, and no. Not at first, not the first day while he explains where we are going to go each day, and what I am going to be allowed to do at the different plants."

"Tell me about the guide."

"He works in the railroad scheduling department. Both embassy women reported he was full of information, and always polite and respectful. They were together five working days, and at hotels five nights. About him personally... beyond helpful and polite, they wrote nothing. Not a single word. I can understand that."

"Elena, you better tell me everything."

"It's complicated."

"That's not an answers. At the party you said you were in a bad mood, a dark funk. You were never like that in Seoul. At the party you were smiling, hugging ladies, making happy talk."

"At a diplomat's party you play your part."

Rolf frowned. "When did this funk start?"

"I think it started back in Moscow when Uncle Lev told me he was sending me here. He warned me to be extra careful all the time because of hidden cameras and hidden microphones, and police and informers everywhere. I am here, I have been putting in long hours with the ambassador and the staff. Not always helpful staff. I'm not happy about this trip around the country, maybe in cold weather, so I've been down."

"Still not an answer. There is more to this?"

"Believe me, there is nothing to worry about."

"Elena, I know you. There is, you better tell me."

She bit her lip and said, "I'm not worried now, but there may be problems later."

"Later?"

"Rolf, in Seoul you were like me. You were on the diplomat side and the trade promotion side. And occasionally other things."

"That's about right. A little diplomacy, mostly trade promotion, and other things occasionally."

"You dealt with Swedish people in trouble. In trouble with the authorities in one way or another."

"Somebody has to help them. Part of the job."

"And here?"

"I have a fancy title, a nice office with a secretary, but my work is much the same here. Some diplomacy, mostly trade promotion, and taking care of Swedish businessmen and tourists in trouble. In Seoul they are arrested, mostly the men, for some offense, put in jail, and told they can face years in jail and a steep fine. The wives call the embassy. I talk to them. I make telephone calls to a police official, or in a serious case, I politely make an appointment to talk to a court official, a magistrate. They pay a fine and are released. I suggest they leave the country. They go to Vladivostok. Aeroflot sells tickets. No publicity of any kind. Here in Pyongyang it can be more difficult."

"Can you tell me more?"

He looked at her seriously and asked, "Elena, why more?"

"I should know."

"What do you want to know?"

"What you do in a serious case here. For someone important. How do you do it here?"

"Do you really want to know? Is there some special reason right now?"

"Yes."

"Yes, what?"

"Rolf, I want to know."

"It's something like this. A Swedish salesman wants a North Korean company to buy some product from his firm. Say a sale equivalent to fifty million kronor. The Korean company wants to buy, but at a lower price. They go back and forth. The Swede does something that he does in Europe when he feels the buyer is playing with him. He suggests to the Korean company exec that his Korean company has done something shady. Something somebody told him. Of course, he doesn't believe it. It is polite blackmail. The Swedish businessman sits in a jail cell facing certain conviction and years in prison at hard labor. In North Korea that is a death sentence. His wife in Stockholm hysterically calls the Pyongyang embassy. The ambassador tells me to take care of him. I go to the jail. I talk to the very scared prisoner. I talk to the Korean company exec. By phone I talk to a Swedish company exec in Stockholm. The sale goes though at a reduced price. The North Korean executive and the Swedish executive are both happy. There is a wire transfer of funds from Stockholm to the embassy. In a serious case I politely ask for an appointment to talk with the magistrate. A substantial fine is paid on the prisoner's behalf. The charges are reduced to disorderly conduct and dropped. The police are happy. Nothing appears in the newspaper or on television. The ambassador is happy. Aeroflot sells a ticket for a flight to Moscow with a connection to Stockholm. The wife is happy even though her husband complains bitterly that the embassy didn't do enough for him soon enough."

"Government people and tourists in North Korea also do stupid things and land in jail. Who pays for them?"

"Government people and tourists in North Korea do many stupid things. They do them here in Pyongyang, and they get drunk and rowdy, sometimes belligerent, at the ski resort. For tourists, parents and relatives pay. Aeroflot sells tickets."

Elena said, "Somebody who cares pays, Aeroflot sells tickets.

That is the realism most of the time for tourists?"

"Sometimes working it out costs more and takes longer. Eventually it is resolved, the money is paid, and Aeroflot sells another ticket."

"What about diplomats? Do they get in trouble, too?

They shared a dark minute before he answered, "They do get in trouble."

"Such as?"

"Should I know why you are asking?"

"Did you ever meet a North Korean diplomat named Ban Chul?"

After a silence he answered, "Yes, I know him. We're friends. What about Chul?"

"Do you know he left the diplomatic service to work for the railroad?"

"Does it matter?"

"It might."

"For you?"

"Yes, for me."

"You better tell me. Why do you want to get into what happened to Chul?"

"Rolf, I am involved. I am going on the third tour around the country. Ban Chul is the guide. I'm going with him."

"Can you get out of it?"

"I can, maybe I can, but I want to go."

"Why?"

"I've looked into it, and I want to go."

"Because of Chul?"

"In part, yes."

"You've met him?"

"No. I've seen his official photograph, and I know quite a bit about him."

"So, you really are… involved?"

"Yes. Has he told you anything about what he is doing working at the railroad?"

"Do you really want to get into what he does working at the railroad?"

"Yes."

"Why?"

"I should know."

Elena, why should you want to know about the railroad?"

"I am going on this five day tour with him, and I should know what I could be getting into."

After another silence he said, "Here in Pyongyang, about a month ago, Chul asked me to go to lunch with him, and at the end of our meal, he told me. He told me he was no longer in the Ministry of Foreign Affairs, and he was in the Ministry of Transportation, mostly working with a complicated computer program doing train scheduling. He is part of the staff scheduling all the passenger and freight traffic."

"Did he tell you why he was escorting Russian embassy ladies around North Korea?"

"Yes. He said it was to help get Russian money and expertise for improving the railroad. He said the tour reports are to show Russian officials the need to upgrade the North Korean railroad. Put in engineers and money. Big money. For Chul, beyond his new work, nothing was certain."

"Nothing was certain. What does that mean to you?"

"Elena, if you are asking if Chul was asking me for help, I can tell you not to worry. Chul is smart, he is resourceful. He is working his way through what is probably a temporary bump. In a career over many years things happen to you. If you can't get along well with the people you work for, it can be for the best if you leave. If you are in government, talented and trusted, there usually is a place for you. Chul is very personable, and he is trusted. You are a diplomat going on this sponsored tour with him, that tells you he is trusted. Nothing bad is going to happen to you, and nothing bad is about to happen to him."

"Until the tour is over?"

"For the foreseeable future."

"You really think so?"

"Nothing bad is going to happen to him. He's valuable where he is, and he is a captain in the army reserve, in logistics, and he's trusted to take you around the country, treat you very well, expecting to be rewarded with a glowing report by you about the urgent need to help improve the railroad no matter how much it costs North Korea, and also costs Russia."

"Nothing bad is going to happen? You are that sure?"

"I am that sure. Elena, believe me, nothing bad is going to happen to Chul. He is smart, he is personable, he is valuable. He could end up any number of important positions, and nothing bad is going to happen to him."

She slowly nodded twice, took both his hands, looked at them held in her hands, smiled again and said, "Can I ask you a personal question?"

"You can ask anything, but don't hold it against me if I don't know how to answer."

"You will know."

"Ask, and I will answer."

"Will you sleep over?"

He smiled. "You're serious?"

"Yes."

"I will, gladly, on one condition."

"What's that?"

"That you don't worry about Chul all night."

"I can try."

"You shouldn't. When I saw Chul he was fine. No change. He looked fine, he acted fine. He said he probably was not going to get back to the Ministry of Foreign Affairs, but that wasn't the end of the world."

She got up, came around the table, and kissed him. "You're wonderful. I feel so much better. Really, I do."

"Really?"

"Yes, my darling, really. Let's eat, let's drink, and we will go to bed like a married couple."

He smiled. "Now I will ask you a question."

"Ask, and I will answer."

"We will go to bed like an old run down married couple, or will it be like a newly married young couple on the first night of their honeymoon?"

She kissed him again. "There is a little piece in Shakespeare that goes like this. *Come, woo me, woo me, for I am in a holiday mood and most likely will agree.*"

"That's famous. It's from Act 1 of *As You Like It*. Rosalind is flirting with Orlando. She goes on, *What would you say to me if I told you that I am really yours?* He says, *I would kiss you before I answered.*"

"Rolf, you're amazing!"

"Maybe I remember it because I love you, and I've known that I love you ever since I met you at the Hyatt in Seoul. That seems like years ago."

"I've loved you, too. I must have shown it."

"You did."

"Do you know how to woo me?"

"What are you thinking?"

Elena asked, "Do you know Act Two of Swan Lake? The prince goes to the forest carrying his new hunting crossbow. He finds this magical swan beside the lake, and she sees him and dances for him, and then dances with him. When he supports her he is strong, and when he bends and kisses her, he is gentle."

"When I was in Moscow about three years ago, maybe four, the Kirov performed Swan Lake. It was marvelous. The music, the orchestra, the dancing, they were all marvelous. The Act II pas de deux by the lake was magic. I've never forgotten it."

"Then, my darling, you do know how to woo me."

"Couldn't that be a little... risky?"

"Not tonight. Come, my love, woo me, woo me, for I am in a holiday mood."

"I have to kiss you first."

"Indeed, you do."

After a long kiss and a long silence, he took hold of her hands, looked in her face, and said seriously, "Elena, we've found each other. Now what's going to happen to us?"

"Rolf, my darling, can I ask you the same question?"

"How can I answer?"

"Rolf, we are both roving diplomats. We come from families of roving diplomats. Posting here, a year or two, and posting somewhere else for another year or two, sometimes a little longer, and so on and on. It is what our families do."

"Elena, that's true. It is what our families in Stockholm and Moscow wanted. We knew it from when we were children. And so it is what we wanted so badly. It is what we worked for with all our heart and might. It is the prize we won."

"Yes, my dear one, it is the prize we won. You in Stockholm, and me in Moscow, it is the same prize. And so, my dear roving Swede, we will love each other while we are here and together."

"And then?"

"We will love each other afterwards wherever we are together again. Our lives and our careers will go on, but we will always stay in touch. That's the reality for couples like us, that's the reality, and I will tell you that my uncle who has lived his life as a roving diplomat has had his share of love that way."

"And, in my Swedish family. Diplomats are realists, and they arrange their lives. The people around them are realists, and they arrange their lives. Their friends and families have to accept that."

"Do they?"

"For the most part, they do."

"Has it always been that way? I suppose it has."

"It has, Elena, and if we want to be realists, it has always been that way. For Sweden and Russia, for five hundred years since Gustavus Adolphus and Pyotr the Great."

"So, Rolf, let's celebrate Swedish and Russian history, wonderful and crazy history."

"That it is."

"Let's eat and drink, toast to being together again, and go to bed."

"Like newlyweds?"

"Yes, my love, like loving newlyweds."

CHAPTER 19

October 3, 2016

At nine in the morning, conservatively dressed with no makeup beyond pale lipstick, and carrying a slender briefcase, Elena approached the main door of the six story building that housed the Ministry of Transportation. A guard expecting her arrival beckoned her to come inside and led her to a hallway where two other guards awaited her. One guard examined the contents of her briefcase, the other reviewed her embassy identification, and asked her to sign a visitor registry before going through the metal detector and then into an office at the end of the hallway.

A few minutes later a smiling well-dressed man came striding in to greet her. She thought that he looked about forty, somewhat older than his official photo. Speaking fluent Russian, he smiled and said, "You are Elena Marloff from the Russian embassy?"

"Yes, Elena Marloff from the Russian embassy."

"And you are here to begin the third tour of the rail and bus transport system?"

"The transportation tour, yes."

He smiled again. "Please, come with me. We will go into the interview room and let us sit down by the table. We have a pot of good coffee."

When they were seated with their coffee he went on, "Let me welcome you to the Ministry of Transportation. My name is Ban

Chul. As I expect you have been told, I will be your guide as I have been for Mrs. Orlova and Mrs. Volkova."

"Yes, I've been told."

"And, as I expect you have also been told, most of the time I will be with you as your guide to help you become more educated, and I hope enthusiastic, about further improving our national transport system."

"Yes, I've been told."

"For this morning we will have our picture taken for the newspapers. You know, two interested public officials, shaking hands and friendly smiles, and then we will start to get acquainted with the tour outline."

"I would appreciate that."

"The Ministry of Transportation has jurisdiction over the railroad, Air Koryo, and some marine activity. Here in this headquarters building there is the planning department, purchasing, maintenance, and operations which includes all scheduling. There is also a smaller section that you will be interested in. It deals with international travel coordination."

"I've heard of such international coordination, but I don't know how it works."

"We have reciprocal coordination agreements for rail, air, and marine navigation with Russia to the north and to the south and east, South Korea, China, Vietnam, Myanmar, Japan, and the other Southeast Asia countries. We will visit the departments and meet their chiefs as time allows. Then you must have lunch with me in our restaurant. When you are ready to leave I will give you a package of papers about the Ministry of Transportation. You may have seen them before, but you should have the latest ones. I will also find one for you about the international coordination agreements."

"That should be helpful. Thank you. Regarding the daily operation of the reciprocal coordination agreements, the one with Russia, can you give me an example?"

"Obtaining copies of the documents would be a chore, and going through them with you would take days, but we will see the daily results. When we are traveling along the coastline you will hear the planes overhead. Air Koryo, our state owned national airline, Korean Air, the South Korea flag airline, Singapore

Airlines, Miramar Airlines, and the other regional airlines, including Qantas from Australia, and NZ Air from New Zealand. During the day, if it is clear, you will see them, but they fly so high that you will not be able to determine their nationality.

"Aeroflot has a subsidiary, Aurora, that runs a Southeast Asia schedule from Vladivostok to Seoul, Shanghai, and Hong Kong every day of the week. During the summer, both morning and afternoon flights. Every day those planes from Southeast Asia airlines are carrying thousands of passengers, and tons of freight. They fly over our coast land and our territorial waters. Air traffic controllers keep all the planes safely separated by distance between planes and different altitudes. Air Koryo serves the entire country and has some international service to China, Beijing Capital International Airport, and Ulaanbaatar, Mongolia, Chinggis Khann International Airport. Not all international service is daily. Air Koryo planes are from two countries, the Russian Tupolev and Ilyushin, and the Ukrainian Antonov. They are all modern turbojets, and they are all expertly maintained at all times, so they are safe, and they are reliable."

"I didn't know about the Ukrainian planes."

"The international coordination section deals with air and marine traffic control, and the other daily operations under these reciprocal agreements. At one level you may correctly say all the coordination agreements are diplomatic matters. On the day by day operational level they are very technical, and they must change with changing conditions, and they do change without diplomats reviewing and approving the changes."

Elena nodded. "The diplomats I know would rather not get involved, but can you give me an example? Once a month I fly to Vladivostok. How does your hands on changing international air traffic control system work to help keep me safe going to Vladivostok and returning?"

"Vladivostok is a good example. The air traffic control centers here in Pyongyang, and Sinuiju across from China, are responsible for all internal traffic such as Pyongyang to Sinuiju. International flights along the coast to and from Vladivostok are the responsibility of air traffic control centers in Seoul and Vladivostok. So, for your travel to Vladivostok, and your return, it is like this. From takeoff from Pyongyang to the coast, to Wonsan, air traffic control is North Korean, and near Wonsan the flight is handed off to Seoul control, and it is responsible to near the Russian border, where it is handed off to Vladivostok control. It is the reverse responsibility coming back. Vladivostok control hands off to Seoul control, that hands off to Pyongyang control near Wonsan."

"And the international flights? China and Mongolia."

"Flying across China to Beijing the hand off is on the West coast near Dandong. We are a part of this worldwide web of air traffic controllers. Exactly how the controllers using their computer programs safely fit planes into their routes, control them, and hand them off, I have only the vaguest ideas. I'm told it is all about continuous radar identification and location plotting for all the planes being controlled by the centers and all the plane transponders and voice communications from all the planes to the centers. The planes from all airlines, passenger and freight, and all charters, passing through must comply at all times as the requirements are published and made effective."

"Thank you. I see why diplomats want to stay out of air traffic control changes."

"There is our office protocol, and there is practicality. Going through the building we will speak Korean. Our people are very concerned about security, and they are not used to hearing people speaking Russian, or any foreign language. Many of them know other languages, but you understand."

"Yes, of course."

Turning to Korean, he continued, "This morning we will visit some offices and meet some staff, but mostly it will be for giving you an overview of what we will be seeing and what we will be doing during our five days together. As we go through the daily travel itinerary you may have some concerns and questions. We can make changes here now, but it would be best to leave them until we get underway."

"Mr. Ban, I am looking forward to working with you for our mutual benefit."

"Ms. Marloff, you may call me Chul. Anna Volkova did. Irena Orlova did." He smiled. "If it is right for the occasion, I may call you Elena?"

Elena smiled. The icy official correctness melted. "Yes, Chul, of course."

"The tour is important not only for us, but also for your country. There have been years of studies about improving our transportation system, but they do not tell the story in the way you should know it, and I hope that at the end of the trip you will report favorably on our current capability and the value of further joint efforts to improve the system."

"I understand."

"Our experience is that almost everyone who comes here from another country thinks that the transport system in an Asian country like ours with a high mountain range and a volcano must be small, old, and broken down. When they travel around the country, when they go from place to place, they are surprised at how large the country is, and how modern it is compared to some other Asian countries. And they learn how the transport system is all designed to work as one integrated system. We say, quite rightly, that the transportation system with the electrified railroad and Air Koryo with its reliable modern planes, are day by day transforming the country. They fly on clear sunny days, also through rain and snow. Even so, with the railroad we know that we are far from where we should be, and your engineers have elaborately documented this. They show that Russia has generously helped a great deal, and also that we need further Russian help. You may have already looked over some of the recent reports, and some that go back years."

"I have. I don't know much about railroad engineering, but I have spent many hours going through the improvement project files. They are all about the need for a more reliable electric generating system, better track signaling, more and better road crossing guards, more powerful freight and passenger locomotives, many passenger conveniences. They all need improvement."

"They do. I will give you a trip schedule for all five days. I will be with you throughout and do my best to assure your comfort and your safety. We will be away five nights and you will have your own room in a good modern hotel every night. However, if you agree, for the last night we might stay in a modest hotel near a traditional restaurant. All your food, lodging, and incidental expenses are being taken care of by the Ministry."

"Mr. Ban, let me be frank. You want favorable reports. Anna

and Irena both had problems. I read their reports and spoke with them. They both speak Korean, but they felt that they did not have sufficient opportunity to talk to the people who day by day use the transport system. At times they wanted to go off on their own and talk to the people in business, people in the factories, and small shops. They wanted to ask what kind of transportation they felt they needed, and how much they felt they could afford day by day to pay for it. They praised the engineering efforts, and the government's increased subsidy for the railroad and bus lines, and that is in their reports, too."

"We are a country that has many subsidies to fund every year, and we are a country that officially is still at war with South Korea. There is much less secrecy than there used to be, but in sensitive areas, there can be problems."

"Am I going to have the same problems?"

He smiled. "We will work it out day by day as we go along. Wherever tourists can go alone, you can go off on your own without me. You can go into the shops, you can talk to the people in the street. At the seaports you can go down to the docks and talk to the people working there. Except in restricted areas, you can take photos all across the country, from the demilitarized free trade zone in the South to the seaport near the Russian border in the North. In some areas you will be able to go off on your own for short periods. An hour or so. When you do you will be as free as any tourist."

"That's just what they were complaining about."

"I know. In some areas you will need to stay with me. In those places you must put your notebook and camera away. I will remind you if you forget."

She smiled. "So, you are to be my official guide, and also my minder?"

"We will work it out. I am your guide, and to use your word, I will also be your minder. I am supposed to look after you so that you go to all the right places, and also see that you don't go to any of the wrong places and get into trouble. As best we can, we will work out your access to all sorts of people in all sorts of areas. Realistically, outside of restricted areas there is little to hide. Even inside the restricted areas, there is little to hide because of the low orbit satellite photography. Military satellite photography, and now also civilian low altitude satellite photography. It is amazing. You must have seen the pictures of the supposed missile sites on television and in the newspapers."

"Holes in the ground around a central building don't mean anything to me."

He smiled again. "Nor to me. I am your guide and your minder, but I hope that I can also be your friend while we explore the country together."

Elena smiled again. "You talk like a French fellow I was sitting next to on a plane from Moscow to Paris. An hour after takeoff he ordered a French wine for both of us and started asking if there was anything he could do to make the trip more comfortable for me, and by the time we were nearing Paris he absolutely insisted that I was going to be his dear friend, he had a reservation at a fine hotel near Galleries Lafayette, just a couple of short blocks away, and if I would let him, he would take very good care of me. He went on that after some time picking up a few nice presents for me we could go to his grand beautifully furnished house in one of the most fashionable parts of the city."

Chul put his hand on his cheek, looked down, and shook his head. "I know the type. If I have offended you, I apologize." He paused. "Elena, I want to take good care of you. I want to do it in the right way, the most informative way. I want to do it for all the right reasons."

"Which means?"

"Whenever possible we will take our meals and stay at places where we can have French wine instead of soju or beer. Which also means, if you agree, we will add a day. We will start tomorrow in the morning with something different for us from the other trips. I will get a car. We will drive to a section of the demilitarized zone about twenty kilometers from the commercial crossing where the trucks line up on both sides to cross. Shall we go to the demilitarized zone tomorrow and start the train trip the next day?"

Elena responded brightly, "Yes, by all means."

"Good! Now we must get our picture done. Tomorrow dress warm, heavy top, pants, coat and gloves. The weather is going to be cold during the day, cloudy with some possible light rain possible at night. I will bring umbrellas for both of us. I will pick you up at your embassy at nine. We will stop for lunch, and we should be at the DMZ by two."

"And coming back?"

"We should leave before dark. We can stop for a meal if you want to."

Under a cold threatening sky Ban Chul passed the binoculars to Elena and directed her to a spot on the other side of the demilitarized zone.

"Elena, we are looking at history. History. Frightful war history. The Second World War officially ended on September 2, 1945, with a surrender signing ceremony aboard the USS Missouri in Tokyo Bay. The People's Republic of North Korea was proclaimed in Pyongyang three years later, in September 1948. The Korean War armistice was signed five years later, in July 1953. It set up the demilitarized zone winding for 250 kilometers across the Korean peninsula. It intersects the 38th parallel and is about four kilometers wide."

"So, a sizable area."

"It was almost immediately fortified all along the North and South sides, including thousands of land mines, and so it has remained with lookout guard posts all these years."

Pointing to a spot on the other side, he said, "Look over there and you will see a pair of soldiers with binoculars standing on a platform. Two soldiers are always there scanning this way and that way. They are supposed to be looking for intruders, but they are bored stiff, and mostly they are looking for the wildlife in the area. The DMZ has become a 250 kilometers long wildlife park. The birds and animals don't mind the land mines. Every year some young people get an irresistible urge to cross, and they somehow manage to get across unharmed, which says something about the guards and the soggy old landmines."

"Why do they cross?"

"They have family to go to, they are looking for a better job, they are going to a girlfriend. All the usual reasons. In addition to the usual birds and animals that live in the area there are rare ones, red-crested cranes and white-napped cranes. There have been reports of a tiger."

"Can the guards on the other side see us distinctly from so far away?"

"Yes, in clear weather, and from time to time one of the guards will turn his field glasses towards this spot. Today we are showing ourselves, it is clear enough now, and if he wants to, he will be able to see us looking at him."

"From over there, what do you suppose he will think when he sees us?"

"He will scowl. They are young fellows full of patriotism paid to scowl at us, just as our young fellows are paid to scowl back at them."

"So sad."

"I will tell you a story, supposedly true. One day one of our boys waved and the other fellow waved back. Maybe they were related and knew each other. A week later the same thing happened. They were caught, tried and convicted of dereliction of duty. There were prison sentences on both sides for waving instead of scowling. Elena, it is so sad. The fellows on both sides are Korean, same stock, same language, same culture, same literature, same history for a thousand years."

"Wars and foreign occupations that go on for many years can eventually change all that."

"They can change some things in some ways, and when the war ends, and the occupying army goes home, they can mostly change back to the old ways. I think that is going to be the history of this war and its results."

"Why do you say that?"

"What happened to Korea was not a conquest and occupation by the army of a foreign country. What happened was a civil war. It was a civil war sponsored by outsiders fighting a long standing bitter ideological war. The war began in June 1950 and ended three years later with the armistice in July 1953. North Korea was helped by China and Russia, and South Korea was defended by a United Nations force that was mostly American. The armistice stopped the fighting, provided for the return of prisoners, and divided the country along the 38th parallel into two zones of occupation that became the Democratic People's Republic of Korea in the North, and shortly after that, the. Republic of Korea in the South."

"You were in the Ministry of Foreign Affairs."

"I was."

"From what you know, between the leaders in the North and South, has there ever been an understanding, a diplomatic agreement, that amounted to a move from the armistice to an unofficial peace treaty?"

"An understanding? A diplomatic agreement? I can only tell you, that as far as I know from my years with the Ministry of Foreign Affairs, there has been no peace treaty, publicly or privately, and technically North Korea and South Korea are still at war."

"While the fighting was going on it was a horrible war."

"It was. It was a war with modern weapons. American planes bombed one North Korean seaport, Sinuiju, to break the flow of war supplies from China, and break the will of the people there. There were massacres by both sides. Thousands of suspected communists were killed by the South, and the North tortured and starved prisoners. Over thirty thousand Americans died. It was terrible. Terrible."

"In time, will the North and South unite again?"

"Elena, they will unite, but this is not the time and place to talk about reuniting the North and the South into one country. I wanted you to see the demilitarized zone. I wanted you to personally experience the division of Korea."

"It's cold, and it will be getting dark soon. Are we going to stay much longer?"

"We will leave, but just a few more minutes." Ban Chul raised his binoculars and slowly scanned across the other side. "There he is. He is looking our way, and he is scowling. It's so depressing. Let's get going."

"Chul, let me have the glasses one more time. I want to look at the soldier on the other side. When I looked last time he was looking back at me. I think he was smiling. I think that he saw a woman, and he was smiling."

"You want to smile back?"

"I would like to, but I'll just wave."

"No, no!"

"Just a little wave. Like waving to a friend across a room at a party. If he waves back it will be just a little wave. Same little friendly greeting. Like this." She raised her hand and fluttered her fingers. "He won't tell anybody, and I won't tell you, so no harm will be done."

"Elena, I am supposed to be looking after you, and your fluttering fingers could start an incident that could get you in trouble, and get me in trouble. Besides, it is starting to rain."

"Give me the glasses," she said sharply. "Let's see if I can get him to wave back. It's nothing, nothing is going to happen."

Chul started to frown, stopped, looked at her, smiled and said, "Here, take the glasses."

"I'm sorry. I was rude."

"No need to apologize. If that's the worst for us this trip, we will get along just fine."

Elena scanned for several minutes, returned the binoculars, and said, "He's gone. Nobody's watching."

"That happens on both sides."

"Sometimes intentionally?"

"Probably sometimes."

"Chul, you didn't have to bring me here. You had a reason that's more than having me experiencing history. You did. Do you want to talk?"

"Not now. We have to leave."

Starting back to Pyongyang in light rain Chul turned on the car's headlights and windshield wipers. After a few kilometers he looked over at Elena and said, "If you want to talk, we can talk on our way back."

"Not while you're driving."

"There is a grocery with lighted parking ahead. About half an hour. I can pull off there."

"Let's do it. Meanwhile, keep your eyes on the road."

Chul stopped at the side of the grocery parking area and turned off the engine and headlights. A few shoppers, head down, hurried past. As the rain blurred the car windows he sat silent, hands in his lap.

After a few minutes looking straight ahead he turned to her and said, "So we are alone."

"Yes, we are alone."

He turned to her and said, "You asked if we might talk. We are safe, we can talk."

She turned to meet his gaze. "Cars can have ears. Cars in a grocery parking lot can have ears."

"This Volvo is a Ministry car. Even so, I checked all through it. We can talk."

"You know from experience what to look for, and where and how to look?"

'Yes. From army logistics. I have searched cars, trucks, railroad cars. We can talk."

"Chul, to talk about anything *serious*, it takes two. Two willing people."

He nodded. "Two willing people, and for us to start, something not too controversial."

"Then let's start with something worth thinking about that is serious, but for us, not too controversial. We could start talking about reuniting the country. How it could happen. Not now, in the future."

"Elena, now for us here, reuniting the country sometime in the future, is a very big and very controversial subject made up of many parts. Some parts, however, are less difficult to talk about than other parts."

"At the border there is a separation zone with big trucks going back and forth every day."

"That's right. I think of it as flowing commerce in hundreds of essential products being more important for all of Korea than any temporary politics."

"And yet, next to the separation zone, on both sides, there are scowling guards and landmines to stop people from crossing without permission. What does that mean for the ordinary people of Korea? A generation of Koreans are growing up with Korea cut apart by such politics. How long do you think it might be before the armistice ends, there is no more demilitarized zone on the 38th parallel, and the North and South are united under one government?"

"It is really the same question but let me try to answer. First, are you asking whether it will be accomplished by force or peacefully?"

"Peacefully."

"Elena, every Korean politician, young and old, North and

South, has always said that eventually Korea will be reunited. It will be reunited because it must be reunited. The question is how and when."

"Chul, what do you think?"

"I believe Korea will be one country again in about twenty years. Maybe much less."

"Why?"

"There are several intertwined reasons. The prosperity of South Korea is based on access to the American market, and to a lesser extent, European and Chinese markets. Those markets have been given to Seoul in return for political agreements and military alliances looking to protect South Korea from being united with the North. In the background there is history, and there is the economic side and the political side."

"How do you see all that."

"In Asia there were the British, French, and Dutch colonies, and in Russia the Communist overthrow of the Czar. Around the world there have been different kinds of governments undergoing great changes to deal with."

"Very different."

"On the economic side, America and Europe will not continue to absorb the huge flows of imports from Asia, mostly from China, Taiwan, Japan, and South Korea. These continuing imports, while good for American and European consumers, are at the expense of American and European industries. It has meant importing billions in cheap goods from Asia and exporting millions of good high paid factory jobs to much lower wage Asia. Over time the balance will shift more and more to local production and national protection. In the United States and all across Europe there will be generous subsidies for their local industries, and the Asian imports will be greatly curtailed by targeted and strictly enforced stiff tariffs. So perhaps not twenty years, but sooner or later, the Chinese, Japanese, and South Korean export bubbles will start to burst. As that happens the costly military protection of South Korea by the American Army, Navy, and Air Force will little by little fade away, and for both the North and South, traditional unitary politics will be reestablished."

"And other reasons?"

"Korea has its traditional enemies. China has subjugated Korea for centuries. The Empire of Japan ruled Korea from 1910 to 1945. As the American protection of South Korea fades our entire country, South and North, will fear, for good reason, another bloody invasion, another horrible war, another heroic defense for a year or two, and then an inevitable surrender followed by another long brutal foreign occupation. Whatever the cost, whatever the obstacles, Koreans North and South with modern economic tools and impressive military weapons will inevitably push to reunite to further their own interests."

"And the results are inevitable?"

"Nothing we can predict is inevitable, but with atomic weapons, and long range missiles, a united Korea might manage to stay free for a while."

Elena sighed. "Chul. I'll never forget this. Korean history expertly explained to me by a Korean diplomat in a parked car at night in the rain."

"Elena, in a way it's a good place for us."

"Not all diplomats explain history like that. You are very knowledgeable and very thoughtful."

"Karl Marx wrote that economics and class struggle will drive an inevitable history and produce the victory of the proletariat. Your Uncle Lev would say now that because of the proliferation of atomic weapons and long range missiles there is no inevitable history, that now guns and economics together do not drive an inevitable history, and that all good generals, admirals, and right thinking diplomats know it."

"Chul, you sound so much like my Uncle Lev."

"I am a stranger who used to be a diplomat. Your uncle is a great diplomat. I am most honored to hear you say that in some way I am like him."

She reached across and took his hand. "Chul, you are not a stranger to me."

"Really?"

"He talked to me about you when he was sending me to Pyongyang. He told me that you had been an honorable diplomat. He said that in negotiations you were knowledgeable and courteous, you could be stubborn, but unlike others, when you gave your word, you stuck by it."

"Negotiating with an opponent that acts another way amounts to playing a game. Good faith negotiating is not a game. Always doing what I believed was honorable may be why I gained an honorable reputation, and perhaps why I may have had some negotiating success, and also why I lost my position."

After a silence Elena said, "Before your railroad position you were highly regarded within the Ministry of Foreign Affairs. You were a busy respected North Korean diplomat."

"If I still were, Elena," he said after a long pause, "how interesting it could be for us."

"Interesting for us?"

"How interesting it would be for us to sit across a table and negotiate a deal."

"Chul, there are many kinds of deals. What kind of deal would interest us?"

"What a question."

"Go on, we're safe here, tell me."

"Elena, we might decide to make a deal to exchange Russian railway equipment for Korean minerals such as coal, iron, cobalt, nickel, or even uranium ore."

"Why uranium ore?"

"Uranium ore is valuable. When the ore is purified, and one of its isotopes is sufficiently enriched in a centrifuge, it produces weapons grade uranium, and when highly enriched uranium is adequately processed in a nuclear reactor it produces weapons grade plutonium, which is also valuable. Where there is good value on both sides, such as trading away weapons for a chance for safety and peace, there can be a deal. First a small deal, and later a more comprehensive one with inspections. Elena, you know it is much more complicated, but you know what I mean."

"Chul, I know about you, the fine diplomat, but I know nothing about you the man, the person."

"I have to think you know a good deal about me."

"I know that Ban Chul was a North Korean diplomat. He negotiated at home and elsewhere. There were many very important negotiations. Tariffs, taxation. There's much more to a diplomat's life than that."

"Yes, of course. That's not for now."

"How much do you know about Elena Marloff?"

"I know the official record. I know you went to university at

Pyotrsburg, graduated from the Academy in Moscow, and joined the Russian Ministry of Foreign Affairs. I assume that after your year in Moscow it was your uncle who posted you to Seoul. I know nothing about your private life." He paused, and then continued, "This is our first day together. We are here in a car in the dark just starting to get to know each other, and for now we cannot talk more about serious matters... or personal matters."

"So, tell me more about the trip around the country, our five day tour."

"It is a working week. And it can be more than that for us. By tomorrow the rain will stop. Cold, cloudy, windy, but no rain. We will take the train to Wonsan on the East coast. It is a major city and a major seaport. We will visit the port and the seafood processing plant. The second day we will start early. We will take the train north to Tanchon, another major city and seaport halfway to the Russian border. We will get off for lunch at the station. We will continue going north to Najin, a seaport very close to the Russian border."

"Will be able to see Russia from there?"

"We will rent a car and drive to the border, and you will see the railroad bridge over the Tumen River to Khasan. The bridge joins us to Russia, and it joins Russia to us. All sorts of freight, tons of it, go both ways, every day. We will not have exit papers, so we will not get on the train and cross the bridge to Khasan. There are always controls on both sides. If we managed to get past Najin with expertly forged exit papers we would be stopped at Khasan and sent back because our Russian entry papers were not valid, not expertly enough forged. Without expertly forged North Korean papers, and expertly forged Russian papers, Najin, even with substantial bribes, is the end of the line. Realistically, some wealthy and clever people do get through, but it would be foolish to rely on that. Sad, sometimes very sad. Enough about that?"

"More than enough."

"After that we will go south. We will take our time and go off on more side trips by bus as things interest you. Bus service is also very important to the country. It is mostly reliable and mostly comfortable."

"Meaning that the bus service all around the country needs some improvement?"

"It does. You can talk to the passengers. They will give you an earful."

"I will likely smile and listen like a good tourist."

"We will travel by train to Sinuiju. It is a major modern industrial city on the Yalu River across from Dandong, a Chinese industrial city."

"Quite an adventure."

"I hope it will be an enjoyable and worthwhile adventure for both of us."

Elena smiled. "I'm all for that. A worthwhile enjoyable adventure for both of us."

"So, we will start tomorrow morning? At the embassy. Nine o'clock."

"Why not my apartment? I'll give you my address and phone number."

"At your apartment. Nine o'clock. I will be dressed casually, you should, too. Warm travel clothes. A notebook. A couple of pens and pencils. One valise, no valuables. You can bring a small camera, but you cannot use it in restricted areas. If you are in doubt, any doubt, don't. Bring your official identification but leave your diplomatic passport at the embassy. If you don't have it with you, it can't be lost or stolen."

"So, I can take notes about what I see?"

"Yes."

"I can talk to the people in the cities, and small towns, the people at the railroad stations and bus stations?"

"Yes, all you want. Rubbing shoulders with ordinary people may not always be comfortable, they have all sorts of big and little complaints, but for you it can be the best way to learn about the country. It will be interesting, informative, and, Elena, if we let it, here and there it can be more than an official tour with me explaining and you taking notes. It can be fun, fun for both of us."

Elena gave him a knowing smile and said lightly, "Chul, I am not being paid to have lots of fun sightseeing around the country. Neither are you."

He smiled. "True, true, but for us, from time to time, if we relax and let it, here and there, it could happen."

"If we can both have a little fun along the way, I'm all for it. Just don't get carried away like that French fellow on my flight to

Charles de Gaulle."

Turning serious, Chul said, "Elena, you can travel anywhere in the world. London, Paris, Rome, Madrid, Washington. I cannot travel anywhere outside this country anymore. My passport has been canceled. I have no exit papers."

"You could apply?"

"At this time, for various reasons, it would not be prudent for me to apply."

"You were a diplomat. You used to travel. You used to travel around the world."

"When I was with the Ministry of Foreign Affairs I traveled. I traveled frequently on my diplomatic passport just as you travel on yours."

"Yes, of course."

"I speak several languages, and I had posts in Russia, China, and France. I did my work as a trusted diplomat. I had many conferences and informal negotiations, but everywhere there was more. Day by day, I saw, I read, I *tasted*, how others like me live their lives. There is everywhere, and always has been, this sense of national belonging, national pride, but from country to country there is a real difference in the freedom of thought and freedom of action."

"Could you perhaps, in time, be asked to travel for your country again?"

He shook his head. "Elena, possibly, but it seems me that is unlikely."

After a long silence Elena said, "Let me ask you a question for tomorrow."

"All right. Ask."

"When we get to the train station, when we are on the train, when we are talking between ourselves, should we always speak Korean, or if no one is close by, could we sometimes speak Russian?"

"On the train we will speak Korean, otherwise we would stand out, but if there is a situation where we might not want to be understood, and there was no one seated close to us, there was no one passing by, then we might slip into Russian for a minute or two. Enough for now?"

"Yes. We should get back."

"We could stop for dinner."

"No, I would rather get home early."

Chul started the engine, put on the heater, headlights, and windshield wipers and turned back on to the highway. Driving through the rain they were warm, silent, comfortable with each other until they reached Elena's apartment. Chul fetched an umbrella from the back. At the door he smiled and said, "All in all, Elena, I would say a very good start. I learned that we can talk to each other. Not just talk, but very important, we can talk freely and intelligently."

"I am very glad to hear you say that. All in all, Chul, I think it has been a good start, too."

"Tomorrow at nine I will call for you here with the taxi. The train leaves at ten."

She smiled. "Tomorrow morning. Taxi at nine o'clock. I'll be ready."

"Elena, we will make it a good start, and a good day. The first of five good days."

"Five good days, Chul. I'm all for that."

CHAPTER 20

The train was less than half full when it started. In their first class car there were mostly middle aged couples and younger women with children. A dozen or so older men were together at the back. Elena sat by the window dressed in a modest top, pants and long jacket. By the aisle Ban Chul in casual clothes sat beside her in silence.

Half an hour later the train passed into the hilly countryside. Elena turned to Chul and speaking in Korean said, "I was looking forward to you telling me about the green valleys with crops and treed slopes that have been sliding by, and about the lovely hilly area we are going to be going through... or we can talk about something else like why there are so few older passengers on our first class car?"

"We can talk about Korean history, what is centuries old, what is new in our century. We can talk about how well most older people are getting along, and about whether for most people, young and old, their lives are so different and much better now with reliable electricity and indoor plumbing."

"I would think much different in some ways and little different in others."

"In many ways, factory jobs, refrigerators, lights at night, telephones, television, their lives are quite different. Especially for our younger couples with enough money to be able to live on their own. For them it is very much better. Most older people cannot afford to go first class, but for some of our older people, like those old men in the back who are able to afford first class tickets, it is also much better."

"What else could we talk about?"

"We can talk about what we will see that is interesting. Factories, farms, harvested crops, food processing."

"Anything else?"

"We can talk about where we will stay each night."

"So tell me where we will stay. The cities, their size, their history. Old, new, changing, or not."

"We have five nights away. In every city we visit, we are supposed to stay at a modern hotel in the business section." He paused and looked at her meaningfully, then continued, "However, on our last night, in Sinuiju, if you agree, we could stay in the historic part of the city at a small hotel near a traditional restaurant. You can sample traditional dishes and also order from the tourist menu with good wine."

"You mentioned that before. I am looking forward to the hotel and the restaurant."

"Good."

"Tell me why Sinuiju is historic, and what is new. Tell me what the people do. Tell me about the old and new groceries, pharmacies, hardware, clothing, and other stores."

"Sinuiju is an industrial city, light industry, on the Yalu River. On some maps it is the Armok River. It has a population of nearly four hundred thousand. A bridge connects Sinuiju, and its nearby port, to the Chinese port of Dandong on the other side."

"You told me Dandong has air traffic controllers for Air Koryo flights to Beijing."

"What a remarkable memory you have."

"Chul, I listen carefully to your every word."

He smiled and said, "I listen to you, too."

She smiled. "As it should be. Go on."

"There are factories on both sides of the river. Trucks cross the bridge all day and all night."

"Tell me more about Sinuiju."

"Sinuiju is an old city joined to the new city that was developed during the colonial period, the Japanese occupation. As I told you at the DMZ, the port and parts of the city were destroyed by American bombing during the war, and have been rebuilt. The old areas have all kinds of little shops and restaurants. The new part has modern factories and a fancy new hotel. You can read about the new parts of the city in the literature."

"Tell me about how the people live."

"Elena, it would be better if we were not seen talking so much here. So for now, stop asking questions, notice how steep the hills are becoming, and get ready for the long tunnels through the mountains."

They toured the country on the rail system and in cities and small towns on new and old buses and old and new taxis. They went to a textile factory. They visited a cooperative farm and a food processing plants. Elena twice went off on her own to take photos, make notes, and talk to young and old people. They heard patriotic praise for the government and mild complaints. They stayed away from army bases and navy installations.

Before dinner on the fourth night they sat together in a small park. It was almost empty. In the twilight they talked about what they had seen that day, what they had missed the day before, what was coming tomorrow in Sinuiju.

Elena said, "Chul, tomorrow we will be in Sinuiju. You've scheduled a full day for us. It will be our last day away... and you must know that since our talk in the car coming back from the DMZ I've been waiting for you to tell me more about your life as a diplomat."

"I know."

"You know me now. Will you tell me?"

"Elena, is my life story that important to you?"

"Chul, it is."

"What's to talk about? What's to remember?"

"Talk about you. Talk about me. Talk about us. Remember the nearly deserted little shopping area on the way back from the DMZ. Talk about us. Talk about us starting to get to know each other in the Volvo in the rain."

"Elena, believe me, I remember."

"You told me it was a Ministry car. You remember?"

237

"I remember."

"You told me you had searched the whole car for bugs. The windows were blurry from the rain, it was dark. You said it was safe to talk. I tried to get you to talk about your life as a diplomat, and all you would say was that this wasn't the time, this was our first day together, and when we got to know each other, it would be interesting if we could negotiate a deal."

"Yes. I remember."

"You meant it would be interesting if we could be at a table and negotiate like diplomats."

"Yes."

"I asked you what kind of a deal, and you said something about North Korea mining uranium ore and processing it into enriched uranium and then into enriched plutonium, and that I knew all about that."

"Elena, we were just beginning… beginning to reach out… beginning to know each other."

She took his hand and said, "So now, even though it has been only a few days, now we know each other."

"In a way."

"Chul, it has been only a few days, very full long days, enough so that we do know each other."

"Yes, in some ways."

"So tell me about your life as a diplomat."

After a long pause he began, "I had a professional position with the Ministry of Foreign Affairs. I was an active diplomat. I was respected and participated in important negotiations. It's all gone.… What does it matter now?"

"Chul, it matters. It does. If I lost my position tomorrow, my service for my country as a diplomat is an honor that can never be taken away from me."

"I know. I think about it."

"Your service as a diplomat for your country is an honor that can never be taken away from you."

"Elena, for you and for me, that is true. For everyone else, you know the expression, honor, like dishonor, is in the eye of the beholder."

Elena took his other hand and said, "Chul, enough evading, enough philosophy."

"What philosophy?"

"Tell me what you have done as a professional diplomat. Tell me how you got along with other diplomats."

"You really want to know?"

"I do. I want to know."

"It means that much to you?"

She squeezed his hand. "It means that much. To me. To you. *To us. It does.*"

"Truly, Elena?"

"Truly, Chul," she said softly.

He looked down and soberly began again. "Not long ago I was like you. Like you, Elena, a working diplomat. A diplomat like you."

"Go on."

"With every posting I promoted my county in accordance with the policies made by the country's leaders as I understood them. I had quick promotions. I thought, foolishly, that I had a good and secure future."

"What happened?"

"I will never know. I will tell you that I never felt comfortable with one of my seniors. From my first day under him."

"Why?"

"We were dealing with thorny issues. Difficult, contentious. You know what I mean."

"Can you give me an example? Nothing detailed, just the area, just the type."

"We were dealing with taxation of foreign businesses, sole ownerships, corporations, and partnerships, a franchise tax based on gross income from North Korean operations, and a supplement tax based on the percentage of total worldwide gross revenue from North Korean operations. The concepts you know are straight forward, but the implementing accounting and reporting provisions are not. Frankly, it soon became apparent that my senior who thought of himself as an expert on taxation of foreign companies did not fully understand the cost and income shifting techniques used by most multinational companies to reduce or avoid such taxes. He had little regard for the great difficulty in enforcing full payment based on the taxation agreements that we were trying to achieve for both countries by our negotiations. The result was that his objectives and my objectives were largely the same, but we often disagreed. I wasn't deliberately defying him. In every case when I told him that I disagreed it was for what I considered compelling reasons."

"My uncle told me you have a good reputation as a negotiating diplomat."

"I am honored. As to my frustrations, I should add that there was the usual inside push and pull between the juniors looking for promotions and the seniors trying to hold on. That's always going to be there."

"That sounds so familiar. One senior I worked under near the end of my first year was difficult, more than difficult, he was maddening. You went into his office to talk to him and after two minutes he cut you off and waved his arm as his way of telling you to get out."

"Maddening, but you survived."

"I survived. He retired."

"You were able to stand up to a senior officer and prevail. I didn't."

"With your colleagues you did?"

"With my colleagues I also had repeated disagreements, but I did find a way to work out most of our disagreements. No hard feelings on either side. We were colleagues, the men and the women, and we were friends. We were friends, and we were patriots working for the same cause."

"And you were also friends with younger diplomats from other countries?"

"When I was with a younger diplomat of another country, a man or a woman, we sometimes had something in common. Big ideas about how all governments should work. Grand ideas about democratic government from the Greek golden age. Years later in another place we would meet again. We found the time and place where we would talk about our work, and then, even. after that time apart, we would talk about what happened in our lives, and it was still a strong personal bond as well as a strong professional one. We found that we could still talk long and frankly, and we felt we could still trust each other."

"There were times that you could, and did, really trust each other?"

"Yes, for certain matters. Not everything, I don't mean that, but for certain matters."

After a long silence Elena said softly, "Chul, when you tell me about trusting colleagues, that there were times for trusting colleagues, you are talking about us."

After a pause, he said, "I suppose so."

"You were transferred from the foreign service to the Ministry of Transportation. What happened?"

"Not here."

"Chul, we are alone. There's no one near us. No one is watching us. What happened?"

"Several things."

"Trust me, I should know."

"It is painful, it is all done and over with, and it doesn't matter now."

"I should know. Tell me."

He nodded slowly and then, speaking slowly, he began, "There was always the problem of exactly following instructions from higher authority, especially when the instructions were incomplete, ambiguous, or it seemed to me, even contradictory. Especially during a crisis. My senior reported me for not following his instructions. I had made some commitments. I had given my word, and my opposition had relied on it and changed his position. I explained that it was the right position, it wasn't crucial, and I couldn't change. He was furious. He reported that I did not follow his orders, and I refused to change my obstinate behavior. He also complained that I was not pure Korean, that my ancestry was not racially pure. All of that and more in the two weeks before I was dismissed."

"Without a chance to justify your work?"

"One morning when I came to my building the guard pulled me aside, told me I couldn't enter, and gave me an envelope. The letter said I was to report to a work assignment office. For three weeks I sat there in a hard chair with a hundred others with nothing to do but wait for my name to be called. Then one morning I was called and ordered to report to the Ministry of Transportation building. There I was interviewed several times before I was assigned to learn train scheduling."

"Your senior officer was your enemy. You acted honorably,

and you were brave. You stood up to him. It threatened him. Also, he is a racial bigot."

"Unfortunately, Elena, in Korea, North and South, race is often used that way. It always has. For centuries Korean ancestry, Korean racial purity, has been central to keeping Koreans separate from invaders. Central, but not fully effective. Over the centuries it was one invasion and conquest after another. The hated Chinese, the despised Japanese. It is the same old story, the officers and soldiers took the women they wanted, and their many children become part of the population."

"I understand."

"I don't look like most Koreans. I am taller and broader boned than most Koreans. If I have a Russian grandfather, perhaps an officer, an aviator, perhaps a foot soldier, what does it matter? Anything else?"

"There are a dozen ministries and departments, there are hundreds of positions, why the Ministry of Transportation and the train scheduling department?"

"I am almost sure I know the answer. In the army reserve I am a captain in a transportation brigade, I still am, and I have considerable experience in trucking and railroad logistics. Moving hundreds of troops and freight cars filled with ammunition and supplies. Also, I have dealt with Russian diplomats, men and women, so it was logical to use me for the railroad tours with the Russian foreign service ladies."

"You were chosen above everyone else for what your government considers a very important job."

"Important?"

"I think so. My uncle thinks so. Chul, you're proud that you were chosen."

"Elena, how can you say that?"

"You've shown it in the way you treated Anna, and the way you treated Irina."

"I tried."

"And you've shown it again and again in the way you're treating me. You continually give courtesy and respect."

"Thank you, I try."

"And you expect courtesy and respect in return."

"I am not good enough, and not loyal enough, to be a diplomat, but I am good enough, and loyal enough, to be a captain in the army reserve. I am loyal enough to know what is happening on the railroad, and I am loyal enough to escort Russian embassy ladies around the country. Show them what they should see, explain what should be explained, all while keeping them comfortable and safe. I used to be in the foreign service, a negotiating diplomat. What am I now?"

"You should be proud to be an army captain. You should be proud to be working with the railroad. Chul, you are proud being here next to me... just as I am proud sitting here next to you and holding your hand."

"Elena, I was a working diplomat, and now I am looking after coal trains."

"Tell me what you do."

"You know."

"I have only a vague idea."

"I schedule trains, regular and special. Along with the rest of our crew I make the transport system operate as intended."

"Tell me what's involved, and how you do it."

"I put a hold on the local so the express gets through. I give priority to the coal trains headed for the port at Nampo on the west coast. If a special trip must be fit into the next week's schedules I put on holds to make space in the schedule and find the temporarily free locomotive, the unused right kind of freight cars, and the available crew."

"That is a great responsibility. That is far more than ordinary day by day scheduling."

"It is kind of you to think of me that way. From time to time there are changes for maintenance and repair work that have to be carefully planned out. Also, special trains can require adjustments. But most of the work is routine."

"Whether it is planning or routine, it is a great responsibility, and an honor."

"Elena, believe me, holding your hand, and talking with you like this, is a far greater honor."

"Chul, there must be more to your life. Your family, how you grew up, your education, how you came to the foreign service and became a diplomat."

"I come from an ordinary Korean family. My family owned a

little clothing shop in Sinuiju where I went to grade school and high school.. My past life doesn't matter."

"It does. Tell me."

"There's nothing to tell."

"That's no answer. Start with your schooling. Tell me more about your life."

"It doesn't matter."

"It does. Tell me."

"Elena, I was fortunate."

"So tell me how."

"Why should you care about me?"

"Because my uncle cares about you… and I care about you."

"Because I was also a diplomat?"

"Yes, because you were a diplomat like me, an honorable good one, and because that is still in you."

"Elena, you are very kind."

She gently squeezed his hand and said, "Tell me more about your family, about growing up, about schooling, and what happened after that."

"I was an honor student. When I was seventeen I was selected at my school to go to college and become an army officer. I was told that it was because I had the best grades, that I could write well, and that I did not just repeat what was in the book. In my writing I did not say anything against the government. Even then, I knew better. After college I was selected to enroll in the University of Foreign Studies in Pyongyang. We had many patriotic history lectures, and we studied world history and foreign languages. At graduation I was put in the Ministry of Foreign Affairs, and I was made a lieutenant in the army reserve. I was told that if I gained weight I would lose my officer rank and I would stay in the army as a private. So I started my exercising. Like many Koreans, I still exercise to stay fit."

"I would think that there must be several young women that found you attractive."

"Perhaps."

"You are being modest. Are you married?"

"No."

"Have you ever been married?"

"No."

"Are you living with someone?"

"Do you really want to know?"

"Chul, I want to know. I really want to know."

"Why?"

"Because I am really interested in you."

"That is very kind. At the University of Foreign Studies I had a woman friend, a few years older, a junior professor, who taught modern European history. For Russian history that meant for her since 1672 when Pyotr the Great was born. She would talk about the readings she was assigning, and the lectures she was giving, and how her students were having their eyes opened to what really went on. She said she was impressing on them that there was a contract kind of serfdom for most of the population in Korea for centuries, and Russia for centuries was far behind Western Europe in civil liberties. They didn't know that in England, Elizabeth I officially ended serfdom in 1500 and Russia didn't officially end serfdom until 1723, over two hundred years later."

"An interesting, well informed woman, with a civil liberties mission."

"Very much so. You should also understand that she was telling her students that diplomats have to be able to represent the government when alliances change, as they will over a lifetime of service. Korea was fearful of Russia in the past. With the defeat of Japan in 1945 that changed, and now we are friends. That could change, and we might want political and military alliances with China. We might want alliances instead with the United States, England and the European Union. She was telling her students that diplomats have to know a lot of history, and they have to respect the lessons of history."

"That is what we were also taught at the Russian foreign service academy. While you were with her, and hearing all this, were you happy together?"

"I was happy with her. I was content with my life with her. For a while she was happy with me, but after a year she was no longer happy with me."

"Why?"

"She would complain that I did not pay enough attention to her, that I spent too much time with my books. She said that for England I had to know Winston Churchill, but not Henry V. For

France I needed to know Clementson and Charles de Gaulle, but not Louis XIV. For Russia, Lenin and Stalin, but not Stravinsky, Pushkin, and Dostoevski."

"Music?"

"I enjoyed Western classical music, Vivaldi, Mozart, Brahms, Chopin, Vaughan Williams, Rachmaninoff, and Prokofiev. She didn't appreciate classical music. She would listen with me to all of them, but she didn't enjoy any of them. We could get along, but we were not interested enough in the same things to want to make our lives together."

"You must have had young women friends when you were posted to other countries."

"Casual women friends, yes, of course."

"Close women friends?"

"I would have liked to, but at my level it was against the rules. The ambassadors and a few senior officers could have their wives and school age children with them. They could even have so called local temporary wives, but at my level anything like that was forbidden. Strictly forbidden. Yet men are men, and it often happened."

"And now?"

"If all goes well, in time I will find a young woman I love and who loves me. I will find a loving woman to marry, perhaps here, perhaps in another country. For now, that part of my life is... suspended."

"You might leave the country to find a loving wife?"

"Yes."

"When? How?"

"That is not something to start on now."

"Chul, our time is short."

"We will have all day in Sinuiju."

"Tomorrow in Sinuiju we will be busy. Our free time will be very short. Talking in a meaningful way takes time. It takes a lot of time."

"It does, and it also takes the right place. It will soon be getting dark. Good North Korean people are at home, they do not sit in a park at night and talk."

"Good people do talk when they need to."

"They do."

"In Sinuiju?"

"In Sinuiju… the time and place may come."

"Chul, we both have our personal security concerns."

"We do."

"Hotel rooms for tourists are not always a good place to talk. In Sinuiju, as elsewhere, they may not be secure for talking about serious things… or about anything personal."

"That's true, all of it, and that is why, if you still agree, we will be going to a small out of the way traditional hotel with clean modern bathroom facilities in the hall. Nearby there is a small high quality traditional restaurant with a tourist menu that serves wine."

"I agree. You talked about it the first day."

"You do have a good memory."

CHAPTER 21

At the Sinuiju station they took a taxi to their hotel in the old part of the city. When they entered Chul spoke to the manager, showed his identification, and paid for two rooms. The manager gave them keys to adjoining rooms on the second floor.

Elena's room, twelve by fourteen, was clean, had a bare wooden floor, one double bed, two wooden chairs with thin cushions, a wash basin with a mirror above, a bar of soap, two towels, a bench next to the basin, two glasses, one small chest of drawers, a rod with wire hangers for clothes, and for light, a window with curtains and a lamp by a chair.

They went off to tour the city. They returned in the early evening. Elena turned on the lamp in her room, looked all around, opened the lock on her valise, and put it under the hangers. She sat down in the chair by the lamp to wait for Chul's knock on the door. When she opened the door he asked if she was ready to walk a few short blocks for her traditional dinner.

She said it was just what she wanted. Chul ordered a traditional Korean dinner and a bottle of Australian wine. Elena ordered traditional food and European dishes from the tourist menu. Chul poured the wine for both of them, ate his food slowly, and was unusually quiet. Waiting for their dessert with his glass almost empty Chul started to talk about how much alike they were alike in so many ways, and yet, how different. Same hopes and dreams, same kind of careers, different outcomes. There were dark clouds for him now, but there was always hope, there could be a bright future. As he went on he was alternately hopeful and pessimistic.

Elena told him they really were not that different. Her day by day life wasn't always so bright, and her working life was sometimes hard and dark.

He listened thoughtfully, then said their differences, the ones that counted now, were not of the same kind, and she knew it.

Elena responded, "Chul, I know it, but listen to me. Our personal circumstances change, and what goes on around us changes. There is the past, we remember it, we know we can't change a day of it, and there is the future. We have to make the future for ourselves as best we can."

He said he had seen too much change already. He told stories about diplomats getting into troubles with young women. Old men with wives and grown children. He went on about senior men and juniors who got royally drunk at a rowdy party and started telling secrets. Foolish old stupid men. Hotheaded youngsters getting even, throwing away their careers and their lives because they didn't think their lives were worth living the way they had been reduced to groveling to keep their position and make a living.

He picked up the bottle to refill her glass. Elena took hold of the bottle and pushed it down. Anguished, she looked at him and then said softly, "Chul, you are upset. No more. We have to pay the bill and leave."

"We haven't finished our wine, we haven't had our dessert."

"You're upset. We have to leave. We have to get back to the hotel."

"We will go back, but first we will go to the store. It is just a block away."

"I don't want more wine when we get back. You don't need more wine."

"Elena, I keep telling you, I'm supposed to be taking care of you, and instead you are still taking care of me."

"Chul, we have been taking care of each other. We have been taking care of each other from the day we met."

"It is kind of you to say that."

"Chul, it was never *you and me*, it has always been *we and us*."

"You really mean it?"

"Yes. Of course, I mean it. I really mean it."

"So...are you ready to tell me what we have to do?"

"I don't need to. You have made your decision, you know what I mean, and it is hard to start. Hard for both of us. I enjoy being here with you, it is wonderful just being with you, but we have to leave. Pay the bill. We'll go back and talk in my room."

She unlocked the door, gestured for him to come in, turned on the lamp, took both his hands and speaking slowly said, "Chul, you have made your decision. I have made my decision. There is no going back for either of us. The time has come for both of us."

"For both of us?"

"Yes. Chul, for both of us. We have a bond. We have a strong professional bond and a strong personal bond. I know it, and you know it. It is more than a Russian kind of bond, or a Korean kind of bond, it is a personal bond. It is between us. Do I need to find other words?"

"No, Elena, I understand."

"If we are going to talk about scheduling special trains, and serious matters, and I am going to listen to you, go to your room, get a firm grip on yourself, decide what you are going to say, and how you are going to say it. And come back in half an hour."

Chul knocked three times quickly. Elena opened the door for him, then locked it.

She took both his hands. "So, because we should talk, and we have a special bond, we are both going to talk about important matters. Special trains and serious matters important to both of us."

"Yes, it's time."

"This is about the railroad, and about moving uranium and plutonium, and beyond that it is about airfreight to some other country."

"Yes."

"And we are going to talk about how, and where, you are going to live the rest of your life."

"Yes, we can talk about that, too."

"Then you had better search the room. Close the curtains tight and search the room."

"We're safe. No one knows we were coming here."

"Other have been here. Who knows why? Old walls can have eyes and ears. For both of us, search the room."

Chul looked around the room for several minutes then said, "Plaster walls and ceiling, solid plank flooring, no upholstered furniture, thin curtains, a radiator for heat, no chandelier, one electric outlet for the lamp, one for something else. There is no place to hide anything."

"The mirror hanging on the wall. Is there anything behind the mirror?"

Chul took the mirror off the hook on the wall, replaced it and said, "Solid glass. There's nothing on the back. Just plaster wall. Anything else?"

"The chair cushions."

"They are old and thin."

"The mattress."

He took off the covers and felt the mattress. "It is also old and thin."

"The plug for the lamp. The other one, too."

"I'll have to unplug the lamp, get off the cover plates, and feel around the wires."

"Never mind. I don't want you to get a shock."

"Anything else?"

"The only other thing we are supposed to do is search our clothes. You can look through the clothes in my valise, but I am not going to undress so you can rummage through the clothes I'm wearing."

"I'm not asking you to."

"And you are not going to take your clothes off."

Elena sat down, Chul pulled the other chair over and sat down opposite her. " Anything else?"

"What we have to talk about can involve your safety. You may have to leave the country. I may be able to help you, I can't make any promises."

"I understand."

"Even if I could, I can't control what happens."

"I understand."

"Chul, I don't know where to start. What should I know? What do you have to tell me?"

"Most of what I can tell you other people must already know."

"Really?"

"There is going to be a railroad shipment of uranium and plutonium, and a lot of railroad people and soldiers must be involved with that."

"How do you know?"

"That takes some explanation."

"We have all night. Tell me."

"The uranium complex, Military Facility 178, and the plutonium complex, Military Facility 206, are very close together on the same rail line. There are no regularly scheduled trains to that location. Each train is scheduled separately. From the work I do putting special trains together, and making the schedules, I know what the train will be like, when the train is scheduled to run, the day and hour, how many cars, what kind of cars, how long it is scheduled to be at the location, and where it is to go afterwards."

"It's very important, do you know, can you know, when the train will run?"

"I know what the train schedule is. I know the transport order for the operation. I do not know if what happens will be exactly in accord with the schedule and order. Special trains almost never stay on schedule."

"Who knows what's happening?"

"There is the scheduling we do and there is the transport order. The daily operations section makes the transport order and gets the operation completion report on the special train. I know the people, I am friendly with them, but our work is different, we don't talk about it except in general terms. They do not make transport orders for the daily scheduled rail operations and the Air Koryo daily operations."

"Start with the rail scheduling system. What is it? How does it work?"

"There are three operators and a supervisor on duty around the clock. Everything is in the computer system. All regularly scheduled passenger trains are in the computer. All regularly scheduled freight trains are in the computer. All special trains are in the computer. Air Koryo scheduled flights are also in the computer. The computer gives an alert if there will be any scheduling interference. The daily rail and air schedules are continuously updated for the next thirty days."

"Tell me about the special trains."

"We are only concerned with one special train. It is the train with a car for guards that has been scheduled for the uranium and plutonium storage areas on the twenty-first. The transport order says the cargo will be metal crates of different weight and dimensions on pallets to be loaded by forklift into the freight car and secured there."

"Does this transport order say anything at all about radiation danger?"

"It is standard language. It doesn't mention radiation."

"Go on."

"The train is to leave the loading dock at two and arrive at the Pyongyang freight rail yard around five. I can't remember the times exactly. The crates are to be unloaded by forklift and loaded on an army truck that will carry them to the airport freight receiving area and unloaded. When that's done there will be a report that the transport order has been completed."

"Is there any information about the destination of any airfreight shipment?"

"Not in the computer system. Not in the transport order."

"Do you have any ideas about the airfreight shipment?"

"I believe there will be an Air Koryo airfreight delivery to Iran, somewhere in Iran. The Air Koryo Ilyushin 76 will leave soon after dark on the twenty-first."

"How do you know?"

"Elena, I don't know. That is what I think is most likely to happen."

"Tell me."

"The special train with guards is moving uranium and plutonium on the twenty-first, and it is going somewhere by airfreight. Probably also with guards, and far away. Probably by Air Koryo. The Air Koryo Ilyushin 76 is the best plane for that."

"And Iran?"

"Iran wants to build an atomic bomb. The JCPOA negotiations are at a stalemate, and Iran continues to talks about getting atomic weapons. And Iran can afford to pay."

"When will the plane leave?"

"The Ilyushin will probably leave when it is dark to try to avoid any watchers reporting on it."

"And so…"

"Elena, this flight will not be secret. Too many people are involved. It cannot be kept secret. This flight must be stopped. It will be stopped."

"You will be suspected."

"Everyone in the scheduling section and operations section will be suspected. I will requisition the engine and order the cars. Operations will arrange the transfer from the freight yard to the airport freight terminal."

"You will have to leave the country."

"I know it."

"You said you don't have papers. Do you know where you can buy papers?"

"Yes, but probably not good enough to get to Russia."

"Will you go to China?"

"Never. They would be alerted to watch for me. They would send me back in chains."

"South Korea?"

"I might bribe my way into the back of a truck and get across. I probably could, but what kind of a life would I have there? They would track me down and take me back, or just stick a knife in me. Until then I might work in a miserable factory and live in a slum dormitory."

"Chul, you have thought and thought about every part of this very carefully. What will you do?"

"Even with good papers I can't cross the Tumen bridge to Russia, the border guards will be on alert, but I can get across the river at night."

"There must be guards against that, too. You could be shot."

"I can find a raft to get across at night, or make a raft, and in the morning I can get to Khasan."

"Then what?"

"Elena, tell your uncle that from Khasan I want to go to Moscow. I do not want to go to Siberia."

"Do you want to stay in Moscow? Do you want to have a job in Moscow?"

"I will stay in Moscow if I can fit in. Make a decent life for myself. If not, I speak English, I will go to England, Canada, or Australia, and I will find a position teaching history or political affairs. For now, I need to get to Khasan."

"When will you leave?"

"I will leave when the uranium and plutonium leave. If I leave a day before it will be a signal that something is wrong."

"And if you are brought back and questioned?"

"I will say that I love my country, but I left because I was very dissatisfied with my job. I will say I know nothing about any special shipment or transport order, and I never talked to anyone about anything like that."

"You know they will not believe you. You know what can happen to you."

"Elena, realize where we both are. We have been together for five days with all that time for us to share this kind of information and make plans. I cannot stay, and you cannot stay."

"I have diplomatic immunity."

"What happens to me will be intentional. What happens to you will be an unfortunate accident. Or you did it to yourself. You must be on a plane before the twenty first."

"How long before?"

"Several days. You develop a severe headache. It is unlike any pain in the head you have ever had before. Your ambassador insists that you fly to Moscow immediately for medical attention. The embassy arranges tickets for you and an escort, an embassy woman escort. An embassy officer drives the two of you in an embassy car to the Seoul airport. You and your escort are put on the first flight to Vladivostok. Your escort stays with you on your connecting flight to Moscow where you will be met by a staff officer."

"When you leave it will be a signal that something is wrong. I will be safe in Moscow, and you will be crossing the river at night."

"Elena, you said we have some things in common. We have a bond. We do. We also know that atomic bombs are much more important than either of us will ever be. Small so-called tactical ones, and big ones. We both know that is what this is all about. I haven't said the words, and you haven't said the words, yet we have both known it from the moment you walked into the Ministry of Transport building and we met."

"Yes, of course. It has always been there. And the risks for both of us have always been there."

"I know my risk. You know your risk."

"I will be safe with my family in Moscow. What about your family? What will happen to them?"

"We will not go into that."

"Chul, that is not an answer. They are sure to be brought in and questioned for hours."

"We will not go into it."

After a long pause she asked, "Could they be helped in some way?"

"No. Don't go near them. Don't let anyone contact them in any way or go near them. They know nothing about any of this. Nothing. The authorities will understand that from the way they answer their question. I must trust that they will be safe."

There was a silence and then Elena asked, "Is there anything more to talk about?"

"No, I've told you everything. You must tell your uncle everything about the railroad and what I think about the plane. The Ilyushin 76 freight plane. The plane will fly, it will, and the plane will be stopped. One way or another, it will be stopped, as it must be."

They sat in a somber silence until Elena reached across to Chul, took both of his hands, looked into his face, and said softly, "Do you know that I care for you?"

"Elena, I have had my dreams, but I didn't dare hope."

"Didn't you know? Haven't I showed you?"

"You have. Several times."

"How?"

"Elena, the way you speak, the way you smile when you raise your glass to mine."

She stood up pulling Chul to her. "We have tonight."

Chul wrapped his arms around her, kissed her softly, and said, "Dreams really can come true."

Elena softly returned his kiss and said, "Tell me your dreams."

"You really do care? You really do want to know?"

"Chul, I care, and I want to know."

After a long pause, he began, "I might say I have loved you ever since you came to Korea."

"How can that be?"

"Two years ago, when you first posted to Seoul, your embassy sent out an announcement and a picture of you for the foreign service community. I was in Paris, but a month or so after that I saw your picture, and I thought that you were beautiful. The next day I went back and looked at your picture again. I looked, and the next day after that I looked again. I looked at you and I dreamed that someday I might meet you. I thought you were very beautiful. And you are. I could never have dreamed that I would hold you. Hold you close. Hold you in my arms."

"What else?"

"What you should expect."

"Tell me."

"I dreamt of being with you in a grand hotel, bouquets of flowers, champagne."

"Where?"

"I was in Paris, so where else? I dreamed of being with you in Paris."

"Where in Paris?"

"Paris at the George V Four Seasons. The finest room with bouquets of flowers high up with a view of the city and the Eiffel Tower."

"In your dreams, what would you do?"

"I would ask you if you would like to go to the summit of the Eiffel tower.'"

"What else?"

"I would ask you if you would like to go to the opera. I would ask you if you would like to go to the theatre. I would ask you if you would like to spend a day at a museum, the Louvre, or the Monet or Rodin museums."

"What else?"

"I would ask you if you would like to go to Giverny and see Monet's house and gardens and with me think of him pouring his soul into those paintings."

"What else?"

"I would recite poetry for you."

"What poetry?"

"A famous Pushkin love poem."

"You know it in Russian?"
"Yes."
"Then do it."
"I'll mess it up."
"You won't. Do it for me."

I still recall the wondrous moment
When you appeared before my sight
As though a brief and fleeting omen,
Pure phantom in enchanting light.

In sorrow, when I felt unwell,
Caught in the bustle, in a daze,
I fell under your voice's spell,
And dreamt the features of your face.

Years passed and gales had dispelled
My former hopes, and in those days,
I lost your voice's sacred spell,

The holy features of your face.
Detained in darkness, isolation,
My days began to drag in strife.
Without faith and inspiration,
Without tears, and love and life.

My soul attained its waking moment:
You reappeared before my sight,
As though a brief and fleeting omen,
Pure phantom in enchanting light.

And now, my heart, with fascination,
Beats rapidly and finds revived
Devout faith and inspiration,
And tender tears and love and life."

"Thank you. I know it, but it never had such meaning."
"And, Elena, such meaning for me."
"Chul, we don't need Paris, we don't need the flowers, we don't

need the museums, we are here, and the bed is here."

"Really?"

"Yes, really."

"I have to protect you. It might be an hour."

"I'll be waiting for you."

The train left at ten thirty for Pyongyang. Elena sat by the window with Chul beside her. After an hour watching the green countryside slide by she closed her eyes and tried to sleep. Sleep refused to come. Her reverie of the night with Chul beside her in bed turned dark as she thought of what was ahead for her -- telling and retelling her story to a recorder and too eager ears. Then she thought of Chul at night looking and looking for a place to cross the river, finding some sort of a raft, starting to cross, falling off, and being swept away in the dark cold river.

To put a brake on her dark thoughts she asked Chul when they would get to Pyongyang. He told her she looked very sad, and they shouldn't be seen talking because people might think they had been quarreling.

She looked out and saw that the coastland little by little was turning into steep hills and sharp valleys. From time to time a town or village swept by, several times with a car or tractor waiting for the train to pass. On and on for over an hour. Again, she closed her eyes, tried to remember the night, tried to sleep. Again, sleep refused to come.

Passing a village the moving picture slowed, and then stopped. She was concerned. She took Chul's hand and asked if this was a scheduled stop, or whether something could be wrong with the train.

He answered, "This isn't a scheduled stop. It's probably not anything wrong with the train."

"Then why?"

"It could be almost anything. Something on the track ahead, big rocks sliding off a hill, something has gone wrong with the signal system ahead, a car or truck is stuck on the crossing. If we are going to be here for a while a conductor should come by and tell us."

Half an hour later a conductor came into their car and in a loud voice said there had been a car accident, the car would be moved out of the way, they would leave when the track was clear. It may take an hour or more. Meanwhile, no one should leave the train unless told to leave.

Elena felt a chill come over her. She clasped her arms in front of her, lowered her head, and closed her eyes. She was remembering the car accident in Moscow that killed Uncle Lev's wife, Angelina, and hurt her mother. Too much vodka, they said. After the funeral her mother took her to church and told her when something like this happens, that's the time for prayers, prayers in church with the priest, or alone, a silent prayer. Chul was sitting beside her letting the time slip by. She wondered what he was thinking. Better she didn't know. She could not stop the thought that she might have to say a prayer for him.

An hour later, without any explanation, the train started again. She didn't want to know what had happened.

CHAPTER 22

October 9, 2016

Six-thirty in the evening at the President's working office in the Executive Office Building. With the President: Admiral Michael Mullin, Chairman, Joint Chiefs of Staff; Howard Elliot, CIA; Major General Jeffery Levy.

Three manila folders with EXECUTIVE SECRET on the front and back were on the President's desk.

The folders contained an eight page CIA analysis of the flight of an Ilyushin 76, followed by maps of Korea, the Korean coastline north of Wonsan, maps of a flight route across Russia and Mongolia to Tabriz, and other supporting materials.

The four page response of the Secretary of State, followed by United Nations resolutions on freedom of the sea navigation, freedom of the air navigation, and other supporting materials.

The three page legal opinion by General Levy, followed by Supreme Court cases and academic texts on the President's authority in foreign affairs.

Barack Obama picked up the State Department folder, turned to Howard Elliot and said, "The Secretary of State is furious that you reached out to Russian intelligence before going to him. He says you are going around him. And doing it needlessly. From what I see, he is right. You have your responsibility, but it is also the Secretary's territory, and you haven't kept him informed. If he were here he would chop your head off."

"Mr. President, I am sure he would. Under the circumstances, the CIA has acted responsibly."

"He doesn't think so. He is worried that the Russians will shoot down the wrong plane. Or that the Russians will shoot down the right plane over land, and some of the radioactive cargo will end up in the wrong hands and could cause some historic catastrophe."

"Mr. President, we have acted responsibly."

The President dropped the folder and continued, "Howard, he is right, you didn't tell him what you were doing even though you knew there are big risks that could affect many countries."

"Sir," Elliot answered, "of course there are risks, but the Russians don't want the Ilyushin coming back from Tabriz empty. Neither do we."

"He's saying give diplomacy a chance to work and Iran may agree to IAEA inspections again because their whole economy is in a bad way, their inflation is running wild, and there have been big open protests against Ayatollah Khamenei continuing to run the country."

"Sir, Ayatollah Khamenei is running the country with the backing of the army. He is not about to be deposed, and he is not scaling back on supporting terrorist proxies, and he is not limiting his atomic ambitions. He will buy uranium and plutonium when and where he can get it and afford it. He will tuck it away in a cave in the desert until he's ready to use it."

"Or the army is making the deal with Kim and running the country with the backing of Khamenei?"

"Mr. President, we believe that is actually what is happening, but in this situation, it doesn't matter."

"No, it doesn't."

The President turned to General Levy. "General, as I read your opinion you want me to forget about international air navigation agreements."

"Mr. President, I haven't forgotten. The continued authenticity of every air navigation agreement depends on the agreement and the nature of the threats and actions of those involved at the time."

"Can Air Koryo fly airfreight from Pyongyang to Tabriz if it scrupulously follows aircraft identification and air traffic control rules?"

"Mr. President, the answer is yes, it can. It can fly to Iran, or any other country, like any other airfreight carrier if it is carrying a commercial cargo."

"Why isn't this sale and delivery by North Korea to Iran a commercial transaction? France for many years has been selling enriched uranium to many countries for their old and new nuclear power plants. Some of that may not go into power plants."

"Mr. President, my opinion concludes that this arrangement between North Korea and Iran is not a commercial sale under international law because Iran is flagrantly breaking international law. For many years Iran has been running militias in the Middle East, and Iran's Supreme Leader has repeatedly called for the destruction of the United States of America and the death of the State of Israel. Wipe Israel off the face of the earth. He means it. His followers mean it. If he gets atomic weapons he may use them. The constitutional powers of the American President in support of the national defense will support a decision to prevent this shipment of weapons grade uranium and plutonium from North Korea to Iran. Prevent it in any way necessary."

"The UN isn't going to buy that."

"Mr. President, the Russians without our help will shoot down the Ilyushin. When it gets out that we sent a plane, a Super Hornet, with a Russian speaking pilot to an airbase near Vladivostok, the United Nations won't care what our legal position is."

"And if the UN calls for US criminal responsibility under UN interpretation of international law?"

"Mr. President, as for American criminal responsibility, as interpreted by the UN, or otherwise, the United States does not recognize United Nations authority over American officials acting for American interests under the President's orders. That has always been our position and it won't change."

"Did you have much trouble writing the opinion?"

"Sir, the lawyer part of me, no. No other decision was possible. But it is troubling. It is a night attack, and the wrong plane could be attacked, and a lot of innocent people killed. That bothers me. There is only a small attack zone over the ocean. That bothers me. If the Ilyushin is shot down over land some of the uranium or plutonium might end up with terrorists, and tens of thousands of people could be seriously affected. If not right away, within a few months, and because we are dealing with long lasting radioactivity, they could be seriously affected for a long time. That bothers me."

The President turned to Admiral Mitchell. "Admiral, do you see any practical alternative to a fighter attack, Russian or ours, from the Vladivostok air base?"

"Mr. President, I don't. Our plane will not take part. The Russians have decided our pilot was not qualified. We have no plans to find another Russian speaking fighter pilot. The Russians know the risks, they will be careful."

"Should we bring the Chinese on board?"

"Mr. President, my view is that Chinese intelligence, and so the Chinese leadership, know what is going on. Not in detail, but in a general way. When they don't want something like this sale of uranium and plutonium to happen, they don't hesitate to tell you. I am against saying anything to the Chinese. The Russians shouldn't need them."

"Has Kim responded?"

"Mr. President, the Russians have warned him. He didn't respond."

The President pushed the folders to the side and stood up, followed by the others.

"Send me a report."

CHAPTER 23

October 18, 2016
Minutes of Nuclear Proliferation Committee

Vladivostok tracked Ilyushin 76 based on air traffic control, Ilyushin's transponder, aircraft radar and ship radar.

Ilyushin departed Pyongyang International at 2012. Under Pyongyang air traffic control Ilyushin flew East to coast. At 2054, under Vladivostok air traffic control, Ilyushin flew North towards Vladivostok. Ilyushin was calculated to fly over Sea of Japan from 2122 to 2139. At 2126 target with external blinking lights was sighted. At 2129 the target identity was confirmed. At 2133 target was attacked with Russian missile. Target was destroyed.

Visual location of the crash site was not possible. Russian calculated location was 12.25 kilometers over ocean.

The fighter left attack area at 2136 and returned to Uglovoye airbase.

American fighter returned from Uglovoye airbase to US without incident.

CHAPTER 24

December 23, 2016

Elena's father tapped his glass with a spoon and the round of conversation and laughter subsided. Another tap and there was silence as Elena's mother stood up.

"Lev and Sonia, Pyotr and Elena, Alex and Veronika, we are delighted to have you all here at our family home. This is marvelous. I thank Lev for arranging to have us all here together. Raise your glasses for Lev." The table resounded with raised glasses and approval. When it subsided Lev Marloff smiled and looked around the table.

"It's a happy moment for me to be here with all of you. We all have much to be thankful for. I am thankful that we are all here in good health. I am thankful that we have these two wonderful couples together here with us."

Turning serious, he continued, "You have doubtless all heard the news on the radio and television that North Korea has accused our country of shooting down one of its freight planes that was flying from Pyongyang to Najin, a city near the Russian border. Privately, it has accused Elena of being involved in the attack because shortly before the incident Elena left the country and an acquaintance disappeared. We have not seen fit to answer these complaints. Should any of you be asked about any of this you know nothing beyond what is on the news."

In the silence that followed Elena lowered her head and repeated her silent prayer for Chul.

After the silence Lev Marloff went on cheerfully, "And now I have better news. Elena is not returning to Pyongyang. She will be spending some time here in Moscow polishing her English, and then she will be posted to London where she can do good work and help me when I have business there. There's more. The London embassy needs Pyotr to head its computer and code operations, and he will be there with Elena. It will be a well-earned year for them together in London. Perhaps longer. Raise your glasses for our toast. To Russia, to the best of Russia."

And the toast rang out around the table, "*To Russia, to the best of Russia.*"

CHAPTER 25

February 2, 2017

Habig met Lev Marloff, as the last time they met, in the same small office on the nineteenth floor. Marloff told Habig he was glad he could come again, opened a bottle of wine, poured two glasses, and they sat down to talk.

Habig told Marloff that his information was that North Korea never returned the payment it received from the Credit Suisse escrow and ventured that might be the most fortunate part of the whole affair. Marloff nodded.

Habig asked about Ban Chul. Marloff told him that his information was that Ban Chul disappeared around the time of the attack on the Ilyushin, and beyond that he did not know what happened to him. He added that he was prepared to give him refuge if he surfaced in Russia, but until then there was nothing he could do.

"Any chance he got out somehow?" Habig asked.

"My information is they searched along the river for miles. Didn't find a body. We were alerted that he might try to get across and we were watching. No doubt he thought about it, and in the end didn't try. There are no reports of him crossing into South Korea or China. In a year or so he may show up."

"This Navy pilot, Lieutenant Alan Rostov, do you know anything about him?"

"I understand he was in Vladivostok but never got close to North Korea."

Habig continued, "When he was in Vladivostok he got himself mixed up somehow in the Ilyushin affair. Any idea what that was about? What he might have been doing there? Who he might have talked to?"

"No. What has he been doing since then?"

"He's leaving the Navy for the State Department."

"Smart fellow."

"Do you think Kim will try again?"

"Probably."

"Air freight again?"

"Probably. Let me know if you hear something."

"I will."

Marloff poured more wine. "Before you go we must have our toast." They raised their glasses. "*To Russia, the best of Russia. To America, the best of America.*"

ABOUT THE AUTHOR

Herbert Leonard Cohen is a retired attorney. He is a graduate of the School of Law, University of California, Berkeley, and had a distinguished career as an officer in the United States Air Force Judge Advocate General Corps, and as Chief Counsel of the Department of Food and Agriculture of the State of California.

In his historical novels he draws on that experience and examines the actions of good men and women in position of high authority who bend the rules when confronted with extreme pressure, and the consequences for them, those they love, and for the country.

He lives in Sacramento, California.

Made in the USA
Las Vegas, NV
17 January 2025

16573116R00163